WHAT I HAVE TO TELL YOU
Mary Elsie Robertson

"Never has a character tried harder to separate herself from her family or be more unlikable than Jessie Farquarson. . . . Yet Robertson tempers this view with her straightforward, compassionate, sometimes humorous treatment of Jessie's story . . . Robertson's skill is to make us care about the fate of a difficult woman who has made a lifetime's work out of not caring about herself."
                                                    —*The Washington Post*

"Compelling . . . you believe in Mary Elsie Robertson's characters and their lives, no matter how many bizarre curves she throws at you."   —*The Edmonton Journal*

"Keeps you guessing . . . a real adventure, all the more rewarding when you realize you've journeyed nearly to the end without a hint as to how it will resolve itself."   —*Arkansas Sunday Gazette*

"Engrossing . . . a fine trip down life's odd road. . . . There is nothing quite like the sensation of being dropped headfirst into a story . . . before you can surface for air . . . you are already in for the swim, swept downstream and away in the currents and cross currents of a most unusual and compelling book." —*Orlando Sentinel*

What I Have to Tell You

QUANTITY SALES

Most Dell books are available at special quantity discounts when purchased in bulk by corporations, organizations, and special-interest groups. Custom imprinting or excerpting can also be done to fit special needs. For details write: Dell Publishing, 666 Fifth Avenue, New York, NY 10103. Attn.: Special Sales Department.

INDIVIDUAL SALES

Are there any Dell books you want but cannot find in your local stores? If so, you can order them directly from us. You can get any Dell book in print. Simply include the book's title, author, and ISBN number if you have it, along with a check or money order (no cash can be accepted) for the full retail price plus $2.00 to cover shipping and handling. Mail to: Dell Readers Service, P.O. Box 5057, Des Plaines, IL 60017.

What I Have
to Tell
You

Mary Elsie Robertson

A LAUREL TRADE PAPERBACK
Published by Dell Publishing
a division of
Bantam Doubleday Dell Publishing Group, Inc.
666 Fifth Avenue
New York, New York 10103

ISBN: 0-440-50383-3

Reprinted by arrangement with Doubleday, New York, New York.

Printed in the United States of America

Published simultaneously in Canada

July 1991

10 9 8 7 6 5 4 3 2 1

RRH

For Jenny and Piers

Part I

1

Of course I was desperate about Dwayne, wondering if he was dead or alive, or I wouldn't ever have gone to a psychic, the one whose card I found on the corner of the bulletin board in the laundrymat—a little card smudged like a cat with muddy feet had slid across it—half-hidden behind a notice for Tai Chi lessons. PHOEBE JEWKES, it said. PSYCHIC READER. DO YOU WANT TO BE FREE? KNOW THE TRUTH. A box number for one of the islands, not even a telephone number. Anybody wanting to find Phoebe Jewkes was going to have to struggle, that was clear. I went back three times to look at the card while my clothes were going around and around in the dryer before I finally stole it and slid it in the back pocket of my jeans. Every time I leaned forward I could feel it back there, giving me a nudge. But I'd made up my mind before I stole the card. I was going to see Phoebe Jewkes. I felt from the minute I saw that card hanging on the bulletin board at an angle, it was meant for me. Something fate had chosen to drop in front of my face, the way a cat likes to show off a mouse before she eats it.

I waited until Monday, my day off, to make the trip, and it took me an hour and a half to find Phoebe, not counting the ferry ride from Anacortes. It was raining, as it usually was up in that corner of Washington State, and as I pedaled my bicycle, water dripped from the bottom of my poncho and fell into my socks. My glasses went so blurry I had to stop and peer at each mailbox, and long before I got to Phoebe's house I wanted to turn back and give up on the whole thing. But my feet were wet, it was forty minutes back to the ferry, and I'd have a wait after I got there. It was just then, when I felt most discouraged, that I saw the mailbox I'd been looking for, a lopsided ninety painted on it in blue, with paint drops making little tear tracks from the top of the zero.

While I was peering at the mailbox, a man came barreling down the driveway on a motorcycle, hunched over the handlebars, a yellow slicker streaming behind, giving me an impassive Buddha look as he passed. When he had, I could see his little braid, thin as a rat's tail and drawn back so tightly it curled like a scorpion ready to strike.

At the back door, where I propped my bicycle, a rusty gutter sagged low, laboring to hold up under all the water pouring off the roof, and I could see paint peeling back from the corners of the windows. Not much money in giving psychic readings, it looked like.

My knuckles had barely touched the door when it opened—so suddenly I thought somebody must have been standing there, waiting for me. My hand stayed where it was, half-raised, as I looked down at the eyes watching from the crack, searching me up and down. "Phoebe Jewkes?" I said.

There I stood, a tall, bony woman with dark hair sticking to her face and wearing glasses that made her eyes look big as a horse's—oh, I knew what I looked like all right. And that's why I can't stand to be stared at—I get nervous as a dog when somebody does—so there on the stoop, I could feel my lazy eye sliding up to take a look at the sky the way it does when I get uneasy. The door shut a fraction, Phoebe becoming alarmed.

"That's just my lazy eye," I said quickly. "It does that sometimes."

I'm harmless, I wanted to say. I may look strange, but I'm not a scary person.

"It's not even about me I've come!" I said finally in desperation. "It's about Dwayne and whether he's alive or dead. My husband, Dwayne."

The door, on the point of shutting, hesitated. Seconds went by while I could feel Phoebe thinking. Then the door opened, and I was in the house, taking off my wet poncho and drying my glasses on the tail of my shirt. Even seeing the world all blurred without my glasses, I could tell Phoebe wasn't much more than half my size. One of those small, delicate people who make me feel heavy and clumsy. In fact Phoebe wasn't much bigger than a child. The flannel shirt she was wearing reached practically to her knees, and I supposed it must have belonged to the Buddha with a pigtail.

It was only when I put my glasses back on that I saw the baby riding her hip, a naked baby boy with a face as round as the clock he was holding in his hands—one of those big silver-colored alarm clocks with a bell on the top. The baby was shaking the clock so the bell kept giving throttled *jings,* like something being tortured, a noise that made the baby chuckle and bounce. Phoebe looked a little overpowered by that big baby, and the sight of the two of them together was so odd I wondered if I was supposed to make something of it, the naked baby shaking the clock and the woman with a beatific smile, her blond hair lying in small ringlets around her face from the damp—a woman who reminded me from the first of somebody else though I couldn't say who. But if it was a test, I failed.

All the time I was looking at her, Phoebe had her gaze fixed on some point a little beyond my left shoulder, which gave me such a strange feeling I had to take a quick look behind me. But there was nothing in the corner except a broom propped on its handle and a blue satin basketball jacket hanging on a hook.

"Whoever he is with you, didn't he want to come in too?" Phoebe said in a clear, little-girl voice. It was exactly the kind of voice I would have expected her to have.

"There's nobody with me," I told her.

"When you were on the stoop. Right *there!*" she said, pointing.

I shook my head no.

"A double?" she said then. "Don't you have a double?"

"A what?" I said, and the eerie feeling came over me again, only much stronger than before.

"Oh, like," she said, still looking at me with those sky blue eyes that stared straight through mine and to something beyond, "do you have a twin?"

Well, I just looked at her and felt the hairs on my arms rising. "It so happens I *do* have a twin," I said. "My brother Jordan. But it's not anything to do with him that I've come."

When she shifted the baby on her hip, I saw there were things hanging from strings around her neck. Rock crystal and a burl of wood as convoluted as the brain of some small animal, a black curved claw that might have belonged to a bear once. Everything about Phoebe made me uneasy, and I was close to leaving then, even in the rain, only at that moment she put the baby down on the kitchen table to put a diaper on him and asked me to hand her the powder. The baby was kicking his legs back and forth like pistons, grinning the whole time so it was impossible not to grin back. He looked a lot like the Buddha on the motorcycle, and a healthier looking baby it would be hard to imagine, just as down-to-earth as a turnip. It seemed to me, with a baby like that, Phoebe was probably a lot more ordinary than I'd made her out to be.

So I handed her the powder. "I'm Jessie, by the way," I said. "Jessie Farquarson."

But I could tell Phoebe wasn't listening. All she did was pick up the baby and hold him out to me, smiling a smile so sweet and joyous—it made her face glow—that my knees went weak with apprehension. I had to tell myself only a nature as suspicious and maybe even as twisted as mine could find something scary in a smile an angel might have had. And so I set my uneasiness aside. She was just a young mother with a baby, trying to get on in the world as best she could. No different from me, though I don't have a baby.

"You can hold Dion a minute," she said. So I took him, jiggling him tentatively against my arm, afraid he'd realize an amateur had taken over, but he was too busy shaking the clock to pay any attention to who was holding him.

"The reason why I'm here," I said then, "is a reading."

Phoebe, free of the baby, stood with her hands on her hips, giving me a look that slid through my eyes and on to something far away, a look she'd no doubt been making people uncomfortable with all her life. But she couldn't help it. I could tell that too, since it was a subject I had reason to know something about.

"No, I won't give you a reading," Phoebe said with such force I looked at her in surprise.

"Why not?"

She shook her head back and forth with her eyes closed, her hair whipping from side to side. I almost expected her to stamp her feet.

I had the very strong feeling Phoebe knew me from somewhere, though I couldn't imagine where she could have seen me. Even if she'd come into Eddie's Oyster Bar some night, she probably wouldn't have seen me in the back putting together salads.

"There's something wrong with the day?" I persisted. "It's the thirteenth or something?" Though I knew perfectly well it was April the twelfth.

A closed look came over Phoebe's face.

"I don't want to give you a reading," she said, and a chill went to my heart. I was certain she knew why I'd come and the question I had to ask, and the answer was all too clear to her. Already she'd seen the pile of bones that used to be Dwayne, washed up on some brushy sandspit of the Rappahannock, back home in Virginia.

"You said on your card, 'Know the Truth,'" I reminded her. "And it's the truth I've come for. Even if it is bad news. I've got to know about Dwayne." Phoebe didn't say anything. She just went over to the stove and poured out two mugs of coffee from a pot left there to keep warm. I followed at her heels.

"Listen," I said. "I've come all the way from Anacortes. In the rain. And you did put that notice up in the laundry-mat. Whatever your price is, I'll pay it."

I could feel my stubbornness rising and knew what Jordan sometimes accused me of was true—I *was* like a tank moving over level ground. If you're a plain woman you can either try to hide away, to disappear into the landscape, or you make yourself bold. And since I'm too big to hide away, I've learned to be persistent.

Phoebe sat with her heels hooked on the rungs of her chair, rubbing one finger around the rim of her coffee mug, looking hangdog and caught out, curly hair falling in front of her face. And it came to me she couldn't give psychic readings any more than I could. It was somebody else who'd put her up to pretending it—the man with the pigtail most likely—and so I'd come all that way for nothing.

But it was at that very moment, when these thoughts were going through my mind, that Phoebe lifted her head and turned in my direction with her eyes closed. "Jessie, when you were little, you slept in a bed with a ram's head carved in the headboard," she said. "A ram with curly horns."

I sank back against my chair, trying to get away from her line of vision. "How did you know that?" I said.

"When you were three, you had a pony named Minnie, and there was another pony too, called Max."

"Max was Jordan's," I said, even before I thought. "That's every word the truth."

I felt awed and all of a sudden shy.

When Phoebe opened her eyes, she was looking straight at me.

"Don't you see, Jessie?" she said. *"That's* why I don't want to give you a reading."

"But whyever not?" I said. "If you can tell all that about me without even trying?"

"Because I knew as soon as I saw you out there on the stoop you were one I shouldn't let in the house. All I had to do was see you standing there with the rain rolling down your glasses, and pictures started coming in my head. Like watching a movie."

"But isn't that *good?*" I said, still not understanding what she was talking about. "You can really *do* this."

I couldn't understand why people weren't lined up outside the door, waiting for fifteen minutes with Phoebe. The Delphi oracle, with all her riddles and double-talk, couldn't have been better than this. And I couldn't believe my luck, to tell the truth, getting in at the beginning before the word got out.

Phoebe reached across the table and put one of her hands over mine. It was a small hand and felt hot, like a dog's tongue. It held tight to my fingers. "Jessie," she said sadly, "I don't want to know your birthday cake when you were three was lemon with cream cheese icing. I don't want to know your mother slapped your hand for taking a third piece and you slapped hers back. I have my own life, don't I?"

Still holding my hand, she leaned over the table looking directly into my face, and I could see her alarm, but I couldn't take it into account. I was back there at my third birthday party—mine and Jordan's—leaning forward to rake my fingers through the icing on the cake, since Mama wouldn't let me have another piece, while she was saying, "Oh, Jessie," in a sad way.

I sat bouncing Dion on my knee, trying to ease my hand from under Phoebe's without her noticing.

But before I could, Phoebe pushed her chair back from the table and stood up, reaching across to take Dion from me. I could tell she was disappointed I didn't take her problems seriously.

But I was disappointed too. And besides, I was a little hurt that Phoebe didn't seem the least bit interested in my life. The way she talked, it might have been a boring novel she put down after a page.

"You oughtn't to have put up that notice in the laundry-mat, then," I said. "Luring people out here for no reason at all."

Phoebe looked surprised. "You really believe I can read everybody the same way I can you? Well, think again, Jessie. If it was like that with everybody, I'd have to shut myself up in the house and never go out. Oh, Jessie! All those people out there with all those lives. I'd go crazy in a week."

"How come you can do this with me, then?" I said.

"I don't know, I don't know," Phoebe said, holding Dion tightly and rocking back and forth. "If anybody ever asked me if I wanted to do this, I'd have spit in their eye. Even in grade school, kids used to draw circles in the air when they saw me coming. They knew there was something funny about me even then."

I felt sorry for her, clutching Dion like a teddy bear. I didn't have to be psychic to know she'd had a tough time in life. Anybody with her gifts was bound to.

"Why listen," I told her. "We're a lot the same. They used to call me 'Goggles' in school. Short for Goggle-Eyes."

I thought Phoebe would be glad to see we had something in common, but she just went on staring at me with that sad, faraway look on her face. I thought maybe she was thinking still about old insults and humiliations.

"Look," I said then, "as far as I'm concerned, my entire past has dropped in a hole and it can stay there for all I care. If I had to go back and live through it all again I'd cut my wrists right here in your sink. It's *Dwayne* I want to know about. Not me at all."

Phoebe took a long breath and looked at me so hard I got nervous. "Remember, Jessie, I did try to tell you," she said. "Do you hear me?"

I said yes, sure, I heard her, though I didn't know just what I was agreeing to. Not then.

I followed Phoebe into the next room, where two cats— one yellow and one brindle—were lying together like yin and yang in front of the dampers of a wood stove, the heat making their fur ripple. "Sun and Moon," Phoebe said, nodding at the cats as she lifted Dion into a playpen where he dropped the clock and grabbed instead a wooden spoon and a measuring cup that he began banging together.

"Dion can't stand toys," Phoebe said. "What he likes are real things, just the same as Keith. All Keith wants to know about is fishing and tearing around on his motorcycle. Things he can get his hands on. Anything else drives him up the wall."

I didn't have to ask who Keith was. I could see *that* in Dion's face.

"Dwayne and Keith would get on just fine, then," I said. "What Dwayne loves is motors and throwing basketballs through hoops." As soon as I said that about Dwayne I felt suddenly lonesome for ordinary talk. For Phoebe and me to sit in front of the fire telling about all the worst and best things in our lives—exchanging secrets.

But even as I was having these thoughts, Phoebe was getting ready for work, lying on the couch with her head in the middle of a cushion. So I brushed cat hairs from a large, ugly chair shaped like the back end of a hippopotamus and sat facing the windows where I could see the rain streaming.

"All right, Jessie," Phoebe said, her eyes shut and her voice already sounding faraway. "You can ask your question."

I cleared my throat, feeling self-conscious though there was nobody to hear except for Dion, the cats, and Phoebe, from whatever place she'd slipped off to.

"What I've got to know," I said finally, "is whether Dwayne's dead or not. Other people think he is, but I don't think so. And now, three times in the last ten days, I've had this same dream. I see Dwayne walking down a highway, his back to me, but I know it's him all right. Same old denim jacket he always wore and a Budweiser cap pulled low. Slouching along with his hands in his pockets, really covering the ground. I'm tickled to see him and start calling out 'Dwayne, Dwayne! Everybody thought you were *dead!'* So then he stops, but when he does, I get this bad feeling like when the scary music starts up in a movie. I don't want to see after all, and stop. But he turns around, and I get a quick close-up: Dwayne grinning an awful, sinister smile like he's really put one over on me this time for sure. And then I wake up scared to death, afraid to go back to sleep."

Even then, telling the tale, I got the shivers. Goddamn Dwayne! Always the one for stupid jokes—Dracula fangs and werewolf claws and fake blood like he was nine years old.

"What does he look like?" Phoebe asked in a slowed-down way that was like hearing sounds underwater.

"Six foot four," I said. "Lanky, with huge hands and feet. Real basketball player-type. Which he was. Top scorer for Sweet Gum Virginia High School his last two years. Hair red, with a little blond in the bright sun, gets a curl to it when he forgets to get a haircut. Freckles. Kind of bony nose and jaw and small, very neat ears that stick close to his head. He has this look about him of a wiry animal. One quick on its feet, if you know what I mean."

"The last thing you know about him?"

"Jackknifing through the guardrail on that bridge over the Rappahannock, going too fast on a highway slick with rain. Right into the water. His truck, at least. It was hauled up from the depths—no question but it was Dwayne's truck—'Humpin' to Please.' One of those with a happy camel on the side, and his lucky silver dollar charm still on the dash. But Dwayne not inside. A half-open window that he could have gotten out of, but no sign of him, dead or alive. Either Dwayne got out, made it to shore and just kept on going, starting a new life as a dead man, or he *is* dead, washed up on some wild brushy place where he's never been found, picked apart by buzzards, maybe. Months since it happened. One thing, though. Dwayne was afraid of water and couldn't do anything more than dog-paddle. No matter how much he might have wanted a new life, it's hard to believe he'd choose that way to do it. He didn't even like *bridges,* to tell the truth, and used to turn a little pale on long ones."

"He wanted a new life?" Phoebe said.

"Oh, I don't know," I said, starting to feel guilty, and not for the first time, either. "Maybe he did. Doesn't everybody want a new life when you get right down to it? I sure wouldn't say no, would you?"

Phoebe didn't answer. "I'll see what I can do now, Jessie," was all she said.

So I sat with my hands in my lap looking out at the rain which, just then, made me think of water rushing up over a windshield and of awful gurgles and bubblings. It gave me the willies, the same as right after the accident when I went over it again and again, imagining that first wild slide across the pavement and then the lunge into water that took my breath every time. It did seem a bad joke that somebody afraid of water should have to drown. If he did.

Over on the couch, Phoebe's eyes were rolling under her

eyelids the same as if she were dreaming, and she was making sharp noises drawing in her breath. I wondered if maybe I should shake her shoulder to make her wake up, but I kept myself from doing it. I wanted too much to know what she was seeing.

After a while, she stopped kicking her feet and her breathing got smoother and I thought she'd gone to sleep, the same way Dion was dozing off in his playpen, curled with his back to the bars and one of the wooden spoons still in his hand.

But then she started speaking.

"The truck came down that hill too fast," Phoebe said. "Dwayne hit the brake, but then he was sliding, twisting around so fast, the wheel no good, just sailing out and him with the brake to the floor and turning the wheel, and then . . ."

"What?" I said, leaning forward to catch every word. "Cold water? Darkness?"

For a long time Phoebe didn't say anything more, although I could still see her eyes moving and a few drops of sweat gleaming on her forehead.

"Nothing," she said at last.

"Dead, you mean?" I asked, my heart sinking.

"I mean *nothing,*" Phoebe said. "I mean it ends right there. Sailing out, flash of gray sky, and then . . . nothing."

"He passed out, maybe?"

"After that minute, sliding toward the bridge, he doesn't want to be followed. A blank wall I can't get through."

"Oh, listen . . ." I said, feeling cheated.

"I can tell you one thing, though," Phoebe went on, ignoring my protest. "He wasn't by himself in that truck. There was another guy, only I can't see him clearly. There's a hat or something, low over his face, but he's tall and kind of skinny."

"Skinny?" I said. "That's the best you can tell me? How many people in the world are skinny?" Though, to be honest, as soon as she said those words I felt nudged, a little jolt of what was trying to find its way to recognition but couldn't make it.

Still, that piece of knowledge didn't seem much for all the trouble I'd gone to. The early morning ferry ride and the long bicycle trek under a lowering sky, the kind that hangs so much of the time over this part of the country up in a corner about as far away from Virginia as I could have gone. And then just to hear that Dwayne wasn't alone when he drowned or whatever it was he'd done. It didn't seem like much. But I was prepared to say thank you anyhow and take my little scrap of information away with me, hiding my disappointment in the name of graciousness. Psychic reader! That was what I got for wanting to believe in magic still, long after a time when other people gave it up.

I was bracing myself against the arms of the chair, ready to get to my feet, when Phoebe started talking again, mumbling something, and I sat back expecting to hear more about Dwayne. But it wasn't Dwayne she was talking about. Or not what I wanted to know. The same way a ball curves down from a high shot straight into the basket, not even touching the net, Phoebe had slipped back to one of those nights in my life I'd most like to forget.

". . . Greyhound bus," she was saying. "And there you

are, Jessie, fourth row on the left, wearing a silk blouse with little seed-pearl buttons, the one you picked up in that Junior League shop in Richmond. You remember the one? And your hair's all mashed up against the seat in a mess, but you aren't paying any attention because you're so upset. Looking at the ceiling of the bus and blinking to keep tears back. And look! There's Dwayne—couldn't be anybody but Dwayne—coming down the aisle looking for a place to sit, and there, now he's seen you . . ."

"No, no, no!" I said, putting my hands over my ears and drumming my heels on the floor.

"He's wearing a baseball cap with the bill turned up," Phoebe went on, as though I'd never said a word. "Sliding into that empty seat beside you like it was something he was supposed to do. Saying . . ."

"I don't want to hear this, Phoebe," I said, loud enough to wake the cats, but by then it was too late, it didn't matter if Phoebe said another thing. Now *I* was the one who couldn't stop it, the one doomed to see the whole thing play through again though I would have given anything to turn it off. Dwayne's sandy-colored eyelashes slowly blinking over those green eyes of his—moss green, money green, not sea or emerald. And those pointed incisors, one slightly crooked, that showed when he smiled. "Shoot, Jessie, I didn't know *you* were going to be on this bus," he was saying, holding onto the luggage rack as he slid down beside me. Now he was going to have somebody from down home to talk to all through the Virginia night, getting to dredge up the times he had to go to the blackboard and stand with his nose in a ring of chalk and the time he got caught in the coat closet kissing Tammy Seifert. Dwayne had known me, sort of, since first grade. Naturally he was pleased. How was he to know he'd just stepped in on one of the worst, most humiliating nights of my life?

But then something gave him warning, I guess, since he leaned forward and pushed the bill of his cap up higher on his head, as though that was what had kept him from seeing before. "Jessie?" he said. "You feel like throwing up or something? Your face looks green as grass."

And there I was, screwing up my eyes tight but tears escaping all the same, while I hit my forehead with the heels of my hands trying to make everything shut off but only crying harder then, since I felt not only humiliated but abused as well.

"Hey, hey," Dwayne kept saying—words of comfort used in his family, I supposed, as though people could be soothed the same way a team of mules could—all the while trying to worm a paper towel into my hand. "Jessie? Hey, Jess?"

But I was past comfort. As helpless as Dwayne in free-fall, turning the useless wheel of the truck right, left, spinning round and around, I forgot all about Phoebe and Dion and the rain streaming down the windows as, eyes closed, I glided through the Virginia night.

2

*P*edaling away from the ferry slip the night I visited
Phoebe, with the rain rolling off the end of my
poncho, I kept hearing a little *swish swish* noise that
seemed to be right behind me, so soft I had to strain
my ears to hear it. *Swish swish. Swish swish.* I suddenly
realized what the sound reminded me of, and the fine
hair on the nape of my neck stirred. That *swish swish*
was exactly the sound windshield wipers make sliding
the rain across glass. And as soon as I realized this,
there Dwayne was, rising up through the gloom, out of
twelve feet of water, showing those sharp teeth on
either side of his grin. I knew going to see Phoebe had
only opened a door that had let Dwayne slip through.

"Oh, Dwayne, why did you disappear?" I said into the

rain. But I was afraid to look over my shoulder for an answer, since if something terrible was following me, I didn't want to see it. I thought if Dwayne was dead, it was probably all the rain that was attracting his spirit since the last thing it had known was water. And here I'd foolishly come to a place where it rained half the time, and even when it wasn't raining, mist hung in the air, drifting through the tops of the trees and angling up the sides of the mountains. Wanting to know what had happened to Dwayne and seeing his drowned face following behind me in the night were two different things.

At Mrs. Chung's house, where I had a room, I yanked my bicycle up the steps, chained it to the railing, and fished the house key from the pocket of my jeans. All the time I was doing these things I kept my head down, afraid to look out into the darkness for fear I'd conjure up Dwayne's drowned face, hair slicked down on his white forehead. I snatched my mail from the box, pushed open the door, and bolted up the stairs, dripping water all the way, leaving brown circles on the dusty oak treads.

For once I was glad to get inside my room which smelled like mushrooms and where mildew had made little dark pockmarks in the plaster. The bed sagged, the lace curtains were tattered. Mrs. Chung had tried to liven up the place by setting milk-glass vases of wax daisies and rosebuds on the dresser, concealing the light bulbs behind pink paper parasols, and putting an ashtray as big as my hand—sporting a picture of the Grand Canyon done in pink, yellow and lavender—on one of the windowsills. Living in that room was like staying on permanently in a Chinese restaurant.

I put the limp mail on the table, hung my wet poncho

over the closet door, and pushed my sneakers off my feet. Safe! Dwayne was shut out there in the rain, Phoebe was off on her island, and I, in Mrs. Chung's moldy house, was safe under the pink parasols. I put a pan of water to boil on the hot plate and went down the hall to the bathroom, knowing that Mrs. Chung would long since have gone to bed and, I supposed, to sleep. Sometimes, when I was going out the door late in the afternoons to my job at Eddie's Oyster Bar, I'd see Mrs. Chung sitting at her kitchen table wearing a kimono with a dragon stretching itself from waist to shoulder, breathing puffs of smoke onto Mrs. Chung's neck while she sipped her tea and looked morosely out the window at her overgrown garden. We didn't have much occasion to talk to each other, but our lives were intertwined all the same. Sometimes when I was in my room during the day, dozing and looking up at the shapes the damp had made on the ceiling, I would hear Mrs. Chung coming down the hallway in her cloth slippers. Outside my doorway the padding would stop, and I'd know she was carefully bending down to look in the keyhole of my door— a good reason to leave the key in the lock. I held my breath until I heard the pad *slap,* pad *slap* of her feet going down the hallway again.

There was no Mr. Chung, but I made up stories about him. I imagined he'd brought Mrs. Chung to this ugly, squat house—a bride speaking no English—and then, one day, he'd walked out the door to buy a Sunday newspaper and had never been heard of since, leaving Mrs. Chung abandoned in a house eaten up with damp and surrounded by a garden grown wild and fervid in its own fertility. I'd seen her one day in the fall, hacking at the suckers of rose bushes with a blunt pair of shears, and had stopped to watch.

"In the house where I grew up there was also a beautiful but ruined garden," I told her, trying to bridge the gap between us. For some reason, whenever I talked to Mrs. Chung, the words came out of my mouth strangely, twisted into odd patterns. I couldn't stop myself sounding like a bad translation, the same way I couldn't stop my eye winking and my mouth twitching when I looked into the face of someone with a nervous tic, or the way I automatically whispered when I was in the presence of someone with no vocal cords. Mrs. Chung only gave me a suspicious look and went on hacking at the rose bushes with the shears. And I knew no matter what the sorrow of our lives might be—two lonesome women rattling around in that big house together—I would never be able to join her at the kitchen table to share a pot of tea while I told the story of Dwayne and she told the story of Mr. Chung.

I would sit upstairs alone, remembering the kitchen at home in Virginia where, as the sun rose as high as the tops of the hedges, the dirt dobbers would come out of their nests under the eaves to bump against the screens and try to get inside the house, which held the early morning smells of baking biscuits and hot coffee. I sighed as I made myself a cup of watery cocoa and took it to bed with me to drink while I looked through the mail. I had become the kind of woman who could take comfort from a cup of cocoa while she read about Turf Builder—that was what loneliness did to a person.

Between the Puget Power bill and an advertisement for lawn chairs on sale, I saw the only envelope that counted—

one that was crisp and white, with the address written across it in Mama's firm handwriting. Mama's handwriting was perfectly legible and did not swing either up or down in its progress across the envelope—the handwriting of someone who believed firmly in what the human will could achieve. I was the one whose world was strange, unpredictable, and often malevolent to no purpose, except that whoever or whatever was in power had a sense of humor I didn't care for. It was no wonder when I was growing up Mama and I had often been at serious cross-purposes with each other. She and Jordan—now comfortably settled as an attorney at Snellgrove, Hardy, and Carstairs in Richmond —had more often seen eye to eye.

The envelope bulged, and I saw Mama had had to put two first-class stamps on it to bring it across the country to me. But this often happened, since in addition to the letter Mama wrote once a week, she often included clippings from the *Sweet Gum Express*—descriptions of weddings and notices of funerals and accounts of birthday parties given for the children of people I'd gone to school with. I just glanced at these and threw them in the wastebasket, not being nearly as curious about the life in Sweet Gum as Mama supposed I was.

This time, however, I saw that the envelope wasn't made heavy by newspaper clippings but rather by an extra letter —one, I saw in an instant, from Jordan. I was in the habit of letting my eyes merely skim over the dutiful notes Jordan sent me, passing over those words the same way my eye flitted over the hard, chunky squares of caramel in a box of chocolates—the kind I never ate. I thought it was sneaky of

Jordan to slip one of his letters in with Mama's where he knew I couldn't ignore it.

But the reasons I didn't read Jordan's letters were not the ones I imagined he thought they were. He probably thought I was too angry with him to want to read anything he might choose to tell me—I would wad up his letters and throw them furiously across the room, to hit the wall before they bounced into the wastebasket. He would never guess the reason I didn't read his letters was that the sight of them seared my heart. I could feel it curl in on itself the way burning paper curls inward before it falls into ashes. To be betrayed by Jordan. That was the one thing I'd never expected.

So I dropped Jordan's letter onto the bed and picked up Mama's. The first page took me through the bluebells and the jonquils and three litters of healthy baby pigs. Then it was Sophie and her back, which was acting up again, and Mama's debate about whether or not she should trade in the Buick this year or wait until next.

The first part of Mama's letters was about the farm, the second part about the town. I didn't always read the town parts of her letters, but this time my eye was caught by the name Eula—Dwayne's mother's name—and so I read on.

Saw Eula Hawkins in Food Lion a couple of days ago. She was fingering the bananas and pretending not to see me, but I stopped right in front of her and said, "Well, hello, Eula," so of course she had to look up. Oh, if looks could kill! Biting nails—that's how sour she was. "Hi," she said finally, her face just like a stove lid. I was

*moving on, my duty done, when to my back, to my back
mind you, she said, "Laying in a store for the weekend?
That boy of yours coming home, I reckon?" I told her yes.
Jordan was coming over from Richmond. "Your boy can
come home for the weekend," she said, her eyes sliding
around everywhere except on my face, "while my boy lies
in a watery grave. And whose fault's that? You tell me." I
just looked at her. "You know very well Dwayne lost
control of that truck on a wet pavement," I told her.
"Dwayne's fault if it's anybody's." I could've killed that
woman, bringing up all this in the middle of Food Lion,
with everybody in produce straining their ears. Even then
she wouldn't let it go. Smiled this ugly smile and said, "I
know and the good Lord knows who drove Dwayne to it.
We know." "Just what is that?" I said, my voice cold as
ice. But naturally she wouldn't answer, rustling around in
the bananas like a big rat of some kind. Oh, it galls me
so, having a woman like that making snide remarks every
time our paths happen to cross.*

I dropped Mama's letter on the bed and put my hand
over my eyes, shutting out the pink light. What had
Dwayne's mother meant when she said I'd driven him to it?
Did she think it was because of me Dwayne drove his truck
into the Rappahannock? This wasn't anything I wanted to
contemplate, lying on Mrs. Chung's bed, shielding my eyes
from the pink parasol.

Instead I picked up Jordan's letter from the bed, holding
it by one edge and almost at arm's length. What leaped out
at me, even from that distance, was this:

What do you think you're trying to prove, running off to a place as far away from Virginia as you can get? You think the truth won't find you out there? Running away from the mess you've made of things, that's so much like you. Never in your life have you been willing to face facts.

I let Jordan's letter drop to the floor. The self-righteousness! The certainty he, and only he, knew the truth! It made me grind my teeth.

And yet, in spite of everything, what I wanted at that moment was to have Jordan sitting in the old bamboo chair that tipped to one side whenever anybody sat in it, and to have him call me JayJay as he'd done when we were five and had a language of our own. I wanted him there sitting hunched over his knees, laughing with his eyes squinched nearly shut, saying, "Oh, JayJay, I couldn't get along without you."

But the Jordan I was thinking about was the Jordan from long ago. The grown-up Jordan, the one I'd get if he came to Washington to pay me a visit, was one I'd rather forget about. *That* Jordan crossed his legs carefully so as not to crush the crease in his trousers, leaning back like a judge, with the tips of his fingers just touching and with a hateful little smile at the corner of his mouth.

"Jessie," I could hear him say, putting on his lawyer voice, "tell the truth now. Why did Dwayne go tearing off that day in his truck, far too fast on a wet pavement? Wouldn't you say he was in an agitated state of mind?"

"No!" I said. "Leave me alone, Jordan."

"Well, wasn't he?" Jordan went on. "Wasn't he so upset his judgment . . ."

"It's not my fault!" I cried. "You want to know whose fault it is? You really want to know? Because listen, Jordan, it all comes straight into your lap from the very beginning. Every bit of it is your fault, that's whose."

But the smile on Jordan's face, I knew, would be totally calm and superior, removed from the fray.

I was the one to take fright, to leap wildly out of bed and run to the closet, root out my duffle bag and drag it into the middle of the room where it lay like a cowed dog. I could throw everything into it and take off in the night for a place it would take both Jordan and Dwayne a lot of time to find. If Dwayne was attracted to water, I could probably lose him in the desert where water seldom fell.

But as I crouched beside the duffle bag, my feet going cold with nothing between them and the floorboards except a thin rug, I calmed down. After all, I knew Jordan wasn't about to come knocking on my door in the middle of the night. He was far too careful, too cautious, for any move like that.

And as for Dwayne, I figured he was safely shut out there in the rain, in his own element. "Listen, Dwayne," I said slyly. "I'll leave you alone if you'll leave me alone. Deal?"

He didn't say yes and he didn't say no. There was no sign out of Dwayne, no white drowned face at the window and no little scratchings on the door. He didn't bother me at all when I got back into bed and pulled the sheet over my head, leaving the light on to make a pink glow.

3

*I*t was a busy time at Eddie's—Friday, when people finish work for the week and want to celebrate—and I was assembling salads, getting orders set up on trays and helping out Fred, the main cook, whenever I had a minute, while my mind clocked through all those things I had to do. And so when Agnes, one of the waitresses, came up to my elbow and said in a low voice, "Somebody wants to see you a minute out front," I just went on slicing radishes over the bowls of salad, not wanting to take my attention away. But it's true, the moment she spoke I thought, Oh Lord. It's Jordan, come from Virginia. I took a handful of croutons and began dropping them over the radishes, giving myself a chance to calm down. But of course the longer I put off going to look the less calm I got, so by the time I wiped my hands on my apron, they were shaking so much I had trouble loosening the tie.

It was Jordan's blond hair I searched for wildly when I came through the side door into the dining area, dancing from one foot to the other in my agitation. If I saw him first, before he saw me, I might make a run for it—past the cashier and on out the door before he got a glimpse. Though what I ought to do was march directly to his table and tell him straight off, "Jordan, you bastard, I'll never forgive you for what you've done to me. Never, never, never. Not if you live to be a hundred."

I was practicing this speech and still looking for blond hair when Agnes, passing by with a loaded tray, caught my eye and tipped her head sideways, toward the door of the restaurant.

Even when I first saw Phoebe, standing beside the coats with Dion asleep over her shoulder, it didn't strike me that she was the one who had come to see me; Jordan was still too firmly in my head.

Only when Phoebe motioned, waving her arm like someone trying to reel in a fish, did I go and pull her beyond the coats so we were in the entrance hallway and out of Eddie's direct line of vision. He didn't like the kitchen workers to go out front when they were on the job.

My thoughts were so much on other things I didn't look closely at Phoebe until we were standing in the hallway with our shoulders pressed against the wall. I didn't notice until then, when she grabbed my wrist, what a freaked-out look she had in her eyes. I would have taken a step backward, only I couldn't, the way she was holding on. She had the bruised, abused look of a child somebody has been mean to.

"Jessie," she said, her eyes looking so far into mine that what they might have been observing was the back of my skull, "I've been seeing things."

"Things?" I said wildly. "What things? What things are you talking about?"

Phoebe shook her head from side to side with a fixed, glassy look in her eyes that alarmed me considerably.

"You've seen Dwayne?" I said, imagining the grinning skull with a tuft or two of red hair still clinging to the crown.

Phoebe leaned against the wall, pushing Dion higher up on her shoulder, where he made snuffling noises in his sleep. "No, no, not Dwayne," she said. "Not Dwayne at all. It's something else."

"Well, what then?" I said, getting exasperated. "What have you been seeing?"

Her head was turned in my direction, but I didn't think it was me she was looking at. "A doorknob," she said in a faraway voice.

*"Door*knob!" I said. "What are you *talk*ing about, Phoebe? You came all this way to tell me you've been seeing doorknobs?"

"One doorknob," Phoebe said.

"Okay. One doorknob. What can be so important about a doorknob that you have to come all this way to tell me about it?"

"It's white," she said, in that faraway voice. "With these little cracks in it and shaped exactly like an eyeball."

As she spoke, a shudder went down my backbone since I knew very well the doorknob she was talking about and I had the feeling I had known too, from the first moment she spoke. I could see it as well as if it were right there above my face, drooping on its long stem, with those brown cracks so tiny not even my fingernail could find them out. I knew if I touched the doorknob it would rattle like everything else in that house with all those boards and joints and pegs and four-sided nails creaking and groaning.

"Oh, I know that doorknob," I said in a bitter voice. "You don't have to tell me what that doorknob looks like."

"And there's this big bed," Phoebe went on in that flat, faraway voice that meant she was going into a trance. "Some kind of animal carved on it. And there's a boy with blond hair. A pretty, pretty boy all flushed with fever . . ."

I shook her, hard, her head bobbing, until I shook that faraway look from her face and she saw me in the here and now, a hangdog expression in her eyes.

"Be quiet, Phoebe," I whispered, easing my hands from her shoulders. "Will you be quiet now?"

I could feel eyes on my back and knew Agnes was watching us as she walked up and down between her tables.

Phoebe rubbed the back of her neck and hoisted Dion higher on her shoulder as she gave me a sickly smile.

"When pictures start coming in my head like that, I have to go on," she said. "I have to *see*. I can't just say stop and they'll stop. Oh, you don't know what it's like, Jessie. And when I get spacey like this, Keith can't stand it. I can see him getting all edgy and I know what he's thinking. All he wants is to jump on his motorcycle and go. Far off distances in his eyes."

She put her hand on my arm, that warm, damp little hand, and it made my skin crawl, the way she held on.

"Oh no," I told her. "You can't dump this in my lap. Whatever crazy thoughts you get in your head don't have anything to do with me. They aren't my fault."

"You know I didn't want to let you in the house when you came to see me," Phoebe said, and to my horror I could see tears welling up in her eyes. "But I did, didn't I? I opened the door, and you came right in."

"Eddie's got his eye on you," Agnes said over my shoulder. But it was Phoebe she stared at.

"I'm coming," I said, waving my hand to show I was doing what I could. "Listen, Phoebe," I told her. "You can see I'm at work. I've got to go."

"I think maybe I've missed the last ferry," she said in a miserable voice, and I said oh shit, but I could see I was caught, trapped, and couldn't just tell her to get lost.

"Look, here's my key," I said, digging deep in the pocket of my jeans to find it. "You can sleep in my room tonight and catch the first ferry in the morning."

I told her how to find Mrs. Chung's house, and she nodded her head to show she understood, but she didn't look either pleased with my offer or grateful. And this made me feel sour.

"Who was *that?*" Agnes said, cornering me by the serving station on my way through the kitchen.

"Oh, just somebody I know," I said as offhand as I could. Agnes meant well, but she was a busybody too, keeping her eye on everybody else's business.

"She putting the make on you for money?" Agnes said, giving me a sharp look as she slid her order onto her tray.

"She's got this baby . . ." I started, but Agnes didn't let me get far.

"Oh, I know her type. One of those leftover '60s people," she said in disdain. "You have to watch out for those. Real cases, a lot of them are."

I wondered what Agnes thought about me, if she didn't think I was a case of some kind too. But if she thought so, at least she kept this to herself.

4

*W*hen I got back to my room at Mrs. Chung's at midnight, I expected to find Phoebe waiting up for me, ready to start in again about the eyeball-shaped doorknob that was haunting her, and I'd braced myself for this, getting more and more irate as I climbed the stairs two at a time, avoiding the middle of the tread where the creak was the loudest. But when I flung open the door to my room, all ready to speak my piece, I found Phoebe and Dion sprawled on my bed, so deeply asleep neither of them stirred when I turned on the light.

That baby just better not pee on my mattress was what I thought, looking down at them. Phoebe at least could have taken the sofa, and she would have, in my

opinion, if she was a person who gave any thought to another's comfort. But she wasn't. I could already have
guessed that. Of course, she was like a child, taking what
she could get, thinking to give back only on rare occasions.
It wouldn't have occurred to *her* to wonder how I was going
to fit on that sofa, tall as I am, and the sofa one of those
old-fashioned kinds with high, rolled arms. Phoebe could
probably have fit on that sofa without even bending her
knees, but *me!* I would have to lie with my knees pulled up
to my chin.

I had my hand out, just reaching for her shoulder to
shake it so I could say, Wake up, you bed hog, I choose
sleeping with a wet baby to folding myself up like a praying
mantis, but she was sleeping so soundly, with her mouth
open against the pillow, I didn't have the heart to do it.

Instead I took the top blanket and wrapped myself in it
like a mummy with only my face showing and folded myself up on the sofa. I didn't expect to sleep like that, but I
must have, since I had one dream after another, and in all
of them I moved through the rooms of Clearwater, back
home in Virginia, where Sophie was stirring up bad-smell-
ing doctoring on the stove. I could hear Mama and Jordan
whispering together in the corners of the house as I stalked
them through the upstairs hallway with Daddy's pistol in
my hand and a sinking feeling in my heart, knowing this
time I was going to shoot them both dead. I knew, even in
the dream, I'd already fastened my hand over that cool,
slick doorknob, the one shaped like an eye, and the door
had swung open.

When I opened my eyes at first light, it was to hear
Phoebe say, using Mama's inflections exactly, "Are you two

going to get out there and feed those horses or am I going to have to do that too, along with everything else?" and I groaned as I looked over at her nursing Dion, who was grunting and snuffling. Her eyes held that fixed, distant look, and I knew exactly how Keith felt when all he wanted was to jump on his motorcycle and keep going, any direction except the one where Phoebe talked in that faraway dream voice about what she could see under her closed eyelids.

"Phoebe!" I yelled at her. "Snap out of it."

"Sophie, those biscuits are ready to come out of the oven," Phoebe told me, Virginia perfect in her voice. It was spooky.

I shook her until she said, "What's the matter, Jessie?" in her own little-girl voice.

"You sounded exactly like Mama just now," I told her.

"If I shut my eyes, there I am," Phoebe said. "There's the stable, the pond, I can see the hay fields . . ."

"You don't have to tell me what's there, I know every inch," I told her. "But that's no sign I want to hear about it every minute."

"I never asked for this either. You think I did? Remember, I didn't want to let you in the house in the first place. I warned you, didn't I?"

"Big deal," I said. "Did I know what you meant? Of course I didn't."

We glared at each other, both feeling hard done by, while Phoebe expertly shifted Dion from one breast to the other, pushing the crystal and bear claw around her neck to one side while Dion made frustrated squealing noises, exactly the way shoats carried on at the trough.

"People always act like it's my fault when this happens," Phoebe said, and I could see she was going to cry again. "But it's not! I can't help it! I can't get those pictures out of my head, and they drive me crazy."

"Well, they drive me crazy too," I said, but Phoebe was crying again, as I'd known she was going to, with tears falling onto her shirt.

I turned on my hot plate so I could at least make us coffee before Phoebe caught the ferry, telling myself to watch it. Be careful. I thought there was a real chance every word Phoebe said might have been an act of some kind, part of some scheme she'd hatched up to get money out of me, just the way Agnes suggested. And I was suspicious, though I didn't know which direction the danger lay.

"Phoebe?" I said, as casually as I could while I measured coffee into cups. "Where did I used to go and hide when I didn't want to be found by anybody? Back home, I'm talking about now."

She didn't have to shut her eyes for that one. She knew right away.

"You'd go under the hedge in that overgrown part of the yard where the fish pond was. Crawling under there to talk to that statue of a boy that got hidden by the bushes. Little wings sticking out of his shoulders. Wild Boy, you called him."

"What was Mama's favorite kind of pie?"

"Chess."

"Jordan's?"

"Key lime."

"What did Sophie keep in the cupboard above the stove, left-hand side?"

"Sassafras roots. Dried cocklebur leaves. Jimsonweed flowers. Stuff she boiled up for doctoring when she didn't feel good."

I pondered the next one, trying to come up with something harder.

"Tell me what MawMaw said that time she came to visit after Jordan and I had scarlet fever. Say what Mama said and what MawMaw said, and what I felt about it all."

Phoebe waited a few seconds on that one, sitting very still with her eyes shut.

"Well, MawMaw came in and sat down in the wing chair by the fireplace, and you and Jordan had to go kiss her, and then she said, 'Why, Sarah Eve, whatever has happened to Jessie? She's gone plain as a post, poor child,' and Mama said, 'It's just a lazy eye that will probably straighten up in time.' And MawMaw said, 'Why you've let Jordan run away with all the looks. Far more good looks than a boy ought to have. You ought to get his picture painted.' And, Jessie, you hadn't known until that moment right then that you and Jordan didn't look alike and, besides, that he was beautiful and you were ugly."

"All right," I said grimly. "That's enough."

I handed Phoebe a cup of coffee without asking her about cream or sugar. I was not feeling generous toward her at that moment.

I took my own cup over to the window and sat on the bamboo chair, looking out over the water turning rosy as the sun came up, blowing on my coffee in a brooding kind of way and avoiding even looking in Phoebe's direction. I wasn't afraid of her exactly, but she gave me the creeps. Even her beauty had taken on a sinister cast.

Oddly enough, she didn't seem to know how I was feeling toward her. As much as she knew about some things, there were others she was dim about.

"I know how your daddy died," she said in a happy voice. "I can see that plain as plain. You and Jordan are crawling across the floor in his room, daring each other to touch that brass horse on the little table under the window. You think he's asleep but all of a sudden you hear him making awful 'Eeeeee' noises, and when you whirl around he's pushing himself up out of his chair, his bulgy eyes looking right at you, still saying 'Eeeee' and turning brick red in the face, purple almost, and then he falls straight to the floor like a tree blowing over in a wind and you and Jordan jump up and run like rabbits, making little crying noises because you're so scared."

I knew at that moment it wasn't trickery I had to deal with in Phoebe. Uncanny was what it was. I could see the goose bumps on my arms.

"I have never told another soul about seeing Daddy die, and Jordan hasn't either. At the time we thought it was our fault. Though of course it was a stroke, really. I do not see how you could know what you seem to."

"I told you I could see everything," Phoebe said, looking pleased with herself. "I'm batting a thousand, Jessie. Ask me another."

I blew on my coffee and looked out the window. I didn't like it, the way Phoebe had come into my life knowing all she did. Nothing safe. I didn't even want to look at her, she gave me such a strange feeling.

"So tell me where Dwayne is," I said. "If you know everything else. That's the one thing I want to know."

"It's you I can tell things about. Not Dwayne. Ask me one about you."

"Tell me why I hate Jordan, then," I said. "Tell me that one if you know so much."

Phoebe was silent, looking suddenly downcast and sad, all the joy gone from her face.

"You don't want me to tell you that. You only asked that question because you want me to leave."

I went on looking out the window. I didn't say no.

Sadly she lowered Dion to the bed and reached underneath for her sneakers. "I can just catch the first ferry if I go now," she said, though even then she sat with her sneakers in her hands, hesitating to put them on.

I knew she wanted me to say, Oh, stay a little longer, Phoebe. Stay and eat some breakfast at least. The look she gave me as she tied her laces was pleading. But I didn't say anything. I didn't want her in my room another second, telling about things I wanted to forget.

"Jessie?" she said at the door.

But I told her to hurry or she'd miss the ferry. And when she heard that hard note in my voice, she went on out and shut the door softly behind her.

5

*O*nce Phoebe reminded me of that doorknob shaped like an eyeball, the doorknob to the door of the bedroom I'd shared with Jordan until we were well past ten and Mama suddenly decided we were too old to sleep together anymore, it kept coming back to me at unexpected moments—not just the doorknob itself, of course, but the entire life hidden away behind it.

Sitting on the bus on one of my trips to the supermarket, I would suddenly see the satisfied, catlike look on Jordan's face as Aunt Lillian drew him over to the chair where she was sitting, giving him a hug without once losing the train of what she was talking about to Mama, while I stood rocking back and forth in the doorway, watching, a black rage in my heart, a scowl on my lips.

Slicing radishes at Eddie's, I suddenly saw two honey-colored heads of hair, bent down together—Jordan and Mama walking down the lane to the stable on a summer evening, laughing together, no time for anybody else.

"Oh shit," I said, and instantly cut my finger with the slicing knife so I had to bind up the loose flap of skin with two Band-Aids and wear a disposable glove on one hand.

I snarled at waitresses wanting their orders, once even waving a knife in the air in a menacing way when Mandy, who was small and dimpled and cute, told me to hurry up —table six had been waiting nearly ten minutes for their salads.

Eddie kept an eye on me in a musing kind of way, and only Agnes, who was subject to moodiness herself, ignored my bad temper.

It's peculiar, when I look back, that I didn't realize until the time MawMaw paid a visit after Jordan and I had scarlet fever that, even though we were twins, Jordan and I didn't look the least bit alike. I think this fact was lost on me because when we were very little Mama dressed us just the same—tartan shorts for Jordan, tartan skirt for me, blue velvet jacket for Jordan, blue velvet jacket for me—so when people saw us they always said, "Oh, *twins!* Aren't they cute," lumping us together.

When we were babies, I cried when Jordan did and he cried when I did—making a terrible din, Mama said—but when one of us laughed the other did too. We made up words together that nobody else understood, and I'm certain when we were small we passed thoughts between us so lightning fast we often didn't need words at all. Since I saw far more of Jordan's face than I did of my own, maybe it wasn't surprising I supposed I looked just the way he did. When I looked into his face it was exactly the same as looking into my own—that's what I thought.

I never noticed how my hair was rusty colored while his was like gold, never saw that although his eyes were deep blue, mine were a washed-out hazel. It's true that sometimes after people said how cute we were someone would remark, "Oh, the little girl is bigger than the little boy." But although I heard this remark, it didn't make any impression on me. There was Jordan, every minute of the day and night, as much a part of me as my arm was, or my foot. I didn't notice I was taller.

But after we had scarlet fever and MawMaw came to visit, everything was changed. After that, when I looked into a mirror, I *saw,* and what I saw was somebody with a broad jaw of the kind that in snakes indicates deadliness, a chin and forehead trying to come together with a nose squashed in between, thick glasses that made my eyes look small and squinched.

And I knew this wasn't in the least the way Jordan looked, with his thick, gold-colored hair, his large, heavily lashed blue eyes, a face like an angel on one of my Sunday school cards.

So it was at that moment, when I looked in a mirror and saw what there was to see, I lost Jordan. Everything changed and Jordan became instantly the Youngest Son in all the fairy tales Mama read us at night, the one who would win the hand of the princess and be showered with riches. But I saw I was one of the uglies, the kind who never get anything except their toes cut off or pushed headfirst into an oven while everyone else rejoiced. We remained stupidly and unrepentantly bad no matter what happened to us. We never reformed, never became one of the favored ones. A race apart, separated forever from what Sophie called the Fair-Haired Ones, Sophie who came from the hills and believed in charms and potions, in magical changes.

"I known this old woman once, said a spell on the girl her boy was fixing to marry," Sophie told me while I was helping her roll out pie dough. "And I'm here to tell you that girl's skin turned into a hide like a snake's within the week. Shiny and scaly, just like a snake. No way of covering *that* up with long sleeves. The boy married her anyway, but you know it never worked out."

"Why not?" I wanted to know.

"How would you like to sleep every night in the same bed with a person looking like a snake?" Sophie said. "That old scaly skin right next to yours?"

"I wouldn't do it," I said. "But how did that woman get the girl to turn into a snake in the first place?"

"Things a body says and spells they make."

"You know them?" I asked slyly. "The spells a body says?"

But Sophie just laughed, showing her little brown, knobby teeth.

"Oh, if I put those words in your mouth your MawMaw'd go off from here with her scales shining, wouldn't she?"

"She'd have to scoot out the door on her fat old stomach," I agreed. "And Mama would have to take the hoe to her like she does to snakes that crawl in the stable."

Sophie sometimes winked at me as I watched her mash down the bread dough or layer a chocolate cake, and I was sure she knew I had a black heart the same way she did.

"When I'm ten?" I begged. "Will you tell me the spells when I'm ten?"

But Sophie just laughed, wagging her head back and forth. "You won't need me to tell you, sweetheart," she said. "Oh no, you won't need me, nobody with a heart as black as yours."

I could see it plain, a black valentine giving off a soft sheen like velvet.

But because Sophie and I were two of a kind, she couldn't help teasing me. She was the one who saw the wild, black looks I gave Jordan when Mama gave him a kiss or singled him out to go riding with her late in the afternoons when the serious work of the day was over. Then Sophie would laugh and shake her apron at me and say, "Jessie's eyes just turned green, green. See that? Stick her with a pin and she'll pop."

I went wild when Sophie teased me, but the wildness helped to cover over the mean feelings I had. A gulf lay between Jordan and me, and I felt lost and forlorn, cut off from what had made me happy.

Yet there were times when Jordan was sitting curled up in one of the wing chairs in the sitting room when I would secretly watch him, studying him the same way I stared sometimes at the painting of our great-grandfather hanging above the sideboard. I looked at him so long I seemed to forget what I was staring at was *Jordan's* face and saw it fresh, as I would have seen the face of some total stranger, and when this happened his beauty took my breath and for a few seconds I would fall into a joyful, dreamy state of pleasure. I could have looked at him all day and not gotten tired. And I knew then why he was singled out, and I could even understand it—beautiful things made me happy too. I felt awed by his beauty and, for a brief time, not even jealous of it. Surely there was a reason he'd been chosen for such good fortune, and the reason must be he deserved it somehow.

And when, after I'd been staring at Jordan for a long time, he would finally lift his eyes from his book and smile at me, my heart would swell with joy. I was in the magic circle too. Included! I wished I could always be in that state since then maybe I wouldn't be mean, and the blackness of my heart would fade to something like eggshell color.

But then, in a moment, Jordan would leap to his feet, throw his book into the chair, and tell me not to stare at him like that.

"I know what you're doing," he would say darkly.

"What?" I'd ask, already belligerent, on the defensive.

"Bugging me."

And he would stalk off to be by himself, leaving me raging, my heart growing blacker and blacker until I could feel it glowing like a lump of burning coal inside my chest.

6

"If somebody comes around here looking for me, you'll let me know, won't you?" I said to Agnes a couple of nights after Phoebe came into the restaurant.

"The one that was in here the other night?" she said, giving me a sharp look. "The girl with the baby?"

"Her or anybody else. Woman or man."

"Well naturally I'll let you know," Agnes said. "But you'd better watch out. Getting mixed up with a lot of screwball people."

"I can take care of myself," I told her.

Agnes snorted and gave me a raised-eyebrow look. All single women were in danger of having terrible advantage taken of them—that was what she thought.

So I wasn't surprised when she asked if I didn't want to go on a drive with her the next Monday when Eddie's was closed for the day. I should be keeping better company, should hang out with ordinary, normal people. I knew what she was thinking.

On Monday, then, I sat beside Agnes, who was hunched forward over the steering wheel of her little Fiat, urging it on its steep climb up the Mount Baker highway, its motor making a wheezy humming like the purr of a very old cat.

"You might know Lyle would get the best car when we split," Agnes said. "He told me since it was just me, I didn't need the station wagon. He needed it for Betsy Wetsy and her two little boys. And I didn't say no, big dummy that I am. Naturally he didn't tell me the Fiat needed a ring job though he must have known it, the way he always had his head stuck under the hood. He put one over on me is what he did."

"At least you've *got* a car," I said.

Agnes snorted. "Some car," she said.

We'd reached the snow that lay near the top of the mountain, and the fog hanging above it turned the tops of the fir trees ghostly. That landscape up there, the dark trees and the cliffs of jagged black rock, gave me the creeps.

"See if I've got a cigarette down in my purse somewhere, would you?" Agnes said.

"I'll look," I said quickly. "You just keep your eyes on the road."

Agnes stuck the cigarette I found her between pursed lips, and I lighted it with a lighter. Her eyes squeezed nearly shut as she drew in the smoke.

"You didn't get even a car out of that husband of yours, huh?" she asked when she let the smoke go.

I'd told Agnes early on that I was divorced too, since this was the easiest explanation I could give for my circumstances, and this was the main thing that had induced Agnes to make a friend of me. She saw us as being in the same boat since we were lone women, making our way with a lot of hardship and pain. Of course Agnes was curious about my past. She especially wanted to know what it was about Dwayne that made him impossible to live with—our fights, those were what she wanted to hear in detail—but I was vague about all that, implying it was still too sore in my mind to be talked about.

"Nope," I told her. "No car."

In fact I hadn't even gotten the money on Dwayne's life insurance since his body had never been found.

"Oh, screw 'em," Agnes said, throwing her cigarette over the edge of the mountain. Remembering Lyle's perfidy fueled Agnes' rage, and she forced the little car hard around the curves, wheels singing. I put my hand on the door handle, ready to leap if necessary, though I was pretty sure there wouldn't be time for that if the car did miss a curve and we were flung out. Luckily the mist covered the drop below us so I couldn't see the horrible rocks waiting down there. But just before we reached the top of the mountain, the mist suddenly cleared, and we emerged into sunshine, which lay dazzling on the white tops of the mountains in the distance. It took my breath, and I was afraid to look down where, without even a guardrail to stop us, the car would land if we fell.

"Oh, say, look at that," Agnes said, taking one hand off the wheel to make a proprietary sweep through the air.

"Pretty, pretty," I said, alarmed, my lazy eye sliding upward to fix itself on the ceiling of the car. Fear nearly always made it drift off.

But the sight of the mountains, which filled me with great disquiet, made a gentle look come over Agnes' face. "It helps me to get my head together, to come up here," she said.

All I cared about was that we'd reached the top and were coming into the parking lot among all the cars with ski racks on their roofs, safely away from the edge of the mountain. Relief gave me something to be grateful for, and I grew expansive and talkative. Even a little light-headed.

"I bet I never told you before that I have a twin," I said to Agnes as the little Fiat drew in behind a large Dodge van and came to a stop.

"You're kidding!" Agnes said. "Really? I've never known anybody who was a twin before. Identical?"

"No, no," I said, laughing uneasily. "He's my brother so he couldn't be identical to me, could he? Look. Want to see?"

I'd taken my billfold out of my bag and flipped the plastic holder of photographs until I came to one of Jordan taken in his second year of law school.

I could tell it was only from politeness that Agnes held up the photograph to the light, expecting, no doubt, a male version of me—another square-jawed somebody with a long thin mouth and thick glasses. So of course when she got a good look at Jordan, Agnes made a little throttled noise, like one struck with a tiny poisoned arrow.

"Oh, hey," she said, bending over the picture. "He's better looking than Robert Redford. He's gorgeous."

"Yeah, well, he is, I guess," I said, already disgusted with myself.

From the corner of my eye I could see Jordan looking directly out of the photograph, not bothering to smile. With that straight nose and the thick blond hair falling over his forehead—he'd needed a haircut when the picture was taken—he didn't have to smile.

"Not much of a family resemblance, is there?" I said, reaching out for the photograph and folding it away again.

"Well . . ." Agnes said, but not even politeness could take her further than that.

"I take after Daddy in looks and Jordan takes after Mama," I said. "If we weren't twins it wouldn't be as noticeable, I guess."

"Is he married?" Agnes said, suddenly looking shy. "Your brother?"

"No," I said. "But you're not the first woman to ask."

I always got the same response when I showed somebody Jordan's photograph, which I did with tiresome regularity, using it as a touchstone of some kind, and I was invariably left feeling annoyed and vaguely cheated. Maybe what I was looking for was the person who would take one look at Jordan's photograph and be overcome with horror, understanding in one flash of perfect empathy the truth. What it was really like for me, having Jordan for a brother.

But Agnes was like all the others. As we climbed out of the car, I could tell she regarded me with more respect than she had before, but as for me, she had slipped in my estimation. I could tell she kept looking over at me when my head was turned, checking up to see if maybe she'd missed something earlier. That maybe I was hiding my beauty under a bushel, and if I would just wear my hair in a different way I might be suddenly transformed. But soon a discouraged look came over her face, and she stopped giving me sly looks.

I'd told Agnes that under no circumstances would I attach a couple of waxed boards to my feet, and she'd said that was okay. We'd just hike around and take a look at things. So now she took out of the back of the car a knapsack that I was sure contained chocolate bars and extra sweaters and probably even a compass and flashlight in case we got lost. Agnes made a point of showing she could take care of herself no matter what conditions she found herself in. Just because she was a woman on her own, she wasn't dependent on anyone or anything.

I followed Agnes up the slopes where the cross-country skiers were making their slow, pigeon-toed ascent, and came up to the ridge that lay in a half-circle around the valley. Agnes climbed in front of me in a kind of loose-jointed way that I recognized as being how she moved in the evenings between the tables in the restaurant and the kitchen. There was something about the easy way she swung her hips that said she didn't give a damn; she wasn't about to let anybody bother her. She moved along over the shiny crust of snow without once deigning to look down to see where she'd go if she slipped.

Behind her, I made my slow way, sometimes on all fours like a dog, keeping my eyes on the dents her boots made in the snow. Once or twice I called out "Agnes!" in a wavery voice, but she was too far ahead to hear, and by this time I was more afraid of going back down the slope alone than I was of plodding on ahead. As long as I walked stooped over with my fingers touching the snow, I didn't think I would fall, only look a fool which was, after all, a condition I was used to. My whole life felt to me as precarious as crawling along that icy ridge, and it was this, probably, that gave the scene a kind of nightmarish glow. Even the sky above my head which my lazy eye insisted on studying—a sweet, pure blue untouched by cloud—seemed sinister.

I was panting and sweat was rolling off the tip of my nose by the time I reached the top of the slope, where Agnes was already crouched on her heels, idly studying the skiers down below with a pair of binoculars she'd taken from her pack.

"Some view, huh?" Agnes said as I sank down beside her.

"Oh great, great," I said, keeping my eyes on the far horizon where mountain and sky met.

The feeling in my stomach was the same one I'd felt when I got word about Dwayne's truck going off the bridge.

"It's going to take me a long while to get down again, sliding on my seat," I warned her.

Agnes grinned, her eyes closing to little slits, and reached over to pat me on the leg. "Relax," she said. "From here, don't you think the rest of the world looks small? On top like this, I don't even believe in Lyle or money worries or the car falling apart. I *enjoy* myself up here."

My own thoughts were far from joyous or even easy. I was surrounded by worries and could take my pick.

"Agnes," I said, "would you believe it if somebody took one look and told you they could see your entire past flashing like a movie in front of their face? All those things you'd nearly forgotten yourself?"

"You think I'd fall for something like that?" Agnes said contemptuously. "No way."

"Yeah, but listen," I said. "If you went to somebody like that and the very first thing she told you was you had a twin? When she couldn't have known?"

"Wait a minute," Agnes said. "Hold on. Did she really say, 'You've got a twin?' or did she say something like 'There's someone very close to you, someone . . . it *could* be a relative, but someone you have a very tight relationship with . . .'"

"Her exact words were 'Don't you have a double?'" I said.

"See? See?" Agnes said triumphantly. "A double wouldn't necessarily have to be a twin, would it?"

"She even knew what kind of cake I had for my third birthday party," I said glumly.

"But what kind of use is a little detail like that?" Agnes said, disgusted. "She might as well have told you you were wearing yellow socks your first day of kindergarten. Who cares? What difference does it make?"

"Then she told me Mama slapped my hand when I reached for a third piece of cake, and she's right. I started yelling, and Mama said, 'Oh shoot! Oh damn! I didn't mean to do that. Come here, baby,' But I wouldn't do it. I sulled up for the rest of the day."

Agnes didn't seem impressed with anything I'd told her. She opened up her backpack and handed me one of the chocolate bars she'd brought along. Hershey. Not my favorite. But I peeled back the paper and started eating the bar anyway.

"Listen, Jessie," Agnes said, chewing hard on chocolate like a horse on corn. "You don't want to get mixed up with all that funny stuff. What you want to do is take hold of your life and show it who's boss. The only thing I had to do was just say straight out one day I wasn't going to take any more crap off anybody, not from that moment on. And as soon as I said it, everything fell into place. That very minute I was free."

Suddenly Agnes laid her chocolate bar down on the snow, cupped her hands around her mouth, and shouted loud enough to stir an echo, "You go to hell, Lyle Benson."

Then she looked over at me with her eyebrows raised, waiting for some response. "You say it," she said then.

"I don't even know Lyle," I said. "Why should I tell him to go to hell?"

"Dwayne, dummy," she said, giving me a disgusted look. "Tell Dwayne where he can go."

"Aw, listen," I said. "I don't know . . ."

"Go on, go on!" Agnes said. "Say it! Take hold of your life!"

So against my better judgment, I cupped my hands around my mouth and said feebly, "Go to hell, Dwayne."

"Is that little bleat what you call telling somebody off?" Agnes said, outraged. "Shout it out! Don't sit there and whisper, woman."

With my pride at stake, I put my hands around my mouth again, and this time I shouted loud enough to spin off a frail echo, like the voice of somebody lost out there somewhere in the peaks.

"That's telling him!" Agnes said, clapping me on the back. "Way to go!"

But the moment I spoke, I wanted to snatch my words back. All that space out there was tuned in and had heard every word, and there I was, exposed on the top of a mountain, easily spotted in all that snow. A lightning flash could do it. A heavy blast of wind.

"Can't we go down now?" I pleaded.

But Agnes dropped her wadded-up candy paper back in her pack and took out her binoculars. "What's your hurry?" she said. "Listen to that quiet and feel that sun on your shoulders."

As soon as she spoke, I became aware of how very quiet it was—no birdsong, no voices, no cars or trucks or even airplanes. No sound at all except for the moaning the wind made, rising out of that void at our backs.

But Agnes was perfectly at ease, putting the binoculars to her eyes, focusing on the skiers on the slopes below us.

"Whoa, whoa," she said, watching somebody fall.

"Here! You take a look," she said, lifting the strap from her neck and handing it to me. "Changes the world, looking through those."

So I took the binoculars from her and lifted them uncertainly to my eyes. Immediately a clump of fir trees, far below us, moved so near I could almost have touched them. I sucked in my breath, startled, and fixed the binoculars on one of the cross-country skiers who was making his way up a slope, angling up sideways. I could see how he was holding his bottom lip tightly clamped under his teeth.

"These things are strong," I said. "Everything looks so real through them."

"Real?" Agnes said. "What do you think this is, anyway? The backdrop for a movie?"

"You can see so much," I said lamely, sweeping the binoculars around until they came to rest on a man standing alone at the base of a tree. He was wearing jeans and a denim jacket and a baseball cap pulled low over his forehead. What made him noticeable was how out of place he looked surrounded by all those people in skiing clothes. But it wasn't that which made the little hairs on my arms rise as he lifted his head and looked me—it seemed—full in the face.

"Dwayne!" I screamed. "That's Dwayne down there!"

"What?" Agnes said. "Who? Your ex?"

She grabbed the binoculars from my hands and swept them wildly from side to side.

"Where? Where did you see him?"

"By a tree," I said weakly. "Wearing a denim jacket."

"I don't see anybody like that," Agnes said. "You better look again."

But when I lifted the binoculars to my eyes, I couldn't remember exactly where the tree was—they all looked alike —and all the people I could see were wearing red or blue or green ski jackets.

Suddenly I pushed the binoculars back into Agnes' hands, got to my feet, and began scrambling down the ridge, digging in the heels of my boots to keep from sliding, sometimes waddling close to the ground like a duck.

"I thought your ex was in Virginia," Agnes said behind me. "What's he doing out here anyway? Spying on you?"

"I don't know," I said grimly. All I could think of was that if I could see Dwayne for sure, if I could be certain he hadn't drowned when Humpin' to Please crashed through the bridge railing and into the river, then I wouldn't have to go on feeling guilty. I could put Dwayne out of my head forever.

But already I was full of doubt, nearly sure it was only my guilty conscience that had stood Dwayne under the tree with his cap pulled low.

"I probably just thought I saw him," I said.

"Oh, listen. When Lyle and I first split up I couldn't go in a roomful of people without thinking I saw him in it somewhere. All it took was a glimpse of black hair or somebody with broad shoulders, and wham! My heart would start hammering."

I sat down hard in the snow and shut my eyes. "I'm scared to see Dwayne again," I said.

"Well, I could have told you *that,*" Agnes said. "It's not any family reunion we're talking about here." But Agnes didn't understand. I'd married Dwayne under false pretenses, and whether he was dead or alive, I didn't want to see his face again, the way he'd looked at me before setting out on Humpin' to Please's last trip.

When we got to the car, I slumped in the seat and pulled the sun visor down over the windshield. "Let's get out of here, Agnes," I said.

She gave me one look and gunned the engine, peeling rubber as she headed out of the parking lot. But no matter how fast we moved, I couldn't escape Dwayne's eyes, the look in them the same as on the evening he walked out the door that last time. Hurt and sad they'd been. Very hurt and very sad.

7

*T*he next afternoon, as I came wobbling up to Mrs. Chung's house with the side baskets of my bicycle loaded with groceries, I saw Phoebe on the porch waiting for me, sitting on the top step with Dion between her feet chewing on a rubber ring, and I thought, Well, *that* didn't take long. I was sure she'd come to tell me she'd just had this vision of Dwayne, surrounded by snow, wandering around on the ski slopes of Mount Baker.

But when I came up to the steps, she just gave me a big smile and took one of Dion's hands from his rubber ring so she could flop it up and down in my face. "Dion's waving," she said happily. "We've come to pay you a visit."

"So I see," I told her, as I propped the sacks of groceries against the wall and unlocked the door. Phoebe could have helped, but this didn't seem to occur to her. She followed at my heels with Dion in a Snugli, smiling in a dreamy way in the direction of my shoulder blades.

It was a damp day which made Phoebe's hair even curlier than usual, and I saw she'd tried to subdue it by pulling a blue sweatband behind her ears. The sweatband made even brighter the blue of her eyes, and her cheeks had turned pink in the cool air so she looked more beautiful than ever, a beauty that made me more acutely aware of my own sweaty and bedraggled self, since the damp that turned her hair curly made my hair go stringy and misted up my glasses besides. The mere sight of Phoebe made me cross. Beauty like hers, it seemed to me, must be like having a warm shawl to throw over your shoulders on a cold day, whereas ugliness meant you were always exposed and left shivering. What was more, people thought your threadbare plight was a joke. Something to snigger about.

I pushed open the door to my room, set the groceries on the table, and turned on Phoebe.

"Well?" I said. "You might as well tell me. What have you picked up about Dwayne?"

"Dwayne?" she said, surprised. "I don't know a thing about Dwayne."

"Oh, come off it, Phoebe," I said. "Don't act dumb. Isn't that the reason you came to see me today? To say you'd seen him, standing under a fir tree?"

"I don't know what you're talking about," Phoebe said, looking at me with guileless eyes. "Cross my heart, Jessie.

We just came to pay you a visit. Dion said he wanted to see his Aunt Jessie."

I made a noise in my throat that sounded a good deal like a growl, certain she knew a lot more about Dwayne than she was letting on.

"I thought I saw Dwayne yesterday up on Mount Baker, standing under a fir tree, wearing his old denim jacket," I said, whipping open my midget refrigerator to shove the milk inside.

Phoebe just sat on the sofa, looking at me in a way I could only describe as dim.

"Well?" I said angrily. "Do you think I really saw him or not?"

Phoebe picked up Dion's ring, where he'd dropped it on the floor, wiped it off on the leg of her jeans, and put it back in his mouth.

"If you thought you saw him, then you did," she said. "What's the problem?"

"Because I don't know if it was real or not," I told her, though I knew the moment I spoke that Phoebe was probably the last person on earth to ask that question of.

"Anything you see is real," Phoebe said, as I knew she would. "Didn't he see you?"

"I don't know," I said. "He'd disappeared before I could find him. Are you sure you don't know anything about this?"

"I just wanted to see you," she said, giving me a happy smile. "And I thought you'd be glad to see me and Dion."

"Well, sure," I said, feeling remorseful enough to turn on the hot plate and take two teacups from the shelf behind the curtain. In all these small ways, Mama had raised me well.

On the sofa, Phoebe bounced Dion on her knees and hummed. "Oh, guess what, Jessie," she said. "I know what you and Jordan were scared of at night after you'd gone to bed and the light was off. Those two little sisters of your great-granddaddy's? The ones who died of diphtheria? You could hear them playing in the dark, rolling marbles over the floorboards."

"We weren't really scared of them," I said. "I think we probably knew that noise was the squirrels, rolling acorns in the gutters."

I didn't want to talk about any of it; I didn't want any reminder whatsoever of Clearwater or of anything that had taken place there. But Phoebe wasn't to be deterred.

"And listen," she went on, sounding very pleased with herself, "I picked up this picture so strong. You and Jordan sitting on your daddy's lap, just hating every minute because you couldn't stand how his trousers were all scratchy on your bare legs, and you were scared he'd throw a fit and start drumming his heels against the floor the way he did after he had that stroke and couldn't talk anymore. 'Gobbley, gobbley, gobbley,' was all he could say."

"Oh, Phoebe, I don't want to *hear* it," I said, whipping two tea bags out of a can and slapping them in the cups. "I don't want to *think* about Clearwater. I don't want to be reminded."

But Phoebe was in full flight.

"And the time Jordan told you to look in the pond, he'd seen a fish as big as a wheelbarrow in there, and then when you leaned over to see, he pushed . . ."

"What do you want out of me, Phoebe?" I said, furious, towering over her, angry enough to give her a sock on the jaw.

Phoebe's lower lip began to quiver, her eyes filled with tears, and I saw it had all become my fault somehow, making her miserable and tearful when all she wanted was to pay me a visit and be friendly. There she was with nothing but sweetness in her heart, and I was turning on her for no reason at all, refusing even the simplest kind of friendship.

"I don't want anything," she said in a small, hurt voice, running one finger up and down the arm of the sofa as I dumped boiling water into the teacups with such force some of it splashed into the saucers.

"I think you want me to say how wonderful you are," I said. "So, okay. You're wonderful. Nobody else can do what you do. But could we just have a rest from it for now?"

"I thought you wanted to hear all those things about your childhood," she said, giving me a tragic look. "I wasn't bragging. I never brag. I don't even like being able to do it —I hate it—but I thought I was helping."

"Oh, come off it, Phoebe," I said. "You know you like being able to do something nobody else can. Without that, what would you have left?"

The wide-eyed look Phoebe gave me was astonished. She couldn't believe I'd said those words to her. And, in fact, I hadn't meant to say them either. They just slipped out.

"You don't have to be that way about it," she said, picking up Dion and getting to her feet in a very dignified way. "Ugly like that."

"With me, I guess it just comes built-in," I said. "Being ugly."

Phoebe didn't seem to find anything to laugh about, but I found it pretty funny myself. My spirits were suddenly restored, so I caught the tail of her shirt as she was heading for the door and pulled her back to have her tea.

"It's just that my childhood makes me miserable," I said by way of apology. "Whenever I'm reminded of it, I can't be held responsible."

Phoebe sat down again and took the tea I offered her, but the happiness had gone from her face, and I felt mean to have caused that dimming of her spirits. It was like kicking a dog that only looks at you sadly as it scurries off.

8

*I*t was after midnight when I came out the side door of Eddie's into the dimly lit alley. There were still two dishwashers behind me in the kitchen who would have come running if I'd given a yell, so I wasn't nervous in spite of the late hour and the dimness of the light. But when a man's voice said my name, I froze where I was.

"Jessie?" the voice said again, and this time I said, "Yes?" ready to run if I had to.

A man pushing a motorcycle stepped out of the shadow of the building, and I calmed down since I didn't think someone with his hands on the handlebars of a motorcycle was going to come after me. The guy's shoulders were hunched, and I could tell he was stocky and round faced.

"You remember me?" he said. "Keith?"

I saw then he was the Buddha on a motorcycle who had zoomed past me the day I'd gone to Phoebe's house, but that time his hair had been braided in the back, and this time it was loose and wild-looking. A bulldog wearing a wig.

"Yeah, I remember you," I said.

He took one hand from the handles of the motorcycle to push the hair out of his eyes, and I could see him more clearly, that round, earnest face, looking worried.

"I've been waiting around to catch you," he said. "Phoebe told me where you worked. And I wondered if you could talk a few minutes? Someplace we could get coffee?"

"Denny's is open twenty-four hours," I said, heading in that direction, though I couldn't imagine what Keith could possibly want to talk to me about. I'd been on my feet since 4:30, and all I wanted was to go home and climb into bed. But it was that air Keith had of seriousness—some dogged, morose quality—which made it impossible for me to say no.

It was only after I'd bumped into Keith's saddlebags a time or two that I looked down to see they were bulging, and a sleeping bag was strapped behind the seat.

"Going off on a trip?" I said conversationally. "Camping?"

"Alaska. Fishing season. I've got this friend with a boat."

"That's nice," I said, though I didn't think it was nice at all. If Keith was going to be away for the summer, then guess who Phoebe was going to spend a lot of time visiting?

Keith went on pushing his motorcycle along in a stolid,

ruminating kind of way, and what he most reminded me of was one of Mama's Black Angus steers, with a broad, short head and stocky little legs holding up a chunky body.

"Well, here we are," I said a few minutes later when we'd come into Denny's and were sitting opposite each other in a booth. But the ruminating look on Keith's face didn't change. In fact he didn't say anything at all until the waitress had taken our order. I just sat in a stupor, feeling light-headed from exhaustion and a little distant from all that was taking place, my battery barely charging.

"Well, hey," Keith finally said in a gloomy kind of way. "Phoebe's all the time talking about you."

"She *is?*" I said, genuinely surprised.

"Going on a tear. On and on about this old house with dead kids playing marbles on the floor and some old guy who can't talk good and makes funny noises. Fish ponds back in the weeds full of scum. If you ask me, she's about to pack her suitcase and move right in."

I had no idea what he meant by that last remark and looked at him in a questioning kind of way as he emptied two of the little sugar packets into his coffee so he could stir it around and have something to do.

"I don't understand how she does it," I said. "How she shuts her eyes and sees all those scenes the way the rest of us watch a movie."

"If somebody put her entire brain under a microscope they still wouldn't know, either," Keith said grimly. "Her block is cracked, all right. Plain cracked. I don't mind telling you I've got to get some running distance for a while."

"How's she going to manage?" I said, instantly alarmed.

"Well, see, I went to Alaska awhile last summer too," Keith said, as though this explained everything.

"And Phoebe was okay?"

"Phoebe freaked out," he admitted. "But I'm hoping this time she'll be more used to it."

"I guess you do intend on coming back?" I said, wanting the bad news now if it was going to come.

Keith didn't say anything right away, and when he did, it wasn't in answer to my question. I didn't care for the way his eyes kept avoiding mine.

"Phoebe and me go back a ways," he said finally. "I guess you don't know that. But I've put in my time with Phoebe, let me tell you. Whole lot of shit. Well, but she was such a kid when I first met her. Up on the Cascades highway. My Suzuki had broken down up there—the fall this was, just before they shut down the road for the winter. No traffic. Zilch. So I was figuring on a long walk. And then a truck comes along and stops."

Keith took a mouthful of coffee, a distant look in his eyes.

"Turned out to be Phoebe and the guy she was with then. What's-his-name. I don't even remember what he looked like, because the minute I saw Phoebe it was like the two of us were up on one of those mountains by ourselves. You know how she can do that? Those funny eyes of hers? Some big door closing behind us. Bang! I couldn't take my eyes off her. I thought she looked like an angel."

"Phoebe still looks like an angel," I said, but Keith was motoring down his own stretch of road and didn't hear me.

"Phoebe took one look and pointed a finger straight at my heart. 'When you were five years old, you lived in a house with little skinny windows and two crooked fir trees by the front porch,' she said. First words she ever spoke to me. Shut her eyes, finger still pointing, and saw the entire picture. Me on the steps with my arms around a chow dog, giving him a big hug. Tiger! I couldn't get over it. Nobody, but nobody, had ever seen the things about me Phoebe did."

"Same thing with me."

"Yeah, it's you she's onto now," Keith agreed. "Every little thing about your life. She's just sucking it up with a straw."

"If she keeps on sucking *my* life up with a straw, she's liable to choke on it," I said, enraged.

"Oh, but listen," Keith said, "once she gets going the way she is now there's no stopping her. Like she's got the flu and it'll just have to run its course. She can't help it, I guess. But I'm here to tell you she'll root her way into your life the same way a wood louse roots into dead wood."

Under the rim of the saucer, the tip of Keith's finger took refuge, showing how.

It made me very uneasy, watching Keith's fat finger wriggle under the saucer like a slug.

"We'll see about that," I said grimly.

"Oh, Phoebe's a hard person to say no to. Just like a kid, you know? Wears her heart on her sleeve. You can't help feeling sorry for her. There're things I've found out about Phoebe, over time. How she grew up in this little Michigan town. And how both her parents died when she was real small. Plane crash, would you believe it? So Phoebe had to grow up all over Michigan, spending a little while here, little while there. First one family, then another. Lonesome, lost little kid, she was. And all the time making up stories. Well, with her it was making up a life for herself, you know? One life and then something altogether different. If you ask me, that's what she's doing still, only now she's taken it a lot further than anybody else. Has it down to a fine art. She went off when she was fifteen with a crop duster, because looking down from that little plane on all those rooftops, all those people, that's when she knew for sure what she had was a gift. When she could look down and see somebody and that person's life would come in clear to her, like a radio signal on beam. When she gets tuned in like that, she tends to go a little nuts. Takes it too far. And I've about got where I can't take it anymore."

"So go on and tell me," I said. "Why were you waiting outside Eddie's to catch me tonight?"

Keith stirred his spoon in his cup and looked uncomfortable. I already knew what he was going to say.

"Well, see?" Keith said. "Phoebe's so helpless in a way, you know? And anyway, Jessie, it's just God's truth I'm telling you. Whether you like it or not, you're going to be seeing a lot of Phoebe. She's gotten off on you more than she's gotten off on anybody for a long time. And when she gets onto somebody, she's relentless."

"So you want me to keep an eye on her while you're away," I said. "You want me to take care of her."

"Phoebe won't write letters and she hates telephones," Keith said. "Her idea of staying in touch is coming to see me in a dream."

"Oh, look, Keith," I said. "Phoebe's your responsibility, not mine. It's your baby she's raising. I don't see what I have to do with it."

Keith didn't say anything right away, just drank what was left of his coffee and shifted around uneasily on his seat. I was sure of it—that he'd had all he could take of Phoebe's craziness and wasn't intending to come back from Alaska, ever.

"Jessie?" he said finally, leaning across the little table. "Do you know somebody named Dwayne?"

"What about him?" I said, instantly on guard.

"Phoebe just said something once. She'd seen him? Knew where he was?"

"What were her exact words?" I wanted to know.

"Can't remember. Just something she said made me think you knew him."

I sat back in the booth looking at Keith and trying to decide if it was just chance that made him ask me that question at that minute. He might be much slyer than he looked.

But one thing I was sure of: Phoebe *did* know more about Dwayne than she'd let on.

"Look," Keith said, taking a crumpled piece of paper out of his pocket and scribbling on it. "Here's where you can get ahold of me. Just a postcard now and then to say things are going okay. That's all."

He pushed the paper across the table, and I took it, though I didn't know what I was letting myself in for and felt very uneasy about the whole thing. But Keith had me hooked and he probably knew it; I wasn't going to be able to turn my back on Phoebe, not since she was the only person in the world who could tell me—if she chose to do it—where Dwayne was.

When Keith got up to leave, I followed him out to the

street and watched as he strapped on his helmet and climbed on his motorcycle. As he pumped the starter, his eyes already fixed on some point straight ahead of his handlebars, I had a sudden great urge to climb onto the seat behind him, put my arms around his black jacket, and hang on through the days it would take us to get to Alaska—to leave everything behind the way he was doing, going off without a backward glance. I saw I'd gotten off that bus too soon when I climbed down the steps into this far corner of Washington State. I should have kept going into those dark forests, those barren mountains, on and on to the tundra and snowfields of the arctic where, no matter how hard I might search, not even a breath of my former life could be found.

But of course Keith didn't pat the seat behind him invitingly. He didn't even look back at me, waving. He pulled into the street, gunned the motor, and shot off into the night.

9

I stuck the piece of paper Keith gave me in the
drawer with the candle stubs, a broken can opener,
and a photograph of Mama with one foot in the
stirrup, getting ready to swing onto Lazy Boy's back,
her hair loose and shining over her shoulders. I would
keep the piece of paper with Keith's address even
though, when I thought of it, that visit annoyed me
considerably. I wasn't the person Keith evidently
thought I was, the kind of woman glad to live some
humble little half-life, making boxes of cookies to send
to far-flung relatives, keeping the sheets on the guest
bed changed. When he looked at me, all he probably
saw was BIG UGLY WOMAN, and he figured I was
willing to resign myself to the shadows, whereas the

reality was just the opposite. Sweetness of nature is a luxury somebody like me can't afford.

Still, Keith needn't have worried. No matter how much I might want to, I wouldn't lose touch with Phoebe. She was the only person in the world who could lead me to the place where I could say, once and for all, "Whatever happened to you, Dwayne, it wasn't any fault of mine, so don't go around acting like it was. You drew everything down on your own head when you married me the way you did, and I would like to have that in writing, please. No way am I responsible for you and whatever happened to you. Got that?"

So on my next day off, I was at the ferry early with my bicycle, telling myself I was just going on what Sophie called a joyride on one of those luminous, pearly days with the air soft, the sun burning through the clouds with a golden light. The kind of air that fills your lungs with a cool sweetness. I thought I might see whales making their way down from Alaska to Mexican waters, or bald eagles, soaring in the sky above their nesting places on the islands. But when the ferry stopped at Phoebe's island, I was the first off the boat, pedaling furiously by the time the cars rolled onto firm ground, racing the shadows of the clouds along the road.

I couldn't wait to get there, to say, "Look here, Phoebe. What do you mean telling Keith you knew something about Dwayne? Just what do you know you haven't bothered telling me yet?"

The closer I came to her house, the more indignant I got, since I couldn't see why she was so set on making things hard for me, holding back the information she had, the way I'd always thought Mama kept things from me that she was very free in telling Jordan.

It was no wonder I threw fits sometimes the same way Daddy did, stationed every day in his rocking chair, the world passing before him and he not able to do any more than make gobbley noises at it.

"Oh Lord, I hope he doesn't know what a state he's in," Mama would say, watching Daddy sadly. "It would break my heart to think he knew all he's lost."

But Daddy knew this much: not everybody spent his days in a rocking chair, being moved around with the sun like a potted plant. He had that much sense. Maybe he knew he'd once been a daddy who lifted me up onto Minnie's back and led her around the paddock on a lead rope. And then he was changed overnight into some entirely different person, one who couldn't talk any longer since only gobbley noises came from his mouth when he tried. A person Jordan and I shied away from and secretly wished he would die so we would never have to sit again on the knees of his scratchy suit and say "Night, Daddy," while we kissed his jaw where the little bristles were just starting to sprout, and he touched our cheeks with his dry-as-paper fingers.

Life had dealt him a terrible hand, and I think he knew it and that was why he sometimes drummed his feet on the floor and cried. Daddy and I had things in common we never had any chance to talk about since I wasn't but six when he died, falling onto the floor with his face a terrible shade of purple.

"Hey, Phoebe!" I called as I came up the driveway, the sun sparking light from the metal strip anchoring the garage roof in place. It struck me there was something lonesome about that shaft of light that lit everything for a moment before the clouds swallowed it again, and I knew long before I reached it the house had an empty feel.

When I rattled on the back door, I heard a scrambling under the steps, and Sun and Moon climbed out with dirt on their fur, to begin weaving in and out between my feet, waving their tails in the air. I crouched down to pat them, looking into Sun's golden eyes and Moon's pale green ones while they arched their backs under my hand. It seemed to me they felt skinny, their backbones knobby, and the moment I cautiously pushed open the back door calling, "Phoebe? Phoebe?" they darted inside and went directly to their food bowls which held nothing except a few broken bits of kibble. They began crunching these between their teeth, with their ears laid back and their eyes half shut, and I took the box of Cat Chow from the cabinet and filled the bowls to overflowing.

"Phoebe!" I called once more, my voice not making much headway in the silence, and I hated the eerie way the light came and went, like somebody was sending signals with a flashlight. In my mind's eye, Keith's round baby face, across the table from mine at Denny's, suddenly became scary, and in a flash I could see the hunting knife in his hand and the blood smeared on the walls.

I grabbed the broom from behind the door, and with it under my arm like a lance, ran up the stairs making little shrieking *oh oh oh* noises, knowing if there was something gruesome up there in the bedroom I didn't want to see it. When I opened the door to Phoebe's room, I narrowed my eyes to slits so whatever terrible thing there was to see would be filtered between my eyelashes.

But the room I stepped into when the door opened under my hand was so ordinary I came to an abrupt halt, lowering the broom under my arm. The sun streaming through the south window lay warm and comforting across Phoebe, who was on the bed with her knees drawn up, and Dion, flushed with sleep, sucking noisily on his thumb, curled into the protected place against her chest. I saw all this clearly before I lifted my eyes to Phoebe's face to see her looking directly at me.

"I thought you might be dead up here," I said. "Why didn't you say something when I called?"

"Jessie!" she said in a small, breathy voice only barely above a whisper, "could you be sweet and go tell Sophie to make me a hot lemonade? I'm so thirsty, Jessie."

There were faint blue shadows under her eyes, though the smile that transformed her pale face was luminous. I stared at her, not knowing what to say.

"If there's a lemon around, I can make you some hot lemonade, I guess," I said uneasily as I leaned the broom against the wall, fearing Phoebe had flipped out altogether.

But as I set the kettle on the stove and squeezed a lemon into a glass, I decided I'd probably jumped to a hasty conclusion. I'd just waked Phoebe from one of those deep, disorienting naps that are hard to shake off, and she was still lost in her dream. There was nothing to be alarmed about.

So before I carried the lemonade up to Phoebe, I stuck some arrowroot biscuits in my pocket for Dion since he was always hungry, and I even hummed to myself as I climbed the stairs.

"Ta *dum,*" I said as I came through the door, glass outstretched. Phoebe was sitting up in bed propped on pillows, and Dion, flushed from sleep and with a red mark down one cheek from the folds of the sheet he'd been sleeping on, was sitting drunkenly between her legs.

"Oh, Jessie," Phoebe said, laughing a small, tinkly laugh I was very glad to hear. "What did I *say* just now?"

"Oh, nothing," I said, sitting on the edge of the bed and handing Dion an arrowroot biscuit which he took daintily between two fingers the way a monkey might have taken a cookie from my hand. "You were dreaming."

"I thought I was *home,*" Phoebe said. "Isn't that funny? I knew Sophie was down in the kitchen, and you were coming in from riding, and Jordan . . . I don't know where Jordan was. Sitting in the garage practicing shifting the gears of the car, probably. You remember how he used to do that?"

"You looked very pale when I came in," I told her firmly. It was the only thing I could think of to say.

"I'm pale because Keith's gone," she said, all the light leaving her face. "He's left us, Jessie."

"Oh, I'm sure it's just for the summer," I said, as offhandedly as I could.

"He hates it when I get spacey. Prowls around the house like a cat, looking out the windows with a traveling look in his eyes. I know I really shook him up this time. He couldn't wait to get on his motorcycle and take off."

"He'll be back," I said, mustering as much optimism as I could.

But Phoebe pleated the cloth of Dion's shirt between her fingers and refused to look up. "I think maybe I went too far this time," she said in a sad little voice. "He couldn't stand it, my knowing, oh, everything."

"Knowing what?" I said uneasily.

"Why, you know, Jessie. *Every*thing." She lowered her face and brushed her lips across the fuzz that covered Dion's head.

"No, I don't know, Phoebe. I don't have any idea what you're talking about."

"You do too," Phoebe said, looking up coyly.

"No, I don't."

"Why, about our being sisters," Phoebe said, as though this were the most ordinary statement in the world, beaming me the whole time the full radiance of one of her smiles.

My mouth went dry, my heart speeded up.

"You mean we're *like* sisters," I said carefully. "But surely Keith doesn't mind that?"

"But he does!" she said. "It came as such a surprise, you see. Just out of the blue, one night when I was giving Dion his spinach out of a jar. There I was, spooning spinach into his mouth, and then I *remembered. I* was the one sitting in someone's lap, watching a spoonful of spinach coming toward *my* mouth. *Whose* lap? And then it came to me. I knew. Sophie's lap, of course. 'Open your mouth, sugar,' she was saying just as clear. 'Here comes that old mama bird with a great big worm in her mouth.' " From Phoebe's lips came Virginia hill country drawl, captured perfectly.

"So that was when I knew," Phoebe went on, sounding very pleased with herself. "I was right there, smelling the starch from Sophie's dress, listening to the wind in the chimney, moaning. I was in that room. And I knew everything, everything, *every*thing. Clearer pictures than I've ever had before. I was right inside the story, seeing and hearing everything. So of course, I knew then. I was remembering. I grew up at Clearwater too, same as you and Jordan. And so . . . Oh Jessie, we're sisters!"

All I could do was stare at Phoebe with my mouth gone slack. My strength had left me; if I'd been standing at that moment, my knees would have given way underneath me. Keith had seen all of this coming—he'd seen Phoebe getting kookier and kookier and had skipped out, leaving me to take over. He'd set me up. Now it was too late, I could see it all.

"Phoebe," I said finally, when I could trust myself to speak, "don't you think that's something a person would be inclined to remember? That they had a sister? How could I possibly just forget a fact like that?"

Phoebe looked serenely back at me as though she'd expected my objection and had answered it long before.

"Listen," she said, "that very first time I opened the door to you, didn't I look familiar?"

"No!" I said. "Not a bit."

But as I sank back onto the bed, weakly propped on one elbow, I had to admit that Phoebe's eyes were the exact same shade of blue as Mama's, and I knew I might have taken note of this from the beginning.

"Oh, Jessie!" Phoebe said, grabbing my wrist with her hand and squeezing hard. "It's all crowding in on me, everything coming back at once. How Mama would come through the kitchen with little bits of dried mud flaking off her boots, and Sophie would shake her apron at her. And how Mama used to lean against the door to Daddy's room, with him sitting there like a stump, and say, 'Leonard, I don't like the noises that John Deere's making. It's going to play out on me, I just know it is, and right when I have most need of it too.' "

"Hush!" I said, holding out my hand the way people try to stop traffic on a busy street. "I don't know what's going on here, but you were never at Clearwater. You weren't there when any of those things took place."

"Tell me how come I know all that if I wasn't there, then?" she said belligerently.

"You have a very good imagination," I said feebly. "You're good at putting yourself into a scene. And this isn't even the first time you've done something like this, either, is it?"

I kept thinking about how Keith had told me Phoebe grew up in Michigan. How he had tried, in his own way, to give me warning.

"But I've never seen pictures as clear as these."

Phoebe's fingernails dug into my wrist and held me tight, though I hadn't the strength to pull away at that moment anyway.

"Oh, Jessie, didn't you know how I always looked up to you? I loved the way you galloped Minnie bareback, cutting across the front pasture, not even a saddle. And how you'd swing off the end of the rope into the deepest part of the pond, farther out than Jordan would go . . ."

"Stop it!" I said, snatching my wrist away from her hand. "Stop, stop, stop. It wasn't like that at all. You're making it up."

"Don't you want to be my sister?" Phoebe said, tears

rolling down her cheeks to be soaked up in the fuzz on the top of Dion's head. "What's so terrible about being my sister?"

"Listen to me, Phoebe," I said, talking very fast. "You grew up in some little Michigan town, and you ran off at fifteen with a crop duster because he could give you a God's-eye view of the world. You have never set foot in the state of Virginia."

When I finished talking, Phoebe was silent, and I braced myself for outcries of grief. Her hands were pressed to her mouth, her shoulders shook.

"Oh, Phoebe, Phoebe," I said helplessly, sorry for her in spite of myself.

But at that moment, Phoebe threw herself down on the bed, and I saw she wasn't crying at all. It was laughter making her shoulders shake. "Did Keith visit you to tell you all that stuff?" she said. "How I grew up in Michigan and all the rest? Is that what he said?"

"Why shouldn't he tell me?" I said indignantly. "It's the truth, isn't it?"

"Don't you know Keith was feeling left out? We've been close for so long, and then you came along. His feelings were hurt. Keith hates it when I get spacey because then I lose sight of him. He likes attention, Keith does, the same as anyone else."

What she said made sense, but I didn't believe a word of it. I'd seen that shifty look in Keith's eyes the night in Denny's when he neatly slid the responsibility for Phoebe into my lap.

"Jessie, Jessie, look me straight in the face and tell me

I'm not your sister," Phoebe said, leaning forward so I couldn't avoid looking into those eyes of hers, Mama's even to the way they sat slightly aslant in her face, the eyelashes golden at the tips.

I knew I was sinking fast. Was maybe already lost. Even the sunshine streaming through the window looked suspect. And I thought maybe I wasn't sitting on the bed in the upstairs of Phoebe's house, wasn't watching Dion smear biscuit crumbs over his chin, wasn't on an island, wasn't anywhere near the state of Washington . . .

"No!" I said. "You are not my sister. Never have been, never will be."

"Before I was born, didn't you want a sister? Not even a little bit?"

"Never, never," I told her.

A sister like Phoebe? A sister with those heavy lashes and hair that went to ringlets in the damp, a sister with skin so fine it didn't seem to have a pore in it? A sister perfect in every detail and not just put together with spare parts, which is what I often suspected about myself since Jordan had grabbed everything good for himself, even when we were in Mama's womb together? No, no, no. Of course I didn't want a sister like Phoebe.

"Don't you know it would never have done, me having a sister like you?" I said.

"But I've always looked up to you so!" Phoebe said. "I *love* you, Jessie."

She was crying then, and I was crying too, and Dion started in because he'd dropped his biscuit and couldn't find it, and we were all together in the middle of the bed, wet with tears so the arrowroot biscuit crumbs stuck to our hair and our faces, and I didn't know who was who or what was what, so I yelled, "Stop!" and everything suddenly grew still.

Part II

10

*F*our mornings, practically to the minute, after
Dwayne and I had said goodbye to each other in the
bus station in Washington, D.C., after sharing a seat
together from Charlottesville—the night I'd cried
because of what happened at the spring party at
Jordan's fraternity, and Dwayne, to turn my thoughts,
had told me about how he was going up to Boston to
visit one of his brothers, who'd gotten himself put in
jail—four days after that, there Dwayne stood, in the
hallway outside my apartment, with a scuffed-up
suitcase in one hand and a white sack blotchy with
grease held in the other.

"You said come say hello," he reminded me. "If I

passed through? So I was passing through and here I am."

Dwayne's hair was standing in a peak on his forehead where he had a cowlick, and his tee shirt, the one that said Country Boy and Proud of It, was grimy, but if I'd been living on a bus for twenty-four hours I would have looked a lot worse. All Dwayne had to do to face the day was shake himself like a dog shedding water and there he was. Ready for anything. Those moss green eyes of his bright as a squirrel's.

"Why hi, Dwayne," I said, trying to sound welcoming.

I'd gotten out of bed to come to the door and hated to be seen that way, with my hair uncombed, standing bare-footed and wearing a pink bathrobe that might have been something made out of a chenille bedspread. Not that Dwayne appeared to notice. His eyes held that happy look of someone who has walked for blocks so early on a spring morning that only birds are stirring.

"What time is it, anyway?" I said, holding the door for him to pass through.

"Five-thirty," he said. "I guess you must not of been up yet?"

"See any cows to milk? Any horses to feed?"

But sarcasm was lost on Dwayne.

"I got some doughnuts," he said, holding up the greasy sack for me to see. "The doughnut people were up and around."

The kitchen table was covered with books and papers, but Dwayne took no notice. He dropped his suitcase onto the floor, sat down at the table, and put the sack of dough-nuts on top of my Aristotle.

"Had a crying baby in my ear all night long on the bus,"

he said. "Seems like I can hear it still, but I guess it's just gone to a ringing in my head."

I left him hitting his ears with the palms of his hands to dislodge the crying-baby noise and went off to the bedroom to put on some clothes. First I put on the ones I'd taken off the night before and left lying in the middle of the bedroom floor—nylon jogging pants with the knees sprung and an old gray sweatshirt with the neck pulled out of shape. But when I got a glimpse of myself in the mirror, I yanked off the sweatshirt and put on a bright blue pullover I took from a drawer, knowing the color suited me. I took time to wash my face and brush my hair, but I didn't look in a mirror afterward for fear I'd get discouraged. I'd discovered a long time ago it was better for me not to know too well what I looked like before I appeared in public. If I knew what I looked like, I wouldn't have the heart to go through with making an appearance, whereas if I didn't know, I could pretend I was invisible.

I told myself as I went back to the kitchen that, after all, it was only Dwayne Hawkins from down home. And he, I saw immediately, hadn't even bothered to so much as run a comb through his hair.

In fact, Dwayne hadn't stirred from the chair I'd left him in though now he had Sophocles, in Greek, open in front of his face.

"This the kind of stuff you read?" he said, shaking the book gently up and down as though he thought he might be able to shake some sense into it. "I'd say this idn't even hardly English."

"It *isn't* English," I corrected him.

"That's what I said. This thing idn't even hardly English."

Dwayne opened the sack of doughnuts, tipping it so I could see. Two crullers and two jelly filled. I reached inside and took one of the crullers.

"I knew that's the kind you'd like," Dwayne said, pleased.

I sat down in the other kitchen chair and took a bite of the cruller.

"What's the story on your brother in Boston?" I asked. "The one in jail."

"Trial hadn't come up yet. But you know what I found out when I went to visit him? You know what that poor, crazy sucker did? I told you he tried to hold up a 7-Eleven with a friend of his. But then what happened? You'll never guess."

I shook my head and Dwayne grinned, his eyes full of a happy light.

"They got theirselves mixed up or turned around and ended up heading the wrong way down a one-way street. That's how come they got caught. Going the wrong way down the street with a police car right there."

He whooped with pleasure, sending little crumbs of his jelly doughnut over the table, reaching across to slap me companionably on the shoulder. But I couldn't see anything so funny about the story. It struck me as being a little sad.

"Omer's always been like that," Dwayne said. "Slow on the uptake."

"How long've you got between buses?" I asked him, brushing cruller crumbs from my shirt. "Do you have time for some coffee?"

"Oh, I'm not in any hurry," Dwayne said, leaning back in

his chair and reaching for the other jelly doughnut. "I thought maybe I'd hang around for a few days. All I've ever seen of our country's capital is the bus station."

"It's too bad I don't have a bed to offer you," I said quickly. "A one-bedroom place is all this is."

"Why, what's wrong with sleeping on the floor? I didn't have anything but a pallet at home until I was nearly ten years old and Harold got married and moved out. Sleeping on the floor idn't any trouble at all to me."

"And it's finals week coming up too," I went on. "I'm going to have to study a lot. No time to show you around, I'm afraid."

"With two good legs and a mouth, what else do I need? You don't have to worry about me, Jessie."

"Well, if you want to sleep on the floor, it's yours," I told him.

What else could I do? I'd known Dwayne from the time we started out first grade together, a scrawny little kid wearing hand-me-down clothes. And later on he and Jordan had been on the basketball team together—the one that ended up nearly going to State. And besides all that, I'd already eaten one of his crullers and had my hand in the sack for the other one.

"You could have the couch if you wanted it," I said, being generous.

So Dwayne shoved his beat-up suitcase into a corner of the sitting room, and before I left the apartment for the day, I got a map and pointed out to him the Washington Monument and the White House, writing down the numbers of the buses he would need to ride on if he wanted to see these places. He nodded his head and acted as though he understood everything, but I wasn't sure he did. However, I didn't have time to worry about Dwayne and whether or not he could find his way downtown. I had classes to attend and studying to do in the library, and I didn't give a thought to him all day.

I forgot so completely all about Dwayne and the fact he was staying in my apartment that when I unlocked the door at five-thirty and came into the kitchen to see a man stirring something on the top of my stove, I got a shock.

"Hey," Dwayne said, turning around to show me his grin. "I was wondering when you'd get back. Supper's all ready."

I looked over his arm to see what he was stirring in the pot—a strange colored brownish green stuff.

"What in the world is that, Dwayne?" I wanted to know.

"Two cans of soup I found. You didn't have all that much to pick from, Jessie."

He lifted the cans out of the trash for me to see—pea and ham and cream of tomato.

"Don't you think it's a little funny-looking?" I asked.

"That's what we do all the time at home," he said, sounding a little hurt. "Mix up whatever. Looks okay to me."

They *would* do that in your household, I thought. Any kind of mess might be served up for supper in the Hawkins' kitchen.

But when Dwayne said proudly, "Just sit down, Jessie, while this is hot and waiting," I didn't have the heart to object.

When he put a dipperful of soup in a bowl and handed it

over, I picked up my spoon. It seemed mean to make fun of his efforts.

"See?" Dwayne said. "Tastes fine. What do you usually do when you come in from school? Cook up a big something?"

"Sometimes I go out to eat. Sometimes I make myself a sandwich or boil a couple of eggs."

"Well, see, tonight all you have to do is eat," Dwayne said, pleased with himself.

I declined a second helping and found a package of peanut-butter cookies in the cabinet that we passed back and forth across the table in an amiable way.

"Did you see the White House?" I asked as we ate cookies. "The Washington Monument?"

"I didn't feel like getting on a bus of any kind today," Dwayne said. "Maybe I'll go tomorrow."

I was disappointed with him for having wasted his day, but I wasn't going to make Dwayne's entertainment my responsibility. When I told him after supper I was going to have to study, he said okay, but I could see he was crestfallen.

After I settled myself in the living room, surrounded by books, Dwayne prowled around the chair where I was sitting, sometimes picking up a book to glance at but mostly looking out the windows, which I knew very well gave him a view of nothing except the buildings the apartment was surrounded by.

"Go to a movie," I told him. "Go have a beer somewhere. You're going to drive me nuts, Dwayne."

After awhile he drifted off into the kitchen, where I couldn't hear anything out of him for some time. A paper airplane, sailing in front of my face, was all that gave evidence he was alive and well in there. Only much later, when I was ready to go to bed, I went in the kitchen to see what he was up to and found him sitting on a chair with the broom handle over his knees. Chips of wood lay over the floor around him, his pocket knife was still in his hand. When I came in, he held up the broom handle for me to see, but all I could make out was a long, skinny indentation stretching around its end—a mouth I guessed it was—and two little round eyes.

"Alligator?" I said uncertainly.

"Aw," Dwayne said, disappointed. "Can't you tell it's a snake? I was going to give him fangs, but that's too hard."

"I guess it does look like a snake, now that you say so," I said, feeling I was being encouraging about the artistic endeavors of a backward child whose feelings might be easily hurt.

I gave Dwayne sheets and a blanket so he could make himself up a bed on the couch, but when I had to go to the bathroom in the middle of the night, I saw Dwayne had put the couch cushions on the floor and was sleeping down there, with just a tuft of his red hair sticking out from the blanket. He was much too tall to fit on the couch; even on the floor, his feet stuck out way beyond the last cushion.

The next morning while we ate shredded wheat, I told Dwayne about the places he might want to go that day— the Smithsonian, the National Gallery—but I could tell he wasn't listening.

So I wasn't surprised when I got back to the apartment late in the afternoon to find Dwayne sitting at the kitchen table with his heels caught over the rungs of a chair, munching potato chips out of the bag, a copy of a *Daredevil* comic propped in front of his chin. Just as I came in the door, I saw the way his lips were moving as his eyes went along the page, and I remembered Dwayne in first grade, left stranded at the back of the room at those times our teacher, Mrs. Moberly, played the reading game with us. With five or six members of the class lined up against the back wall, Mrs. Moberly would hold up a card with a word on it for us to identify. The first to call it out could take a step forward, and the first child to reach the front of the room won the game. But Dwayne was always left in the back without ever having taken one step. He would stay back there knocking the window shade pulls against the wall until Mrs. Moberly would tell him the game was over and he could go and take his seat. Since Dwayne never learned to read even *cat* in first grade, it wasn't surprising he had to do the whole thing over. And after he dropped back a grade I saw him only at recess, playing running base or straining to throw an old slick-skinned basketball through the hoop near the swings.

When I came in the kitchen, Dwayne pulled a chair out from the table for me with a flourish. "Supper's all ready," he said. "You don't have to lift a hand."

Out of the refrigerator he took a plate of sandwiches— bologna smeared with Miracle Whip—and a bowl of deviled eggs. The eggs took me by surprise; he'd gone to some trouble with those.

"Did you get to the Smithsonian?" I asked as I helped myself to a sandwich.

"I stayed around here pretty close," Dwayne said, looking shifty eyed.

"But what did you *do?*" I persisted.

"Oh, walked around some," he said, taking a huge bite from a deviled egg. "Played some basketball with kids in that park down at the corner of the block. Fooled around shooting baskets for a while. That's a good place to hang out. Watch the people."

"Any people you might have watched there were either winos or dope pushers or both," I said. "You know what could happen to you in a place like that?"

"Aw, listen," Dwayne said. "What do you think I am, anyway?"

"A big old country boy from Sweet Gum, Virginia," I said. "That's what. That's what anybody else can see too."

"I can take care of myself," Dwayne said, giving me his vampire smile.

After that second day I didn't even bother to tell Dwayne about places of interest he might go in Washington since I knew he wasn't about to go to any of them. He'd spend the day talking to the winos in the park and reading comic books.

But what I couldn't understand was why he wanted to go on staying with me. It couldn't be much fun for him that I could see, and if he wasn't bored out of his skull, that was only because Dwayne was easily entertained.

Every morning when I sat down to my shredded wheat I thought Dwayne would say, "Well, Jessie, I think maybe I'll mosey on down home today." But a week went by and he didn't mention Sweet Gum.

Of course I could have said any time, "Okay. Visit's over. It's time for you to go on home now," the way Mama sometimes had to tell some child who had stayed at our house playing until suppertime. But I didn't do it. It was that happy look on his face, for one thing, and for another, I got a kick out of having Dwayne around.

Every day, when I got off the bus at the corner near the apartment, I had a bet on with myself: what terrible food, favored by Dwayne's family, would be waiting for me that night? One day baked beans and Vienna sausages. On another came sweet potatoes smothered with melted marshmallows. Once he really splurged and went out and bought a bucket of Kentucky Fried Chicken. And every time he showed me, with great pleasure, what we were going to have to eat that night, I always thought, Why of course. *I* should have guessed that one.

With Dwayne around, I got to see the whole of his childhood pass before my eyes. One day he caught some ants in a matchbox in the park and brought them back so we could have ant races across the kitchen table. One hot Sunday afternoon we sat on the fire escape with a bowl of soapy water between us, blowing bubbles between our cupped hands—huge bubbles that floated slowly and majestically up and up, one or two reaching the top of the buildings and disappearing beyond them. I liked sitting companionably beside Dwayne as the soapy water ran off our elbows and soaked our shorts, forgetting all about Homer and Aristotle and Ovid and the finals I was going to have to take shortly. I could have been nine years old again and sitting on top of the garage with Jordan, throwing green pecans at anybody below who came anywhere near us.

Three nights before finals started, I told Dwayne I was going to have to go to the library to study after supper. I couldn't concentrate well enough in the apartment with him prowling around the way he did. I thought a library would be the last place on earth Dwayne would want to go, but he insisted on coming with me, sticking a rolled-up *Silver Surfer* in his back pocket and saying he could keep quiet as well as the next one if he had to. There wasn't anything for it but to let him come.

And he did behave himself. Every time I looked over at him sitting at one of the tables, he was leaning forward on his elbows and going right ahead with his comic book, moving his lips as he always did, ignoring the curious looks he got. Maybe he didn't know people were staring, but he probably did and just didn't care. He kept quiet and didn't get up and prowl around the way I thought he would. Just sat at the table leaning on his elbows with his hands over his ears.

On the way home I suddenly asked him if he wanted a beer, and he said sure, perking up. McGillicudey's was the only place I knew to go for a beer, the place I went some-times with other graduate students in classics. We'd stop off at McGillicudey's some nights after we left the library, drinking draft beer and quoting bawdy passages from *The Satyricon* in Latin. Nobody else ever joined our table, and this wasn't only because we tended to show off, talking only in archaic languages. Our table gave off an aura of oddity which bothered other people. There was something wrong with everybody majoring in classics; this was the main thing that let me know when I became a graduate student that I was in the right place. MacRae MacKinzie, who also came from an old Virginia family, was well under five feet tall, was so small, in fact, she could probably have been classified as a midget, though nobody ever said this to her face. Marshall Fontaine had gone bald when he was ten years old and now, at twenty-four, had the wizened look of a tired monkey. When anything upset Sheila Boston, even something so slight as a remark that she was looking pale that night, she would wring her hands and say, "No, no, no. Not true, not true."

We were used to each other and our peculiarities. We were used to having MacRae stack her books on a chair so she could reach the table, to having Sheila shred napkins into tiny pieces while she whispered to herself. But I didn't know what my friends would make of Dwayne or what he would make of them, and I hoped when we opened the door to McGillicudey's none of them would be there.

But the first thing I saw when we came into the room was MacRae's eyes looking into mine. So of course there was nothing for it but we had to go and sit at the table with her and Marshall and Sheila. Dwayne immediately took himself off to the bar for beer, and I told them he was visiting me for a few days.

"Carrying on a secret life we don't know anything about?" Marshall said with one of his pinched monkeylike smiles.

When Dwayne came back to the table it was with one glass of beer for me and two for himself, one of which he chugalugged right away. "I didn't know if I could do that anymore, it's been so long," he said. "There's a guy I know in the park who can do that with a whole bottle of wine."

"Sociology major, are you?" Marshall said. "Doing research on the urban underclass?"

Marshall was working hard, trying to fit Dwayne into some slot he could understand, but Dwayne wasn't listening. He'd reached across the table to take Sheila's napkin and now he was folding it, turning it this way and that, so when he gently pulled the two opposite corners it suddenly became two little cigarette-shaped babies swinging in a hammock. Sheila laughed her rare laugh and asked him to teach her how to do that. While they had their heads together over the napkin and Marshall was frowning and tapping on his glass at his end of the table, MacRae slid down from her chair and winked at me, our signal she had something to say in private. So I followed her to the women's room.

"Dwayne must be a friend of yours from Sweet Gum," MacRae said as we came into the women's room together.

"Well, of course he is," I said, and we both laughed. MacRae knew a boy from the Virginia hills when she saw one.

"But, oh my, Jessie," she said. "It's a little obvious what you see in him."

"What do you mean what I see in him? What could I possibly see in Dwayne?"

"Don't try to put that innocent stuff over on me," she said. "It's his sexiness I was referring to, as if you didn't know. S-E-X-Y."

"Are you kidding me?" I said in amazement.

"Oh, come off it," MacRae said, giving me a disgusted look. "You know the way he looks at you. You can see it in his eyes. And don't tell me you've just never noticed."

"Well, I haven't," I said crossly, shutting myself up in one of the cubicles.

"Then you'd better take another look," MacRae said

through the partition. "What else has he got but good looks?"

"Dwayne was a friend of my brother's in high school," I said, getting on my high horse. "They were on the basketball team together. And all Dwayne has ever looked to me is kind of half-asleep."

In the next cubicle, MacRae laughed.

When I bent over, I could see the toes of her shoes, barely touching the floor as she sat on the toilet seat.

"Oh, Jessie," she said. "You're so funny."

When I got back to the table, I studied Dwayne over the rim of my beer glass, trying to see him the way someone who'd never set eyes on him before would. And what I saw was that MacRae was right about one thing. Dwayne wasn't bad-looking, exactly. Not handsome as Jordan was, but not bad in a kind of foxy way, with his red hair and freckles and high cheekbones and soft green eyes. But sexy? What would I know about that?

All I knew was that when our eyes happened to meet, Dwayne didn't look away quickly the way most people did. He just kept staring without even blinking, a stare that did give me an odd feeling in the pit of my stomach.

On the way back to my apartment, Dwayne said, "I guess you hadn't had much time to go out while you've been here, have you?"

"Out?" I said. "I go out every day of the world."

"Boyfriends was what I meant," Dwayne said, his eyes for once slipping from mine and studying the heavy leaves of the maple tree we were passing under.

"Graduate school's a lot of work."

Besides that, I could have told Dwayne, I had decided

early on I was going to dedicate myself to Greek and Latin, becoming a crotchety and eccentric teacher at someplace like Hollins where I would spend my life terrorizing my students and taking horses over fences in my spare time, a life, I already knew, I was going to hate. Relationships with men, as far as I could see, would play no part in my life. I had every intention of renouncing men before they could humiliate me.

"Who says you have to work all the time?" Dwayne said, still avoiding my eye. "You have fun with me."

"Yeah, I guess," I said, not wanting him to feel he was an imposition.

And anyway, it was true. I did have fun with Dwayne. Now that Jordan had grown up and become a rat I missed having a boy companion.

That night after I'd gone to bed, I suddenly got the strong feeling Dwayne was standing outside my bedroom door. Just standing there, waiting. I thought I could hear him breathing, and I lay very still myself, not making a sound. After a time, the feeling went away.

The next morning while I was hunched over my cereal bowl, skimming through the *Apologia,* getting ready for a test, Dwayne all of a sudden leaned over the table and lifted my glasses off my nose, away from my face.

"Hey!" I said, outraged.

"Just a minute, just a minute," Dwayne said, holding the glasses in the air out of my reach. "I want to see what you look like without those things on."

I could feel my lazy eye sliding upward to have a look at the ceiling, and I knew what I must look like—wacky. I hated feeling exposed and stared at.

"If you're sitting there feeling sorry for me, you can just keep those sentiments to yourself, buster," I told him.

"Well, I was going to tell you you've got these long eyelashes, but now maybe I won't."

"My eyes are for seeing with," I said indignantly. "And that's all they're for."

I grabbed Plato and my glasses and went off to the bathroom in a huff. But after I'd been sitting on the rim of the bathtub reading again about Socrates drinking the hemlock, I calmed down. I even forgot about Dwayne and wasn't giving him even the edge of my attention. But all the same, right in the middle of a sentence, something came together in my mind with such force I sat straight up, Plato falling to the floor. Right then, I *knew.* All those things Dwayne had been talking about lately—whether or not I had a boyfriend and about my eyelashes—could have only one possible meaning: Dwayne had his sights set on Clearwater—on all those rolling acres of prime Virginia hill country. That big herd of Black Angus cattle and all those Poland China hogs. That old house built in 1809 and those barns and tractors and balers and all the rest. Dwayne might not be very smart, but he was smart enough to figure out that, sooner or later, Jordan and I would inherit all of Clearwater.

Well, well, I thought.

I sat kicking my heels gently against the side of the bathtub while it all came together—all those suppers of canned soup and weiners and baked beans, the looks Dwayne gave me across the table. And I knew why he was staying on day after day in my apartment even though he had no more desire to see Washington, D.C., than some Blue Tick hound dog would. Bent over the tub's rim, looking down at my feet, I laughed.

"What are you doing in there?" Dwayne said, rattling the doorknob. "Are you okay, Jess?"

"I'm just fine," I told him.

It tickled me to know I'd seen through Dwayne, that I'd caught onto his game—which seemed perfectly obvious once I'd thought of it—and now he wouldn't be able to make a move I wouldn't understand instantly. All I had to do was sit back and watch Dwayne blundering on while I enjoyed myself.

I didn't have to wait any longer than that evening.

I was sitting on the couch reading when Dwayne came and sat down beside me. After not more than five seconds, he put his arm over my shoulders. I pretended to take no notice while all the time I was making a bet with myself: now he'd either say something about how pretty my eyes were without my glasses or he'd remark how much he liked tall women.

But when Dwayne spoke, he took me by surprise.

"Jessie?" he said. "What were you crying about that night on the bus? That night we rode up here together?"

"Not a thing I want to talk about," I said, feeling instantly upset.

Dwayne wrapped a strand of my hair around his finger while he leaned down so he was whispering practically in my ear. "Why not?" he wanted to know.

"Because I don't want to, that's why."

I watched as one of his hands came down over mine where it was lying in my lap, and I could feel the calluses from all that work he'd done on car engines rough on my skin. I was surprised to see how much bigger his hand was than mine. No wonder he could palm a basketball.

"You know what, Jessie?" he said. "I remember the first time I came to your house with Jordan to shoot baskets. You were sitting up in a pecan tree watching us, and you had all these little green pecans you kept throwing. Didn't think I saw you, did you? But I did all right, up there in the leaves."

"I'll bet you never saw me. Admit it now. You're making this up."

"I could see your legs swinging back and forth. You had nice long legs and you were barefooted."

When I tried easing my hand from under Dwayne's, he just tightened his hold.

"Let go, Dwayne," I said.

But he wouldn't. He held even tighter to my hand, and when I turned my head to object, he kissed me, his lips just brushing over mine. It was such a quick kiss I thought it was maybe an accident. But when I saw the way he was watching me with that sleepy look in the back of his eyes, I yanked my hand from his and jumped up, putting the coffee table between us.

"You didn't have to do *that,*" I said. "Just because I'm letting you sleep on the floor."

Dwayne watched me from the sofa, giving me a downcast look.

"You think that's why?" he said. "Because I've been sleeping on your floor?"

"Oh come on, Dwayne," I told him. "That is too the reason and you know it."

"You don't know anything," he said, picking up a copy of

The Odyssey that happened to be lying on the floor at his feet, opened it, and pretended to be reading. The copy he had was in English, but I knew he wasn't reading one word even though his eyes went along the line and skipped down to the next.

He was just upset because his little plan hadn't worked out, and he knew he'd blown his chances. By getting impatient he'd ruined everything, and now there'd be no Clearwater for him. No twelve hundred acres.

I thought he might have something to say, but since he just sat there with *The Odyssey* propped on his knees, I went off to my bedroom and closed the door. In five minutes I was in bed, the light out. And a few minutes after that, when I heard the thump of the sofa cushions hitting the floor—Dwayne making himself a place to sleep—I shut my eyes.

When I came awake, suddenly, much later, I knew there was somebody in the room with me. It wasn't a sound I'd heard, only I had a sense I wasn't alone. I held my breath, staring into the darkness.

"Jessie?" Dwayne said in a low voice. "It's just me."

When he stepped in front of the window, I could see it was Dwayne all right, standing beside my bed in his underwear—droopy boxer shorts and an undershirt without sleeves, clothes I figured only old men wore.

"Hey!" I said indignantly. "What do you think you're doing?"

But Dwayne didn't say a word. Maybe, having come this far, all he could think of was to go ahead with what he had in mind. If he hesitated a second, he was lost. So before I could say another thing, he'd lifted the sheet and slipped into bed beside me so I, still groggy with sleep, had a confused notion I was back in the walnut bed with a ram carved into the headboard and it was Jordan pushing me from his side of the bed, scooting me over with his feet.

"You can get yourself out of this bed the same way you got in," I told him. "I thought for a minute you were Jordan." I could feel Dwayne's legs against mine, touching their entire length.

"You never for one minute thought I was Jordan," he said. "Don't be crazy."

His arm was around my shoulder and his mouth so close to mine I could feel his breath. His kiss that time was a lot more than a brushing of lips, and I thought, astonished, Well, he's not going to back off this time. His mind is made up.

When he had to stop to get a breath, I raised my head higher on the pillow, feeling my lazy eye sidling up to study the window, but I knew in the dark Dwayne couldn't tell what my eyes were doing. I couldn't see his face, either. I could just feel his body lying wiry along mine, both of us so tall we had to lie a little crooked on the bed. One of his hands lay on my breast, and I could feel my heart under there, pounding away. One look and MacRae had seen what was on Dwayne's mind, but I was slow on the uptake.

"I know what you're up to, Dwayne," I said.

"What?" he said, his voice muffled by my hair. "What am I doing?"

Trying to get your hands on twelve hundred acres of prime Virginia land, I thought. That's what you're up to. But I didn't say it. Dwayne's hand was moving down from my breast, slowly, finding its way in the dark, and I held my breath, waiting. There'd be plenty of time later to tell Dwayne what I knew; it didn't have to be right then. I just lay there without a word to say, feeling Dwayne's hand slip lower and lower.

At daylight when I woke, there Dwayne still was, lying with his arms over his head and his knees bent like he was shooting baskets in his sleep. While I watched, his eyes opened and he grinned, showing those sharp teeth.

"You look just like a dog when you grin like that," I told him as I got out of bed and made for the bathroom, shutting the door behind me. When I brushed my teeth, I bent down to look in the mirror, wondering if maybe some miracle had happened and a transformation had taken place during the night. Maybe the magic I'd hoped for when I drank some of Sophie's doctoring when I was five had finally taken effect, and I would suddenly, amazingly, look like I belonged in the same family as Mama and Jordan. But what I saw in the mirror was the same sight I saw every morning—that dopey look nearsighted people have without their glasses, my nose, which was too short, turning up the way it always had, my straight mouth, coarse skin, lanky hair pushed behind my ears. Not a trace of beauty that I could see. Nothing to inspire anyone to enthusiasm. I finished brushing my teeth, tightened the belt of my ratty old bathrobe, and went into the kitchen to sit scowling at the table with my heels pressing the rungs of the chair, determined to do every single thing the same way I always did while all the time I wanted to kick myself, to stab my hand with a fork. It was clear to me I'd done a stupid thing.

I was sitting there reading the back of the cereal box

when Dwayne came in with his hair standing on end, humming "Honky Tonk Doll" to himself, pressing the tail of his shirt under the band of his jeans. I felt at a disadvantage in my bathrobe with the threads pulled into long loops and little round dots down the front where drops of milk had dried. I frowned at the cereal box, refusing to give Dwayne even the edge of my attention. If he so much as laughed one note—just *ha*—I was prepared to shout him out of the room. When he poured two glasses of orange juice and set one directly in front of my cereal bowl, I ignored it.

"What's the matter with you?" he said, sitting down across from me and hunching up so he could see my face.

I went on reading and crunching up cereal between my teeth.

"I don't know what you're mad about. I've had my eye on you ever since ʼou were thirteen years old, sitting up in that pecan tree."

"You can't even lie," I told him. "So you better keep quiet."

"I can't lie worth two cents," Dwayne said. "I can't lie a-tall. So you have to believe what I tell you."

"I most certainly do not," I scoffed. "You can't even pretend in a convincing way."

"All right, be cross if you want to. It won't change one thing on my end of the stick."

I stayed cross all day. Whatever bit of cheer Dwayne tried to bring to the day, I crushed. Whenever he smiled, I frowned. When he took me to the little restaurant on the corner of our street for spareribs and potato skins—a great treat as far as Dwayne was concerned—I played with my food. When we got back to the apartment, I went into my bedroom and slammed the door behind me.

But in spite of all that, I had no more than turned off my lamp when the door opened and Dwayne came straight to my bed, so surely that I knew he'd been listening for that little click of the lamp being turned off.

"Just what do you think you're doing, Dwayne Hawkins?" I said. "You go straight back through that door."

But Dwayne lifted the sheet as he had the night before and climbed into bed.

"Dwayne! Do you hear me?"

"Oh hush," Dwayne said, sliding his arm under my head. "Tell me in five minutes to leave and I'll do it. Go on, tell me."

"Think I won't?"

"Yeah. I think you won't," Dwayne said. "You want me to go? You mean it now?"

"I guess you can stay a little while," I said.

For three days things stayed the same. When I had to I went to the campus to take a test, and otherwise I spent my time studying or in bed with Dwayne.

But on the third night, Dwayne moved on to the next step, one that took me by surprise though I knew, later, I should have predicted it.

We lay side by side with my head on Dwayne's arm, which was hard and not very comfortable; he was rubbing his foot up and down my leg in a companionable way, and I was almost asleep when he put his hand on my stomach, where it lay curled like a cat in the sun, and put his mouth against my ear.

"You know what I think, Jessie?" he said, his breath tickling inside my head and sending a shiver down my backbone.

"Um," I said.

"I think we ought to get married."

As soon as he spoke, I stiffened, every muscle on the alert. I hadn't expected him to act so fast, but then, of course, his time was short. He had to make his move before finals week was over, before we both left to go home to Sweet Gum.

"Are you sure, Dwayne?" I asked. "Dead sure?"

I wanted to give him a chance to come clean, to take those words back.

But he didn't hesitate. "Sure I'm sure."

Well, well, I thought. Dwayne was more ambitious than I'd have guessed.

"Don't you think getting married is a pretty rash thing to do? Our interests aren't exactly what you'd call the same, Dwayne."

"Because you read all that funny-looking stuff?" Is that what you're talking about? Because listen, Jessie. That don't bother me one little bit. We have fun. That's all that counts."

"Don't you think it generally takes more than having fun for two people to live together?"

"That right there is more than most people have," he said stubbornly, squeezing my hand. I couldn't deny it. He'd thought it out better than I'd expected.

I'd let Dwayne have his moment of hope, I'd given him every chance to back down, and it was on the tip of my tongue to say, Okay, Dwayne. Game's over. I'm onto you and I've been onto you from day one. I know exactly what's in your foxy head. But Clearwater isn't ever going to be yours so you've wasted your time here, so to speak. Get out of my bed now and we won't mention it again.

I was on the point of saying this when something stopped me. Something grabbed my tongue and held it still. The dawning realization of a completely different story, one so simple and yet so cunning. And as soon as I thought of this other story, my heart speeded up in what I took to be excitement.

What I saw was Dwayne, sitting at the dining room table at Clearwater—at that big mahogany table that had been sitting in that same room since before the Civil War—his hand heavy with a silver fork weighted with its load of roast beef. Sunday dinner. There Dwayne sat, leaning on one elbow, an uneasy grin on his foxy Hawkins face while Mama and Jordan looked on in shock. How horrified Mama and Jordan would be when I told them, "Well, this is who I've married." My husband, Dwayne, who moved his lips when he read and said "Don't make me no nevermind." Oh, I wanted to see that astonishment on their faces. I wanted to hear their cries of outrage.

In a cleft stick, that's where I'd have them. The first time in my entire life that I'd held them there. Their mouths would drop open, but not a sound would come. And that's where I wanted them. Speechless.

This was the only part of the story I thought about, the first part when I would have my say. Beyond this, I didn't consider.

Lying beside Dwayne, I cleared my throat, looking up

into the darkness that concealed the ceiling of my bed-room. Nothing up there gave me any warning.

"Well, Dwayne," I said. "You want to marry me? Okay. I think that's a great idea. We'll get married."

"You will?" Dwayne said. "Right away? Before we go home?"

Oh ho, I thought. You really do believe in striking while the iron's hot, don't you? No dragging feet here. No second thoughts.

"Sure," I said. "As soon as we can."

Dwayne recovered quickly, leaning over to kiss me, though all he could find in the darkness was the top of my head. But he kissed that, his breath as warm on my hair as a cow's.

11

*M*ama was waiting for me in front of the drugstore
when the bus pulled into Sweet Gum on that
Thursday afternoon in May. She slid out of the truck
and stood looking up at the windows of the bus, trying
to see behind the tinted glass. When I climbed down
the steps, her smile stretched.

"Jess!" she called out, waving—anyone could tell she
was being welcoming—but I'd already seen it: Mama
braced for disappointment. If I'd thought getting
married might bring about some changes in me, one
look into Mama's face told me the same old story.
There I stood, the same drab Jessie, my skirt drooping
where the hem had come out, looking down at Mama

with eyes magnified behind my glasses, my hair string-ing.

More than once Mama had said to me, too exasperated to keep her mouth shut, "I wonder if you don't do it on purpose, Jessie. So beaten-down looking. Just to make me feel bad."

But I knew she always had some hope, when she saw me again after an absence, that I might have somehow trans-formed myself while I was away and she would see this stranger coming toward her—a trim and assured stranger with hair making sweet tendrils around her face. I knew about Mama's hopes because I'd seen the flicker of disap-pointment pass over her face so many times.

When she hugged me she had to reach up to pat me between the shoulder blades, though Mama was far from being a short woman. I stood loaded down with books, my winter coat, a bag holding the things—lettuce, half-full bot-tles of catsup and mayonnaise, a nearly complete loaf of bread—I hadn't had the heart to throw out when I emptied my apartment.

"Mama," I said, nudging her with my shoulder, which was the best I could do with my hands full. She'd let her hair grow since I'd seen her at spring break, and it had reached her shoulders. The fullness softened her face and made her look even younger than I remembered, and I was struck all over again by her beauty. That always took me by surprise, just as my plainness did her. A little breeze pushed her hair against my neck as I leaned over, and I thought bitterly, Oh, fairness plays no part in life. It doesn't even enter in.

"Why, hello, Dwayne," Mama said across my shoulder. "Where did you come from? Do you need a ride?"

Dwayne stood there swallowing, and I saw he hadn't realized how it would be, appearing in front of Mama like that. His eyes showed too much white, like a horse's that's about to bolt.

"Dwayne's with me," I said quickly, but naturally the significance of this remark didn't mean a thing to Mama who was hurrying along to oversee the unloading of the suitcases so nothing of mine would be scuffed along the curb. I caught Dwayne's eye in a meaningful way, urging him to say something, but I could tell by the grim set of his mouth he'd gone tongue-tied, and I knew I might as well expect a cat to take charge as hope for anything out of Dwayne.

It was up to me to tell Mama, I saw that clearly, as I put my books and bag of groceries in the back of the truck, but I couldn't seem to decide how to start the sentence that would break the news. I saw, too late, I had done it all wrong from the beginning. I should have gotten off the bus with my arm around Dwayne's shoulder and should have said before I stepped down from the last step, "Mama, I'm married to Dwayne, I've got our marriage certificate right here in my book bag, and there's not a thing you can do about it. So what do you think of that?"

Now I had waited until all three of us were crowded into the cab of the truck with me next to Mama and Dwayne hanging one elbow out the window. It wasn't turning out the way I thought it would at all. But there was nothing for it. I shut my eyes and said very fast, "Dwayne and I were married on Tuesday, Mama. At a justice of the peace in Washington, D.C."

And then I opened my eyes quickly, to see Mama's hands still on the steering wheel and one of mine hanging onto the dash. A doomed feeling came over me.

I looked over at Mama's face expecting to cheer myself up by seeing her shock and horror, waiting for her to say, "Oh no, Jessie. You can't do this. I wouldn't think of letting you. Dwayne Hawkins? Married? Never!" But instead she just stared straight ahead without saying a word. I grew light-headed and thought maybe I'd only imagined telling Mama that Dwayne and I were married, and it was all still left to do.

"Dwayne," Mama said, "I'm going to let you out at your daddy's Sunoco station. I'm afraid I can't take the time to drive you home."

She might just as well have said "Lunge Lazy Boy for me, would you? He needs the exercise," for all she gave away. And there I had been, all prepared for her to place her hand on her heart and say, *"Why,* Jessie? Why are you doing this to me?" A question I had waited, it seemed to me, all my life to answer.

As for Dwayne, I could see I would get no help out of him. I remembered now a fact I had conveniently set aside when I married him, that he had always been in awe of Mama. On those afternoons he had come to our house to play basketball with Jordan, he had stood in the kitchen door afraid to set a foot inside until Mama called out, "Why come on in, Dwayne. Don't stand there with the screen open letting the flies in."

I saw it was hopeless to expect Dwayne to say, "Jessie's

with me now and you can reach us at the Best Western if you want to see us." All he did was whisper in the direction of my ear, "Jessie?"

Mama pulled up to the curb in front of the Sunoco station and waited for Dwayne to get out, keeping her foot harder on the gas than she needed so the gearshift shuddered back and forth between us like something having a fit.

"I'll telephone you later, Dwayne," I said coldly. I could see the anguished look he was giving me, but Dwayne and his hurt feelings were not uppermost in my mind just then.

Finally Dwayne opened the door of the cab and got one leg out, but then he stuck there, half in and half out. I knew he was wondering what he should do. Turn back and kiss me, establishing his claim? Pull me along with him into the street?

But it was indecision that was his undoing, the little hesitation that threw everything off until it was too late for any kind of brave gesture. The best he could do was let his hand fall on my leg before he climbed the rest of the way out the door and took his duffle bag from the back of the truck.

"Don't stand there in the street with your mouth open, Dwayne," I told him out the window. "I'll talk to you later."

I could tell by the dazed look in his eyes it had been a very different story he'd been telling himself as the bus drew near Sweet Gum. He could probably see himself being hugged, welcomed into the family. He could probably just hear Mama saying, "Why, Dwayne, how nice you've married Jessie. A fine boy like you. Did you say you'd like a set of keys to Clearwater? Why, here you are, son."

And instead there he was, abandoned to the exhaust fumes as we sped away. I almost felt sorry for him.

"Mama," I said as we left Dwayne behind, still standing in the middle of the road. "Did you hear me tell you what I told you just now?"

"There's nothing the matter with my hearing I know of," Mama said. And after that her mouth shut tight, her eyes fast on the road.

I was so full of bitter disappointment I could have kicked a hole through the cab door. Of all the things I had imagined Mama doing or saying when she heard my news, this was not one of them.

It wasn't until she pulled the truck up to the side door of the house and brought it to a halt that she turned in her seat to fix me with those steely blue eyes of hers. "I want you to know, Jessie," she said, "that just because you married Dwayne Hawkins in some kind of huff you don't have to stay married to him."

"Is that what you think it is? A huff? Just what kind of a huff do you think it could be that would make me do something like that?"

"You tell me," Mama said, holding my eyes with hers. "You tell me."

Too many words pressed on me at once—you always favored Jordan; you never loved me as much as you do him; you're in cahoots over every single thing, the two of you with your heads together—so I couldn't choose.

"No reason," I said. "No reason, no reason."

"So you're in love with Dwayne?" Mama said. "Is that what I'm to believe?"

I studied the walnut trees out the side window of the truck.

"Well?" Mama said, softly hitting the steering wheel with the palm of her hand, leaning forward trying to get a look full into my face, but I made sure she didn't.

"Just tell me what you hold against me so," she said, and I steeled my heart against the sadness in her voice.

"Why Mama," I said, "whatever makes you think I hold anything against you? Can't I even get married without you taking the blame for it? What gets your goat is I took you by surprise. Can't you just admit it? I took you by surprise."

Mama sighed, a gentle melancholy sigh that could have been aimed at an audience of hundreds. "Sweetheart," she said, reaching out her hand to me. "Oh, sweetheart."

But I was already out of the truck, grabbing two suitcases from the back before I opened the door and walked fast through the kitchen where Sophie watched me pass through, hands on her hips.

"Hey, Sophie," I said as I went past.

The suitcases bumped on the stairs all the way to the top, but I got them into my room and locked the door behind me. The door-locking was only a gesture, however; I knew Mama would never come storming up the stairs behind me, pounding on the door. Begging was something she would never do.

I lay down on the bed with my hands under my head and waited. I knew what I was listening for and late in the afternoon I heard it—the sound Jordan's little BMW made as he turned off the highway and into the long driveway that led to Clearwater where it stood on its hill. I knew the sound of Jordan's car just as well as I knew his footsteps, would recognize either if I were dead and buried.

I unlocked my door and tiptoed to the stair landing in time to hear Mama say, "Jordan! You broke the speed limit all the way here!"

But to my disappointment I couldn't hear anything more than the hush-hush-hush of their voices as they moved into the sitting room, walking with their arms—I was sure— around each other's waist straight to the big wing chairs beside the fireplace where they would sit with their heads nearly touching, leaning forward as people do who have secrets to share.

Mama and Jordan, Jordan and Mama! Even the way their eyebrows grew was exactly the same, accord passing between them like fire traveling down a stick. I could hear the rise and fall of their voices, two people singing the same notes.

If it had been different, I might have run down the stairs and flung myself onto the middle of the rug with my hands clasped in front of my heart while I cried "I didn't mean it! I didn't mean to marry Dwayne! All I wanted was to make you suffer!"

But the sight of the two of them leaning together so conspiratorily would bring me up short, would stop the outcry in my throat. As the one left outside the magic circle, the one pounding on the door begging to be let in, I would rather die than see the pity in their eyes.

And I knew in that moment pride would hold me to Dwayne as tightly as a tick holding to the neck of a dog and nothing would shake me loose. I saw it all with cold clarity —how I would squander my education, as Mama would put it, as profligately as though all those hours of reading Greek and Latin were so much scratch thrown out to the chickens.

A bitter smile curled my lips when I thought of this, and I went silently back to my room and closed the door without making a sound, leaving Mama and Jordan to talk behind my back. Of course the Greek and Latin had been for my pleasure, though they didn't know this.

I knew how, down below, Mama was pouring out two scotches, gently slipping the ice into the glasses without bothering to look down, her eyes never wavering from Jordan's face.

I'd barely shut the door of my room behind me when I heard Jordan climbing up the stairs, two at a time. "Jessie!" he said, rattling the doorknob—that old white porcelain knob with the fine little cracks in it. "Let me in, Jess." He sounded demanding, but I caught the note of anxiety in his voice. I knew as well as if I'd heard the conversation Mama saying, "Oh, you go try talking sense to her, Jordan. You've always been so close, you two. You know she won't listen to anything *I* tell her."

But Jordan knew very well I hadn't said one word to him for a month. Not since the party at the Kappa Sig house when Jordan had said that horrible thing. He knew I held something terrible against him, knew things had changed between us, but still, there he was, pretending nothing had happened.

"We don't have anything to talk about, Jordan," I told him coldly through the door, my heart hammering wildly but my voice calm.

I knew just the way Jordan was standing, leaning toward

the door listening, running his fingers through his hair the wrong way so it stood up in ragged peaks. When he was little and got upset, he would bite on the fleshy part of his thumb until tears came into his eyes, never being able to hide what he was feeling as well as I could.

"Jessie?" he said. *"I* don't have anything against Dwayne. I always liked him fine. I think maybe I understand your doing, um, what you've done."

"Really? You understand my marrying Dwayne? Well, that's amazing, Jordan."

"What's amazing about it?" Jordan said, sounding peeved. There he was, doing his best, and for all he could tell I was making fun of his efforts.

"Did you know Dwayne moves his lips when he reads? Did you know that? Even when he reads a comic book he moves his lips. And anything besides a comic book is beyond him."

"Damn it, Jessie. What's the matter with you, anyway? Why're you acting so strange? If you're mad about something, what is it? Let me in there so we can talk some sense."

"You think this isn't sense? You've just told me it's fine with you if I marry somebody who moves his lips when he reads. That tells me plenty."

It came over me again powerfully, all I'd felt of humiliation and misery, standing behind the column in the Kappa Sig house, listening to what Jordan had never meant me to hear.

The doorknob on its long, loose stem rattled furiously.

"What do you want me to say?" Jordan said angrily "Tell you marrying Dwayne Hawkins was the stupidest thing you've ever done in a long line of stupid things? All right. It's stupid. Is that enough or do you want me to say it again? Stupid, stupid, stupid."

"Oh, don't stop there," I said in a cold, calm voice. "Go on. Tell me all the rest."

"What rest?" Jordan said warily, instantly on the alert. "What're you talking about?"

Betrayal I wanted to cry out. I heard you betray me while I stood behind that column, you mealy-mouthed bastard. I heard it all. Even that laugh of yours I'd know anywhere. But my heart shriveled inside me, and I couldn't speak. All those years when I thought Jordan and I had a special understanding had been nothing but a lie. I didn't know the first thing about Jordan.

The doorknob, on its long stem, turned back and forth. And then it stopped. On the other side of the door, Jordan was silent so long I thought maybe he'd slipped off his shoes and slid away in his stocking feet. But then he spoke, his lips right against the door crack.

"JayJay?" he said so softly I might almost have imagined it. "JayJay?"

It was Jordan's old name for me, the one from the time he'd seemed like a part of my own body—another arm or leg—that name from the beginning, when we'd slept with our heads on the same pillow and had waked every morning looking into the other's face. The one name that could strike me to the heart.

How dare he say that name to me after what he'd done?

"If you don't leave me alone, Jordan, I'll kill you," I said. "I'll take one of Daddy's pistols and shoot you through the heart."

"Very well," he said. "Stew in your own juice, then."

I could hear his footsteps walking away, leaving me alone. It took all my willpower to stop myself from running after him, to cry out, "I didn't mean any of it, Jordan."

But instead I waited where I was until I could hear him at the bottom of the stairs and knew he wasn't going to turn back. Then I grabbed the pillow off my bed, the one Grandmother Carter had made for Jordan and me when we were born, yanked open the top drawer of my dresser, took out my fingernail scissors, and started clipping away at those fine little embroidery stitches—the stitches joining our names together—Jordan and Jessie, in a heart of love intertwined with rosebuds that was meant to link the two of us forever.

By nightfall, the pillowcase was nothing but a rag pierced with hundreds of tiny needle holes, and all around me on the floor were the red and blue and green threads. A small, gaudy bird might have had its feathers plucked at my feet.

The next morning I came to a halt in the doorway of the kitchen, where Mama and Jordan were facing each other across the table, drinking coffee. When they saw me they set their cups back down in the saucers and pushed them aside, out of the line of fire. Clearly they expected a fight. But all I said was, "I have to have the car today."

"The keys are in the glove compartment," Mama said. "But can't you eat breakfast first? You haven't even seen Jordan and now he has to go back to Richmond."

I'd refused to come downstairs the night before for supper, so Mama had left it on a tray outside my door. I was certain they were relieved, getting to have a quiet evening together without me giving them both black looks from my side of the table.

"I've got important things to do today," I said. "I can't waste time just sitting around."

I didn't look back, but I knew Mama and Jordan would sit at the table, not moving a muscle until they heard the engine of the car start, and then they would jump up, help themselves to biscuits hot from the oven, refill their coffee cups, and settle down to talk in peace about me until Jordan had to leave.

I drove straight out to Dwayne's house, six miles into the country over a road oily with shale, where the bushes and scrub oak threatened the little space cars and trucks could call their own. I'd practiced my driving on all those back roads when I was sixteen and I knew them well. This one was lined with overgrown fields and houses with roofs curving down like the backbones of old cows.

The house where Dwayne's family lived was as run-down as any—those boards had never seen paint. In the yard two gutted trucks without wheels had come to permanent rest at the side of the porch, which sheltered a washing machine, a tractor wheel, and two wash kettles filled with dirt where dead petunias and marigolds bowed their heads. Three bony hounds came out from under the house to bark while I sat in the middle of the road blowing the car horn. Heads appeared in the windows and disappeared again—waves of consternation reached me where I sat beside the mailbox—but I kept my face straight ahead until somebody ran over the hard-packed ground, and there was Dwayne, opening the car door.

"You know what?" he said, slamming it behind him.

"When I came in yesterday saying I was married to you, they thought I was making it up. You ought to of heard the carry-on when you drove up."

"There's a carry-on at my house too," I said.

Dwayne opened the car window and the wind rushed through, flattening down his hair. "Hey, Dwayne," I said, patting his knee to cheer him up. We were in cahoots now, and I was glad to see him.

"I thought you were going to call me last night," he said, sounding hurt. "You *said* you would."

"No chance," I told him, though, to tell the truth, Dwayne had hardly entered my thoughts from the time he'd gotten out of the truck at his father's Sunoco station. Other things had taken my attention. "Jordan came over from Richmond, and he and Mama had their heads together about us. That's what they're doing this minute. Sitting at the kitchen table talking us up one side and down the other."

Dwayne looked pleased. "Is that where we're heading for, then? Your house?"

"Are you crazy?" I said. "We've got to find us a place to live. That's what we have to do today."

"I thought we'd stay at your house," Dwayne said, looking disappointed.

"I don't know where you got that idea," I told him. "You sure didn't get it from me."

"Your house is so big," he said, "and just your mama rattling around in it." There was a wistful note in his voice I thought I'd better curb right away.

"You wouldn't last five minutes in that house, Dwayne," I told him cruelly.

"Why not?" he wanted to know. "Your mama always seemed to like me fine."

"Well, why shouldn't she?" I said. "When all you did was come over to our house and throw basketballs around in the afternoons? A far cry from marrying into the family."

I didn't tell him that half the time Mama couldn't remember his given name and referred to him as "That red-headed Hawkins boy."

"But listen," Dwayne said, "all I get, working for Daddy, is a hundred and twenty a week. That's not much to find a place on, is it?"

"We're just going to be poor, then," I told him.

Good was what I added to myself but didn't say. I could see the way I'd trail through town wearing some old shapeless dress, with my cheeks sunken, a sack over my back for putting the aluminum cans I'd find in trash barrels out at the fairgrounds where people sometimes took picnics if they didn't have anything better to do. "You know who *that* is?" people would say, pointing me out as I made my slow way, old basketball sneakers of Dwayne's flapping on my feet like flippers. "Would you believe that's Sarah Eve Farquarson's girl, the one who owns Clearwater?"

"You sure your mama wouldn't give you any money if you asked her?" Dwayne said.

As a matter of fact, I had some money left over from the college fund I'd lived on frugally all those years, but I wasn't about to let Dwayne know I had a penny.

"Listen, Dwayne," I said. "You better get this through your head right now. Mama was furious when she found out I'd married you. So you better forget about any help coming out of that quarter. A cheap place to live is what we're looking for. A very cheap place."

By nightfall we had found one on the top floor of a suitably decrepit house on the side of a hill leading down to Black Creek. The lower half was lived in by Esau Flanagan, whose shoes were held together with baling wire and who had snuff juice dribbling down his chin. The house smelled of vinegar and mice, and when I turned on the hot water tap a thin trickle the color of horse piss came out. I told old man Flanagan we'd take the place.

"Comes furnished," he said aggressively. "Not many places this price come furnished. Bed, soffer, table. Everthing a body needs."

"Fine," I told him. "We'll take it."

"Even gottsuh some skillets and things of that nature. My wife, she was the one to think of that."

"Looks great," I told him.

"Rent due first day of the month," he said warningly. "Not on the second or third but on the *first,* right on the nail."

"We could give you a month's rent right now," I said, giving Dwayne a sharp look so he came to, like somebody who'd just been taking a nap, and took his checkbook out of his back pocket.

Even when he wrote out the check and handed it over, the old man's expression didn't change. "I don't pay no electric or no phone, and what you do with your trash is your lookout," he said.

When the old man finally went back down the stairs, bringing both feet together on each step the way two-year-olds do, Dwayne shut the door behind him.

"You really think this place is okay?" he said doubtfully.

"Sure," I said. "Why not?"

"Looks to me like stuff's been coming off the ceiling," Dwayne said. "You don't think it's kind of run-down?"

"Oh, a little paint will do wonders," I told him airily.

Dwayne cheered up enough to go and look out the windows. "Hey, look, Jessie," he said. "You can see all the way down to that big new development. The one across Black Creek. Suncrest Hills."

I heard the longing in his voice and saw in a flash what he wanted so much—the sprawling ranch house with carpet thick enough to sink to his ankles in, a giant-screen television in the bedroom, a Winnebago the size of a small house in the driveway. If he had all of that, he'd never get over the wonder of it and would be forever showing kinfolks of his through the place like it was the sacred holy. "This here's the microwave," he'd say with awe in his voice. "And see that matching deep freeze and refrigerator? Busy making ice any time you want it."

"This is just a start, idn't it?" Dwayne said, looking hopeful.

He put his arm around me and intertwined his fingers with mine the way he liked to do. "Everybody has to start somewhere."

I told him yes, everybody did.

"So we'll just have to work our way up to something better, won't we, Jessie?" he said, sounding happy.

I didn't tell him no.

12

*B*eing married to Dwayne and living in the big room at the top of old man Flanagan's house reminded me more than anything else of the way it had been when Jordan and I were little and used to make a house for ourselves under the dining room table. With some of the leaves taken out, the table was so shrunken the tablecloth reached nearly to the floor, and once we crawled under it, we had a cozy space for ourselves— a space that we furnished with cracked plates and cups and stewpans without handles. We dragged a quilt from the quilt box and cushions off the living room sofa to make our house comfortable, and Sophie gave me a water glass for the phlox I picked from the garden. When we sat under the table on the cushions, eating our pretend meals, with the light coming through the tablecloth dim and mysterious, I had the feeling we had taken ourselves to some faraway, wonderful place, and not even the sounds of ordinary life I could clearly hear coming from the other side of the tablecloth changed my mind— Sophie singing "When We All Get to Heaven" while she made a crust for chicken pie, and Molly walking around and around our hiding place, her claws clicking on the floor until she finally lifted the cloth with her nose and came into our room to stretch out on the cushions with a sigh. The sun, emerging from cloud, shone through the table-cloth making even the cracked teacups glow, and I thought I'd like to live under there with Jordan forever.

The room Dwayne and I had at the top of old man Flanagan's house had that same feeling for me. We were far away from everything I'd known before, living in a big playhouse.

Dwayne and I painted the walls together, splattering drops of paint on the floor which we then covered up with a crazy-quilt rug I made by sticking squares of carpet sam-ples on heavy tape. It covered nearly the entire floor in many colors—yellow and brown and blue and green—an effect I liked myself, though I caught Dwayne once in the Sears store in Lexington running his hand over the heavy, thick carpets that cost twenty dollars a square foot, touch-ing them in a longing kind of way.

Most of our furniture came from the town dump, Dwayne and I saving it from the fire that raged every two or three days. We weren't quite in time for our heavy arm-chair—it was already smoldering when we pulled it to safety—but we kept it anyway since the hole was in the back cloth and didn't show. It embarrassed Dwayne to be seen loading up our old truck with furniture other people had thrown away, but I was secretly pleased when we were seen at the dump. I was sure they were saying all over town, "Don't you think it's hard of Sarah Eve, cutting off her only daughter without a penny just because she married beneath her?"

It gave me perverse pleasure to stock our room with chairs with broken spindles and uneven legs, a refrigerator that made strange wheezing noises. The curtains I made myself, sewing as Sophie would say "on my fingers," so they were lopsided and had uneven hems, a very amateurish effort. But I got a kick out of it all, being married to Dwayne and living in our upstairs room in the middle of all that broken-down furniture. I knew I could walk down those stairs any time I wanted and keep on going. I wasn't tied to anything I couldn't get out of—that was what I thought. When it stopped being fun, I would just tell Dwayne, "Well, no hard feelings, Dwayne. Fun while it lasted. And now we're even steven, tit for tat." Of course, he wouldn't get Clearwater, or any part of it, and that would be a disappointment, but that was life. You didn't always get what you'd planned on.

We'd been in the apartment less than a week when Mama first came to visit. It had turned hot for late May, but I was spending my afternoon painting one of the chairs we'd found at the dump a bright, shiny red when I heard Mama's footsteps on the stairs.

"Jessie," she said as she came through the door, "this

room is like an oven. You know that paint will never dry in this heat and will always be tacky."

"Then we'll just stick to it every time we sit down," I said. "A minor inconvenience of poverty."

Mama rubbed her hand over an orange chair, one I'd painted a few days before, and gingerly sat on the edge. "Speaking of poverty," she said, "I've just been to the bank and topped up your account."

"Then you can just untop it. We don't intend to take a penny from anybody. We'll live on Dwayne's income."

"Suit yourself," Mama said, a steely note in her voice.

Her hair was loose around her face, she had turned a rosy pink from the heat, and her beauty upset me, as it always did. It rattled me and put me on the defensive, and the fact that she seemed totally unaware of this only made things worse.

"Oh, money," I said meanly. "All you think about is money."

She bent down to pick up one of my books from the floor and fanned herself with the back cover.

"Do you think so?" she said in that cool way that had always made me feel frantic. Nothing I could do or say, it seemed, would make her suffer.

"What about the farm?" I said. "That's not just some wispy cloud, is it, all those acres? You care about it, all right."

"And now you're blaming me for that too? That I've managed to run the farm after your father died?"

Will there be no end to this, all the things you blame me for? was what her tone of voice said.

I went on brushing paint over the rungs of the chair,

paint drops spattering like blood over the newspapers it was sitting on.

"I've never said I blamed you for anything," I said, and Mama made a noise in her throat that she cut off before it could reach full throttle.

I knew exactly what she was planning to tell Jordan the next time she saw him: "Oh Lord, I don't know how much more of that sister of yours I can take. What am I supposed to do with her? You tell me."

"I didn't climb those stairs to come to this oven of a room on a ninety-degree day to argue with you, Jessie, no matter what you may think," she said, slapping the book cover back and forth so fast it made a blur.

I sat back on my heals, the paintbrush like a wand in front of my face.

"You don't approve of one single thing I've done with my life so far, you don't even approve of the way I'm painting this chair, so how could we be in the same room together for more than thirty seconds without arguing?"

"I suppose it's beside the point to ask if you're happy," Mama said.

"Of course I'm happy," I said, tears springing to my eyes. "Happy, happy, happy."

"Fine," Mama said. "I'm glad to hear it. But you know you've always got a home to come back to," she added, setting the book carefully on the floor and standing up.

It was that dignity, that care, that made me come within an inch of throwing the paintbrush, loaded with red paint, straight at her.

If she had torn at her hair, shaken me until the world went fuzzy in front of my eyes, if she'd said, "My God,

Jessie, what are you doing with your life? I won't let you do this crazy thing," I would have been eased. Even content, maybe. But as it was, I was full of turmoil as I watched the door close behind her, and I knew that nothing I could have said would have been enough, not even the most cruel things.

And yet what I'd said to her was true. I wasn't unhappy exactly, living with Dwayne in our upstairs room, though there were times when Dwayne did aggravate me.

He was especially curious for some reason about my daddy, though by the time I married Dwayne, Daddy had been in his grave for over twenty years. Still, when we were lying at our ease, with Dwayne's arm around my shoulder, he tried worming his way into those parts of my life that had nothing whatsoever to do with him.

"Was your daddy like everybody said?" Dwayne whispered in my ear as we lay side by side. "No mind a-tall? Just like some big old bump sitting there?"

"I don't want to talk about it, Dwayne," I warned him.

"If he was still alive, I'd be seeing him all the time practically, wouldn't I? So I think you ought to tell me so I'll know."

"It's not something I want to remember, much less talk about," I told him.

"One thing," Dwayne said, his mouth close to my ear. "The story going around was your daddy couldn't say a single, solitary thing. When he opened his mouth, noises came out sounding more like a turkey gobbler than anything else. Is that the truth, now?"

"All he could do was make noises like a baby learning to

talk," I said. "But we always thought he understood more than he could say."

"And did your mama once throw a bowl of English peas in his face while you all sat at the table and say, 'Why aren't you dead, Leonard? I just can't go on anymore this way?' "

"What?" I said, throwing off Dwayne's arm and sitting straight up in bed. "Where did you ever hear a thing like that? My mother would never in her life say such a thing. Never! Even if she thought it, which she never did, she would never, never have said it. You don't understand the first thing about my mother or anything else about my family if you could think such a thing!"

"It's just what people were saying," Dwayne said defensively.

"Who?" I said.

"Lots of people."

"Lots of people are liars, then," I told him, glaring.

"*I* never believed it," Dwayne said, his eyes going wide to show his innocence. "All I'm telling is the story going around. I need to know the straight of stuff like that, don't I, now I'm one of the family," he added piously.

"If you're going to be part of any family with me in it, you'd better get some sense in your head, Dwayne," I said with such annoyance in my voice he looked crestfallen.

"I never believed those old stories," he said, but I knew he had, the same as the rest of Sweet Gum. People would go to any lengths to make up a good story to keep themselves entertained.

To put things right, the next day Dwayne brought me a car from the station, a car that had been in a wreck so the side was mashed in and one door had to be held in place with a piece of rope. The mats were in shreds and the vinyl on the seats was cracked, but Dwayne said that engine would carry me around the countryside for years to come. I could get out of the house and go visit people.

"Juney Fry?" he said that night while we were waiting for the chicken to finish getting tender. "The one took Home Ec. with you and caught a tea towel on fire once, threw it out the window on Neil Hudson's head? She was in getting her oil changed today and said, 'I sure wish Jessie would come visit me. Here I am every day of the world right where I've always been, living at home and working in Daddy's lumberyard.'"

"I have other things to do in life than entertain Juney Fry," I told him.

Dwayne chipped at the gold-colored foil around the top of a beer bottle with his thumbnail. "I shouldn't maybe ought to say this, Jessie, but you know what people were always saying about you when we were in high school?"

"Nothing I'd want to hear," I said in a bitter voice.

"Well, but I think I ought to tell you this. They said you were stuck up."

"That wasn't the limit of what they had to say, either, was it?" I said, getting impassioned. "I know they never liked me the way they did Jordan because Jordan can joke around with anybody and he was on the basketball team and all, but let me tell you something, Dwayne Hawkins. If it was any contest between Jordan and me over who was the most stuck up, he'd win hands down. He just hides his true feelings better than I do."

"All I said was Juney Fry said come visit. How did Jordan get into this?"

"Though I guess I can't blame other people for not see-ing Jordan's true nature," I went on, as though Dwayne had never opened his mouth. "It took me long enough."

"Come to that, my mama would be tickled if you came to see her. Or Jolene. Shut up in that trailer with the baby."

"I don't lack for entertainment!" I told him. "Have I said one word about being bored? You and my mother, busybodying around."

"We must just want the same thing, then," Dwayne said, leaning over to slide his hand along my arm. "You happy."

Mama didn't waste much time having us over to Clear-water for Sunday dinner. I knew all along she'd have us as soon as she could arrange a time when Jordan could drive over from Richmond, since she would always do the right thing. If there were those in Sweet Gum waiting to see her dip her skirts in the mud, they would have a long wait.

Dwayne, when I told him the news, looked pleased. "I'd been wondering when she'd get around to having us over," he said. "I knew she *would.*" He gave me a meaningful look that meant, I suppose, I'd been wrong when I told him Mama was less than ecstatic having him marry into the family.

"Mama will always do what she considers right. No more, no less."

"I think you sell your mama short," Dwayne said. "She's a lot nicer than you let on."

"Whatever else, I don't sell Mama short," I told him. "That's one thing you can be sure about."

The day we were to go, Dwayne was very cheerful, like a little kid being taken somewhere for a treat. Uh-oh, I wanted to tell him. You haven't got anything to celebrate, Dwayne.

But I didn't have the heart to discourage him, and by eleven o'clock he had shaved, polished his shoes twice, and was starting to get dressed.

I lay on the bed in my pajamas, watching him.

His shirt, a pale blue, was a little generous around the neck, and I was pretty sure he'd borrowed it from one of his brothers the same way he had worn their hand-me-downs when he was in grade school.

"Remember this?" he said, holding up a tie—a yellow one sprinkled with little black horseshoes—the kind that comes pretied on a band of elastic.

"Am I supposed to?"

"Junior-Senior Dance," Dwayne said reproachfully. "You don't remember?"

"Oh, I remember the dance all right," I said. "But I can't say I remember the tie you wore to it."

"I remember what *you* were wearing. Every single thing. A blouse the same color as an eggshell and this long blue skirt. Pearls around your neck."

"Mama dropped those pearls over my head as I was going out the door. I wanted to stay home, but Jordan dragged me along."

"You looked pretty," Dwayne said. "With that ribbon in your hair."

"I did not, and I hated every minute."

It was Jordan I saw clearly, in white trousers and a shirt with tucks down the front, and I remembered how proud of him I'd been. That was when I could still bask in his glory.

"Remember when I danced with you?" Dwayne said.

"Jordan put you up to that, didn't he? The entire basket-ball team danced with me before the evening was up."

"Hey, no, you've got it wrong. It was on my own hook. Jordan didn't have a thing to do with it."

I didn't believe Dwayne, but I thought it was good of him all the same to deny Jordan had twisted his arm.

Dwayne's suit, a shiny blue polyester, was his only one; he'd worn *that* at the Junior-Senior Dance too. I noticed it was short in the sleeves, and I wondered if he'd grown after he got the suit—he had very long arms.

I watched as he combed through his hair very earnestly, bending down to see himself in the mirror above the wash-basin. It was neatness he was aiming for, I could tell, and I suddenly remembered seeing Dwayne when he was seven years old, arriving at a birthday party. I happened to be looking out a window at the time and so had seen Dwayne walk to the door, hesitate, and then run back down the steps to the lawn where he slid the soles of his shoes up and down to clean them off. He'd wanted so much to do the right thing, even when he was a kid. And I knew, watching him leaning down over the mirror, it wasn't van-ity that made him part his hair four times, trying for the best effect. All he wanted was to be acceptable.

When he turned away from the mirror, he had a satis-fied look on his face, his hair sleeked down without a sprig standing up, and his tie so tight around his neck his collar bunched up underneath.

"Shouldn't you get ready?" he said to me. "I don't want to get there late."

"I hate to disappoint you, Dwayne," I said, "but it's not going to take me long to get ready."

In fact, it didn't take me more than three minutes. All I did was pull on a pair of jeans, drop a baggy tee shirt over my head, and pull my black basketball sneakers from the closet.

"Is that how you're going?" Dwayne said, shocked. "To Clearwater? For Sunday dinner?"

For Dwayne, at that moment, going to Buckingham Palace for tea wouldn't have seemed like a bigger deal.

"This is what I always wear," I told him.

"But doesn't your mama care?"

"It's my feet wearing these basketball shoes," I told him. "Not hers. Notice that? You see Mama hanging around in that closet there?"

But even as I spoke, I felt remorse. I knew Dwayne could shine his shoes and slick down his hair until doomsday, trying to make himself acceptable, and it wouldn't do any good.

As we came up the driveway, I watched the worn brick of Clearwater come into view between the overgrown hedges. The formal gardens were in ruins, the woodwork around the windows needed paint, but I liked the looks of that house anyway, on the top of its hill.

Jordan's car was already beside the garage when we pulled in, and I thought it was just like Jordan to burn up the highway between Richmond and Clearwater so he could get there before me. As soon as we came around the corner of the house, I saw Jordan and Mama walking up slowly from the bottom of the lawn, skirting the flower beds, walking so close to one another their shoulders nearly touched, their heads bowed in the intensity of what they were saying.

The sight of the two of them together like that struck me to the heart as it always did, and I thought bitterly they would never miss me if I just disappeared from the face of the earth, my absence swallowed up with hardly a ripple. They so clearly belonged together, Jordan in a white summer suit and Mama in a pale green dress, their hair the same shade of dark gold.

"They're dressed up," Dwayne said reproachfully, and I saw how I was letting him down, leaving him unprotected. But if I couldn't protect myself, how could I protect him?

I grabbed Dwayne's hand and made him run with me to meet them as I might have called a dog to run at my heels. When they saw us, they stopped walking and waited with careful, slightly pained smiles, and I knew exactly how ridiculous we looked in their eyes—me in my jeans and high-topped basketball shoes, hauling an anxious Dwayne along behind me in his shiny suit that pulled tightly across his shoulders as he ran, exposing a wider and wider band of shirt cuff.

I saw it at that moment in Mama's eyes: how pitiful-looking we were.

"Well, here he is," I said defiantly, giving Dwayne a push forward between the shoulder blades. "Here's Dwayne."

There he was all right, gawky, hands hanging from the sleeves of his shirt like something caught on the end of a line.

If this was the scene I'd been waiting for when I married

Dwayne, it had finally come about. But I didn't feel gleeful the way I thought I would as I lay grinning at the ceiling that night Dwayne asked me to marry him. All I felt at that moment was depression.

Mama nodded to Dwayne and said, "Dwayne."

Jordan put out his hand and said, "Hello there, Dwayne," shaking Dwayne's hand on his way to kiss me on the cheek. Jordan's face loomed closer and closer until it blurred, and then I flinched. A traitor's kiss.

Jordan must have felt that flinch, but it didn't stop him from holding me back by the shoulders as Mama walked with Dwayne toward the house.

"How's it going?" he whispered in my ear the way we'd whispered so many things back and forth in the past, his voice both secretive and expectant, the same voice he probably used to ask a client, "Well, *did* you beat your wife? I need to know the truth."

I stood, my heels dug into the ground, keeping my eyes away from Jordan's face.

"Why, it's going just fine, Jordan," I said in the kind of gracious voice I used on Mama's friends when they asked me how college was.

Jordan drew back as though he'd been stung by a hornet, and I could see by the stiffness of his shoulders as he walked to the house without me how upset he was.

Or maybe I was wrong even about that and he wasn't upset at all. Everything I thought I knew about Jordan was undergoing a change since in the most important thing of all I knew Jordan had managed to fool me our entire lives together.

~~~~~~

Ordinarily Mama, Jordan and I ate Sunday dinner at one end of the dining room table, bunched up together like cattle in a field. But this time I saw the plates had been spaced around the table, with two at the ends and two in the middle, so there was a long expanse of polished mahogany making an island around each of us. Mama and Jordan took the places at the head and foot, naturally, leaving the middle ones for Dwayne and me—the children's places, the ones that would have belonged to Jordan and me if Daddy had lived and we'd all four eaten dinner together at that table every Sunday of our lives.

"You're the guest," Mama said to Dwayne, handing him his plate and gesturing toward the sideboard where all the food was sitting, keeping warm over candles, Mama's concession to informality.

Dwayne gave me a desperate look, afraid to go first, so I took his plate. "You want everything, right?" I said, heaping up the roast beef, tiny new potatoes, and Kentucky Wonder beans fresh from the garden. If Dwayne's mouth was full of food, he wouldn't have to say much.

But of course Mama couldn't let Dwayne eat in silence. She had to ask him about his family, so Dwayne sat with his fork poised while he told about Jolene's new baby and how Omer was doing in that jail in Boston, while his ears turned pink with earnestness and he leaned forward over his plate in order to catch any word Mama had to say. I watched as his tie dipped lightly into his gravy. How he wanted to please! The more his head bobbed up and down, agreeing with Mama before she'd even gotten the words out of her mouth, the more fed up with him I got. *Show some pride, Dwayne,* I wanted to yell at him

Under the table, Jordan nudged the edge of my shoe with his, giving the faintest pressure on my little toe. It was our old signal of togetherness which meant, Hey! Funny, huh?

I pulled my foot to the leg of my chair and looked down at my plate. Again Jordan's shoe touched mine, and again I moved, so I was sitting sideways in my chair.

Jordan gave me a baffled look and shot the cuffs of his shirt, the way he did when he was starting to get angry. But I didn't give any indication I'd seen that, either. Jordan might have been invisible for all the attention I gave him, though at the same time, there wasn't the slightest gesture of his that escaped my notice.

While this was going on, Dwayne was giving anxious looks across the table, asking silently if he was doing okay. But Dwayne wasn't uppermost in my mind just then, and I looked straight through his little pleas for help. It was Jordan's face I couldn't keep my eyes from—that straight nose, that elegant jaw, that thick, smooth hair that covered his head like the pelt of some expensive animal—the face I thought I knew as well as I did my own. But as I looked at it now, catching it on the slant, it took on a foreign cast. It could have been the face of someone I'd never seen before. Who was Jordan? Nobody I knew.

"You want more iced tea?" I asked Dwayne abruptly.

"Tea?" he said, giving a scared look at this glass, which was nearly full. He seemed to think I was speaking in a code of some kind.

"Tea," I said again. "I'm going to get some more." And

took my own half-full glass into the kitchen where I left it sitting beside the sink. I couldn't stand it any longer, listening to Dwayne make a fool of himself while down the table Jordan's face turned into some stranger's.

Under the heavy noon sun, I crossed the lawn past the last of the Paul's Scarlet Climbers wilting on the arbor and headed down the lane to the stable, where the ponies and horses were hanging around in the paddock. Taking a handful of Trim from the feed room, I whistled up Minnie, who'd never forgotten me through all the time I'd been away from home.

When I reached through the fence to pat her between the ears, she drew back her gray muzzle and showed thick yellow teeth. Though she ate the Trim from my palm, I saw the wicked gleam in her eye and gave her a quick slap on the nose to let her know I was onto her. I knew too well how satisfying it must be to bite down on a cushion of soft flesh and hear a yelp of pain. Minnie had always been mean and always would be. Life had paid her a dirty trick by making her a miniature horse, a kind of joke, and she wasn't about to forget or forgive. We saw eye to eye, Minnie and I did.

When I came back to the house later, I saw Jordan and Dwayne in front of the garage with their jackets off, their sleeves rolled up, leaning under the opened hood of Jordan's car, passing an oily rag back and forth as they prodded and poked, and I thought bitterly, well, that could have been predicted too. Dwayne would never be willing to hear anything bad about Jordan, his old basketball buddy. It wouldn't make any difference how many times I might say to Dwayne, "He's just condescending to you, Dwayne.

Don't you know that?" he would only look perplexed, a worried furrow between his eyebrows.

"Jordan's your *brother,* Jessie," he'd say, as though this explained everything.

I watched the two of them sourly, jealous of the way Dwayne was being so friendly with Jordan. I thought of Dwayne as being *mine.*

When I got back to the kitchen, Mama was lying in wait for me, doing the dishes by hand, which she did every Sunday no matter what anybody said to her about sticking them in the dishwasher or leaving them for Sophie.

"I'm ashamed of you," she said the moment I came through the door. "Walking out like that and leaving Dwayne alone the very first time you bring him to the house."

"He wasn't exactly alone," I said, opening the refrigerator door and helping myself to a large slice of lemon chiffon pie.

"You know exactly what I mean," Mama said. "And that's another thing. I hope you realize Sophie made that pie especially for you. She always remembers it's your favorite."

"I do realize it," I said, taking a big bite. "That's why I'm having some."

I knew it threw Mama into a depression when I showed myself to be without manners. It made her feel a failure. And this, of course, was what made rudeness irresistible though I could never be rude in a lighthearted way. I was always grim about it, evidence, if Mama chose to see it, that she had taught me all too well.

"And I guess you know too how you were hurting your

brother's feelings during that entire meal. You were so cold to him, Jessie. He was *pained.*"

"Oh, oh," I said, pretending to stab myself in the chest. "Mustn't hurt my dear brother, must I? I don't suppose it entered your head that Jordan could have hurt me first, did it? Oh, surely not Jordan, your consolation prize in this vale of tears."

Mama turned from the sink to give me a hard, straight look that sent my lazy eye immediately on an upward slide.

"Well, has he?" she said. "Has Jordan hurt your feelings?"

"How can you even ask?" I said in a bitter voice. "Haven't I heard you say more times than I can tell what a thoughtful boy Jordan is?"

With every word I spoke, I hated myself more. I wanted to cry out Mama, Mama, Jordan doesn't love me at all, and I loved him so much, but I was trapped by the self I'd made up for Mama—a smart-aleck self so full of toughness nothing could pierce its skin. I couldn't just suddenly become another character.

"A day doesn't go by," Mama said, still fixing me with her steely blue eyes, "when I don't lament Leonard's having had that stroke so young. For your sake more than for anybody else's. You would have been so close, I think, you two."

"Because I look just like him, as everybody is so fond of saying?" I took a huge bite of pie and chewed hard. "Is that why?"

"If your daddy had lived, you might have been happier, I think. You might not have been so . . . I don't know."

"Mean?" I finished for her.

"It grieves me to say it," Mama said, not hesitating a second, "but you have a hard heart. I don't think you have any idea in the world what you've done this time. Marrying that boy without caring a thing in the world about him. Just to be perverse. I saw that clearly by the way you acted at dinner. And then just going off, leaving him dangling like that."

"Don't waste your sympathy on Dwayne," I told her, licking the pie crumbs from my fingers. "He's getting something out of this deal too, you know. Or at least he thinks he is." And I laughed, a short noise that sounded more than anything else like the bark of an anguished dog.

13

*T*he next Sunday afternoon we went to visit
Dwayne's folks. He said it was right we should do that
—a Sunday with my folks, a Sunday with his—and I
couldn't argue with this, though I went with no
enthusiasm. Everybody, Dwayne said, was going to
want to see me—a yardful.

"They all *have* seen me," I said. "It's not like I was
some stranger to Sweet Gum, Dwayne. I can't go in
the hardware store without seeing your sister Jolene,
and there's Jim Dale at the station, and I'm always
running into the others in Food Lion."

"Well, but you know it's different now," Dwayne
said, looking bashful. "They haven't seen you as my
wife. That makes a big difference."

"I haven't turned purple, just because I'm married to you."

It was hard for me to see how some little ceremony, read through by a justice of the peace in six minutes flat, something done on the spur of the moment as a kind of bad joke, could have so much bearing on my life, but I saw that for Dwayne, the little ceremony held great importance.

When we drove up to Dwayne's house on Sunday afternoon, we couldn't get anywhere near the driveway for all the pickup trucks left leaning in the ditches on both sides of the road. Dwayne was right. Everybody in the countryside, it seemed, was at his house and most of them in the backyard where the men were pitching horseshoes and the women sitting in the shade with babies in their laps.

"Here's Dwayne," somebody shouted as we came around the corner of the house. "Here's Dwayne, everybody."

Dwayne grinned, standing with his hands on his hips while he was cuffed on the arm and had his cap yanked down to his eyes, but it was me they were surrounding, everybody trying to be heard.

"I'm Jim Dale's wife. Patsy? And this here's Dwayne's Uncle Barney. And here! You hadn't seen Jolene's new baby, have you?"

I put myself onto automatic pilot so when somebody put a glass of iced tea in my hand I drank it, and when somebody swung a baby in my direction I said, "Hey, big boy," and when somebody said, "How's your ma doing?" I said "Jus' fine."

I was hitting every ball that came my way, and I could have gone on doing it, I was sure, until the cows came home. One of my grandfathers had been a state senator, and I suddenly understood how easy campaigning had probably been for him. It wasn't hard to let your tongue loosen into the country drawl—I'd been doing that all my life—and easy enough to clap hands on shoulders and kiss babies that were thrust into your face. I was doing just fine, getting into the swing of things, when Dwayne said in my ear, "Mama's in the house. We'll have to go see her."

"She sick?" I said. "Why's she in the house?"

Maxine, Dwayne's oldest sister, leaned over Dwayne's shoulder to tell me that Eula had a headache, a pain like a knife between the eyes, and was resting in the house. But she'd impressed on them all that as soon as Dwayne came, we should come on in the house to see her. She was waiting for us.

We found Eula in the living room with her feet on a hassock and a chair runner embroidered with a cross and some lilies held in place with straight pins under her head. She had her eyes shut when we came in the room, but she opened them to fasten onto Dwayne, passing me by. "Well, Son," she said, "I'd about give you out."

"Here's Jessie come to say hello," he said, pushing me forward, though I wasn't bashful. Careful was all I was being.

"I have known Jessie Farquarson since the time she was a baby in a quilt," Eula said, looking at me with little eyes staring from under heavy, wrinkled lids. "There Sarah Eve was, sitting in a car directly in front of the court house, a baby in each arm. 'Come see my twins,' she called out, and I went. Fine heads of hair you both had."

"Hello, Eula," I said. "Of course you know who I am."

"I have known you all your life," Eula agreed, her lips

drawing back to show brown teeth—a gesture that could pass for a smile. "And I want to tell you I liked to have fallen full length on the floor when Dwayne told me you and him had gotten married. I don't know I have recovered to this day. If he'd told me he'd gone and married the Queen of Siam, I wouldn't have been much more taken aback."

"Well, I've known Dwayne since first grade," I said quickly. "It's not like I'm a stranger."

She looked at me from under those wrinkled eyelids, and I held still, hardly moving a muscle, the way a dog will stand still when another dog comes up to sniff. Eula was one of those women who get potbellies from having too many babies, and with her long skinny arms and her big belly what she reminded me most strongly of was a spider.

"Seems like you could have let me know what was on your mind, Dwayne," she said. "Could have dropped a hint anyhow. Gave me such a shock, you coming home with news like that, I thought sure you were funning me. Then come to find out it was all true. That pain I got in my head the very second you told me your news, that pain that went like a knife blade right between my eyes, hadn't let up to this day."

Dwayne stood with his head hanging to one side, looking downcast, but I wasn't fooled. I didn't believe for a minute Eula hadn't known Dwayne's plans well in advance. I was certain they'd all been in on the plan from the beginning, from the afternoon Dwayne lingered at the dinner table and said, "I got this idea how I can make me some money. A whole lot of money."

I took it for part of the performance when Eula looked

more kindly on Dwayne and said, "Son, what're you doing in the house on a fine day like this? You go on out and show the rest of them how to pitch a horseshoe. Jessie will stay in here and keep me company."

Dwayne didn't waste any time clearing out, and I saw I was stuck. The chair I chose to sit in was at least three arms' lengths from Eula, but she didn't hesitate to motion me over closer.

"There's something here I want to show you," she said. "And you can't see a thing sitting way over there."

So I scooted my chair a little closer to hers while Eula lifted a photograph album from the floor and opened it on her lap, smoothing the pages. "I want to show you what you're getting," she said. "What a fine boy my Dwayne is."

"Oh, I know, I know," I said. I was trapped in the house with her and might have said anything.

"No, hon, you don't," Eula said. "You don't know Dwayne the way I do. How could you? I've had him twenty-six years come August, and you haven't lived with him a month. You got a long way to go in knowing Dwayne like I do. Nine children, but I love each and ever one just the same way your mama loves you and your brother. No difference."

"Mothers do generally love their children," I said, feeling a little light-headed. "It's true Medea killed hers, but that wasn't because she didn't love them. She just hated her husband more."

Eula lifted her eyes briefly to my face. "I don't believe I've heard that story you're telling," she said. "Richmond, was it? Doesn't sound like Sweet Gum to me."

"No place close," I told her.

"I don't see how any mother in her right mind could do anything to hurt a baby of hers," she said. "Now just look here. Wouldn't any mother love a baby like that?"

She turned the album sideways so I could get a good view of a gangly-looking baby with little stick arms and legs, propped on a bed pillow. Its eyes were open, squinting idly upward trying to get a view, it appeared, of the tuft of hair, like the crest on a woodpecker, rising above its forehead.

"Oh, cute," I said, though my true opinion was that Dwayne had been one of the homeliest babies I'd ever seen in my life.

"He was a skinny baby," Eula admitted, "but he filled out fast. Here he is, now, just a little while after that."

There Dwayne was, being held on the seat of his daddy's tractor—a baby with a thin, chickenlike neck and sparse hair. And another of him standing on his feet, hanging onto the skirt of a headless and footless somebody.

All I could tell was that Dwayne in those photographs looked as ordinary as ditch water, and I couldn't see why Eula couldn't tell this too.

"Sweetest one of mine when he was a baby," Eula said. "That was Dwayne. Sweet as the day is long and never a minute's trouble. I hope you and him have one halfway as sweet for your first."

She cut her eyes at me, a calculating look I didn't catch at first. And then I thought how Sophie was always bragging about how she could tell just by a glance when somebody was pregnant, the same way she could tell whether or not somebody was harboring a fatal disease, one that might as yet elude a doctor, and I caught Eula's drift.

"A baby is about the last thing on earth we're talking

about right now," I said quickly, to cut off any thoughts Eula might have on the subject. "We're not even settled down yet. A one-room place isn't anywhere to bring a baby."

The mere thought of having a baby gave me the shudders.

"My mama was one of seven in a cabin with a dirt floor, her mama getting started at fourteen," Eula said, nothing stopping her. "The younger you have them, the easier it is. Why, in my day, I was slow off the mark having Omer at eighteen since there was Grace getting ahead of me, having her first at fifteen. Grass is growing under your feet, girl. I bet you're twenty-five if you're a day."

She smiled, showing lots of brown teeth, but her eyes didn't give in to it. And it was those eyes that led me to see what was on her mind. A baby would clinch it. If the Hawkinses could get a baby in the picture, I'd never be able to get rid of them again, no matter what happened between Dwayne and me. A baby would open every door.

"And listen, hon," she said, leaning close. "You want to keep a man at your side, you give him a child, blood of his blood."

"Oh, look at that," I said, pointing to a picture of Dwayne at six, giving a big artificial smile in a school picture to show the gap where his front teeth were missing. "I can remember Dwayne looking that way."

But this, of course, was a lie. I couldn't remember what Dwayne looked like with that gap in his teeth any more than I could remember what I looked like myself with my front teeth missing. What I did remember was the way Dwayne wore a belt far too big for him, and how he curled

the end down into his pocket, giving the other kids something to pull on to make him cry. In first grade, Dwayne
probably would have given anything to have clothes bought
just for him, clothes that didn't make him a laughingstock.

"Oh, he was so sweet," Eula said, looking over my shoulder. "I just hope you know what a treasure you're getting."
She put her hand, like a claw, down hard on my arm, giving
me a sharp little pinch.

14

"*J*essie?" Dwayne said as I was drifting off to sleep. "Don't you think it'd be fun if we had a baby?"

"What?" I said, coming instantly awake. "What put that in your head at that minute? I bet Eula's been in your ear, hasn't she?"

"She has not!" Dwayne said with such vehemence I was sure she had been. "Can't I think of having a baby without Mama getting in her two cents? I think it'd be fun. I keep thinking about it."

"I bet you have," I told him. "And you can just think again."

"But why not, Jess?" he said, spreading his hand over my stomach as though he could already feel a baby inside, swimming around.

It was on the tip of my tongue to say, You ought to *know* why not. This little agreement we've got going between us has nothing at all to say about a baby. Not a word.

"It wouldn't be such a good idea," was all I said.

"Maybe we'd have twins. Like you and Jordan."

"Like me and Jordan!" I said, enraged. "Listen, Dwayne. If that came about, if history repeated itself in that particular way, I'd shoot myself. Nothing on earth would make me go through that or make a daughter of mine go through what I have, either."

"What's so bad about it?" Dwayne said, taking my hand under the sheet. "I always thought it looked like fun, having a twin. I remember you and Jordan in grade school, always sticking up for each other."

"Yeah, well, that was grade school."

"But what's so different now? You act like you've gone off Jordan this last little while."

"Noticed that, have you," I said. "Well, I never pretended to anybody I could hide my feelings."

"But why, Jess?" Dwayne said, propping himself on one elbow so he could look down at my face. "What did Jordan do?"

"Nothing I want to talk about."

Dwayne drew a circle around my lips with one finger. "We're married to each other now," he said. "We can tell each other anything."

I thought it was very sweet of Dwayne to say that; I'd noticed before how he took account of other people's feelings in a way that nobody else I knew did. And I had a glimpse of it at that moment—Dwayne lost in a big family, always wanting the one person to tell secrets to, the one person who would stand up for him at recess when the others were pulling on the loose end of his belt. Of course he'd watched Jordan and me and thought we had it all.

I took his hand and held it under the sheet.

"You won't even believe it if I tell you why I've gone off Jordan," I told him. "You think Jordan's so great. You don't want to hear anything bad about him."

"No, I'd believe it," Dwayne said earnestly. "If you told me, I'd believe it."

"All right," I said grimly. "We'll see. The thing is, Jordan goes around saying he doesn't believe I'm his real sister. He thinks I'm an accident the hospital made."

"Jordan wouldn't say anything like that," Dwayne said, shocked.

"See? I said you wouldn't believe it. I knew you'd stick up for Jordan."

Dwayne squeezed my hand tightly. "I think you must not've heard him right."

"You think I don't know my own brother's voice? That laugh of his?"

"Well, if he said it he must've been making a joke."

"I'm telling you. Jordan said what I've just told you like it was something he'd given a lot of thought to."

"Aw, Jessie," Dwayne said, unconvinced.

"You want to hear the whole thing?" I told him. "Well, here it is." I curled into a ball and put one hand on my jaw as though I had a toothache. "When I went down to Charlottesville to see Jordan during my spring break, his old fraternity where he'd lived when he was an undergraduate was having a party, and he said, 'Oh, come and go with me. You never go anywhere.' And it's true. I don't. I could have stayed in Jordan's apartment by myself and been perfectly happy. But no. I had to go with him. Oh, Dwayne, the thing is, I thought he really wanted me to go with him. And I was flattered."

It made me grind my teeth, remembering how I'd always wanted to please Jordan. Dwayne pulled me over against him and ran his hand over my hair in a soothing kind of way. Dwayne was the only person I'd ever told this story to, and I knew why I'd chosen him. He listened hard and knew what I was feeling.

"Well, we got there early," I went on, "and I wandered into the study room while Jordan went off with some of the others to buy more liquor. When he got back, he probably thought I was still in the study. Or maybe he forgot I was even around. Who knows? But I got tired of being by myself and went into the reception room to see what was going on. When Jordan came in, I was leaning against a column, sort of hidden behind some big potted plants. Jordan didn't know I was standing there. I know that much. I could hear them laughing around as they took bottles out of sacks, and I was just about to leave my column and go help when one of them said, 'Jordan, you sure there wasn't some mix-up in the hospital when you and your sister were born? I mean, come *on!*' "

"I bet you didn't hear it right," Dwayne said. "Across the room that way."

"There's nothing wrong with my hearing," I told him. "And when Jordan gets excited, his voice goes loud. I heard him, Dwayne. No getting around it. 'We don't even look kin, do we?' Jordan said. 'Much less twins. All my life I've had dark suspicions about that hospital, some drunk doctor putting the wrong name on the wrong baby. When I was a little kid, I had this strong feeling my *real* sister was out there somewhere, undiscovered, and someday I'd see her and know. I still get that notion sometimes. One day I'll just look up, and there she'll be. And we'll recognize each other, just like that.' I remember every single word. Burned in my brain, practically."

My voice cracked, and I fell silent while Dwayne patted my hair and made hushing noises the way he had that night on the bus. I rolled against him and pressed my face into his stomach. I could tell how upset he was.

"I don't think he meant it," Dwayne said, but he didn't sound convinced.

"I know what Jordan sounds like when he's joking," I said, my breath making a warm spot on his stomach. "I *know* Jordan."

But of course as soon as I said those words I knew they weren't true. Clearly I knew a lot less about Jordan than I thought I did. The Jordan I thought I knew would never have said what he did with that note of longing in his voice. I'd always known, when I looked into Jordan's eyes, I wanted to see my double looking back, and after the party at the Kappa Sig house I knew Jordan wanted the same thing. Only I wasn't his double.

"Hey, Jess," Dwayne said, trying to be comforting. "I still think it would be fun if we had twins. One for you to hold and one for me. I used to change Jim Dale's diapers when I wasn't any more than seven. I grew up with babies, Jessie."

I blew my nose and rolled over to my part of the bed, turning my back on him. "Oh, listen, Dwayne, there's a lot more to having babies than changing their diapers," I said.

"Things just don't turn out the way you think they will. For instance, look at how my daddy had that stroke when I was four. Whatever he and Mama had in mind about their lives got blown right by the board. I don't want any part of it."

"But you have to do things," Dwayne said. "Even if you don't know how they'll turn out."

I was touched he wanted so much to say the right thing, and I held his hand while he went to sleep, but just thinking about that night when Jordan betrayed me kept me awake, churning this way and that and getting bunched up in the sheet. I could see, as clearly as though I were reading words in a book, how so much of my life had been based on what turned out to be a bunch of lies.

Take, for example, the way I'd majored in classics in college.

That started with the book of Greek myths Aunt Lillian gave Jordan and me for our seventh birthday, a book Mama thought was too old for us, so she put it on the high shelf in her closet where she kept the clothes we hadn't yet grown into. When I climbed on a chair and got the book down to look at the pictures, the first thing I saw was the frontispiece, which happened to be of Artemis and Apollo. Artemis was holding a sickle moon in one hand, and Apollo had the sun. She was dark haired and beautiful, and he was fair haired and beautiful. I knew they were twins, and I thought with excitement, See? There we are. Just like those two. Nothing would do but I had to make my way through the stories about them, even though I skipped half the words. They instantly won out over the Bobbsey twins, whom I'd loved best until then, and it was a direct result of holding that book with the red binding and the gold lettering in my hands on that afternoon when I carried it out of the closet, that I'd spent so much time in later years learning Greek. It was enough to make me sick, when I thought about it. I saw it wasn't those old stories about Artemis and Apollo I should have paid the least bit of attention to, but others I needed to take more to heart—all those that show a person can't rely on happiness, can't be sure until he's on his deathbed that the worst possible thing might not yet happen.

"Dwayne's talking babies," I told Mama the next time I went over to Clearwater. We were in the stable where I was brushing Diana and Mama was brushing Lazy Boy after we'd taken them out for a ride, passing the dandy brush back and forth the way Jordan and I had done hundreds of times while we talked and laughed. And all the time he'd probably been looking sideways at me—at that dish-faced somebody—wishing some stranger in my place.

Mama, bending down on the other side of Lazy Boy, came to attention.

"Dwayne *would* talk babies," she said. "All those Hawkinses reproduce like rabbits."

"Well, I don't want to have a baby," I said, suddenly bursting into tears so I had to wipe my nose on the sleeve of my jacket.

"Oh, sweetheart," Mama said, pity in her voice, straightening up to see me over the top of Lazy Boy's back. "I knew it was a terrible mistake for you to marry Dwayne. But you don't have to stay in that mess. Nothing could be easier. I'll go straight to the house and telephone Jordan this minute."

"Jordan!" I cried, my tears stopping on the instant. "Why in the world would you telephone Jordan?"

"Why, have you forgotten your brother is a lawyer? Jessie, we can have that marriage annulled so fast Dwayne Hawkins won't know what hit him."

"No! Stop!" I cried, running my hands up and down my cheeks to wipe my tears away. "It's got nothing to do with Dwayne."

Mama looked at me, hands on hips, in the same way she would probably have watched someone caught up in a Dionysian frenzy and frothing at the mouth.

"What do you mean it has nothing to do with Dwayne?" she said.

"Leave him out of it," I told her.

A sudden light came into Mama's eyes as she stared at me.

"That boy doesn't hold something over your head, does he? Jessie, he's not mistreating you, is he?"

"Dwayne?" I said. "Good Lord, no."

The thought was so preposterous I laughed, and with that laugh I could see Mama's sympathy for me go. She was sure I was laughing at her, for some obscure reason she couldn't understand. The way she strode back to the house with her shoulders stiff reminded me of an insulted cat.

But of course she had to have one of her secret consultations with Jordan later. I could just hear it, that conversation zinging along the wires between Clearwater and Richmond.

Mama: "Jordan, something must be done about Jessie. She's so unhappy, poor girl. She's made this awful marriage she wants to get out of, but she's too proud to say so. I think we have to intervene."

Jordan: "So what do you want me to do?"

"Get through to her."

Noises of irritation from Jordan's end of the wire.

"Oh God, Mama, why can't you just let Jessie be? But okay, okay. I'll see what I can do."

The next Sunday at dinner, I could feel Jordan's eyes resting on me balefully through the roast duck and on into the angel food pie. I refused to meet them, keeping my gaze firmly fixed just beyond Dwayne's left shoulder, on the muddy painting of a pond overhung with dark and sinister-looking trees that hung above the sideboard. Whatever their other virtues might have been, our ancestors were terrible judges of art. All that painting had ever made me think of was death by drowning.

When we finished our pie, Mama gave Jordan a meaningful look and asked Dwayne if he would come with her to the barn to have a look at a calf she was afraid might have scours. Dwayne got instantly to his feet, looking pleased, thinking no doubt he was being considered one of the family, being consulted on matters of high importance. Dwayne's innocence in these ways drove me crazy, though I found it kind of touching.

The moment the kitchen door shut behind them, I told Jordan I was going to sit on the swing and read the newspaper.

"Mind if I come along?" he said.

"Free country," I said churlishly, heading for sunlight.

I took over the swing, sitting sideways, which took up all the room, leaving Jordan to sit in a wicker chair.

I took the front section of the paper and kept my eyes resolutely on it, tossing Jordan the sports section which he allowed to lie at his feet.

"Whatever it is you're priming yourself up to say, you might as well save your breath," I told him.

Jordan's fingers came together in a peak above his stomach, an old man's gesture I hated. "If you're determined to ruin your life, there's nothing I can do for you," he said. "I told Mama, but she wouldn't listen. If you want any help out of me, though, here I am."

"When we were little, you know how I could always tell when you were about to cheat me at cards?" I said. "You'd open your eyes a little bit too wide, that's how. Every time I saw that innocent look on your face I'd think, Uh-oh."

"What's that supposed to mean?"

"It means whatever you think it does."

I saw Jordan grip the arms of his chair, rise a few inches, sink back down. He could leave with dignity or stay and fight. Those were the choices he had.

I knew when he gave me a sweet-looking smile what he'd decided on.

"Jess?" he said. "Maybe you could tell me something. I've often wondered what you and Dwayne find to talk about when you're all alone and it's just the two of you. Clogged carburetors? Broken alternators?"

I turned a page of the paper without looking up.

"Oh, there are other things in the world to do than talk," I said. "You must know that. Otherwise, how do you stand those little Junior League women you favor?"

The flared part of Jordan's nose went white.

"Broken cars and basketball," he said in an unpleasant

voice. "Those are all Dwayne knows, wouldn't you say? Oh, and how to hit a coffee can at ten paces. How could I have forgotten that?"

I'd lost my temper a long time before, but I was determined not to let it show.

"So what?" I said. "Every baseball player in the country can do the same thing."

"Who would have thought you'd be happy, living with Dwayne Hawkins in one room with furniture dragged in from the dump."

"Not everybody is as materialistic as you are, Jordan."

"Oh, for God's sake," Jordan said, shocked. I could tell he was upset at how far we'd moved into malice, and in just six minutes too.

"Shallow," I said. "That's what you are."

"All right," Jordan said, a dangerous light in his eyes. "Is that the way it's going to go? All right, then. I can tell you a thing or two you're not going to want to hear. Even when we were little kids, you envied me so much you couldn't stand it. You didn't think I knew that, did you? Well, I did."

"You've never known what I was thinking," I told him. "Never, never. So don't flatter yourself."

"Transparent as a pane of glass," Jordan said. "So transparent I couldn't help reading you. And you think that's fun to live with? You really think so?"

"My heart bleeds," I said. "It's dripping here, all over the porch."

"You have a good time with Jordan?" Dwayne asked as we drove back to Sweet Gum in our old truck.

"Oh, a peachy time with Jordan."

"I had fun with your mama. I didn't know she cared so much about those little calves. Tramping around in an old barn in her good dress and everything."

"She cares so much about those little calves she'll sell them soon to the highest bidder who'll take them off and cave their heads in with a sledge hammer," I said bitterly. "If I ever have any say-so about this farm one day, nothing will be grown here but thoroughbred horses."

"Well, that's just farming," Dwayne said in a mild voice, giving me a worried look. "That's just how you have to be, I guess."

"I don't want to hear about it," I told him, angry enough about the entire afternoon I wanted to smash my foot right through the floor of the cab. "Not another word about anything."

So we rode the rest of the way home in silence while I brooded over Jordan, and Dwayne treated me with patience the way he would have if I'd been sick but was feeling a little better.

15

Sometimes, when we'd been fooling around in bed while we waited for our supper to cook, I'd feel Dwayne's eyes on me and would see an uneasy look in them before he could turn away.

"Jessie," he said finally, "I know this isn't the way you're used to living. I mean, we go over on Sundays to your house, and it's got these big rooms, and furniture everywhere and bowls and pictures and rugs. And then just look at this here."

He waved his hand around our room, where the crooked, homemade curtains were billowing and the bedsprings twanging with every move we made.

"I like our place," I said. "I get a kick out of it."

But I knew even as I spoke I couldn't expect Dwayne

to feel the same way about it I did. It all reminded him too much of what he'd just come from and was hoping to escape.

"Aw, but listen, Jessie. All this stuff could just fall apart in the middle of the floor any minute."

"Look, Dwayne. I love Clearwater. Sure. I do love that house and the way it sits on the hill, and I love the pastures and woods and hay fields. But the things you're talking about, the family silver and china, that doesn't mean spit to me."

"There's Jolene and Bob in their trailer, now," Dwayne went on, not listening. "They've got wall-to-wall and a new sofa. Not like this stuff from the dump."

"Well, but we don't have much money, Dwayne," I said sensibly. "Considering what we have to work with, I think we do very well."

I saw the look Dwayne gave me when I said we didn't have much money, but I dismissed it at the time.

So I shouldn't have been surprised one November day when he got home for supper very late, looking pleased with himself.

I had been trying to keep food hot for over an hour and was anything but pleased. When Dwayne said "Guess what?" in a way meant to evoke delight, I only gave him a cold stare.

"This fish I was cooking for supper looks like a cornhusk by now and probably tastes like one too," I told him.

"Oh, forget that fish," Dwayne said, taking the skillet and upturning it over the garbage pail. "I'm taking you out to Western Sizzlin to eat."

"You must have fallen into some money, then," I said,

knowing how he hated to waste food. "Some rich old aunt you didn't even know you had has died and left you a pile."

"Nope," he said, tossing me my jacket from the hook. "Guess again."

"You've been playing the races on the side."

"I got myself a job," he said, sounding proud.

"I know *that,*" I told him as I followed him down the stairs. "You've got a job with your dad."

"Not that one. A new job. Something that's going to pay me a lot of money."

He swung me up in the pickup in such a jaunty way I could see he was enjoying himself.

"You've found yourself a rich wife," I said before I could stop myself. "A sickly rich wife."

He gave me a reproachful look. "I've got myself a job driving a rig," he said.

"A truck? You don't know the first thing about driving a truck, Dwayne. Those things are always losing their brakes on hills and jackknifing on ice. You'll get yourself killed."

"I have to take this course and pass a test, but I figure I can do it. I've known truck drivers, and they don't seem any smarter than I am."

"You don't even like being away from home, Dwayne, so why do you want to drive a truck for a living?"

"I want to make us more money so we can get ahead in the world. Buy us a house. Well, why not? Other people do. And after we get ourselves a house, who knows?" He goosed me in the thigh with a knuckle.

"Even if we had a house, it wouldn't change anything," I said quickly, giving him warning.

But Dwayne was off and running, not hearing anything I

might have to say. I could tell it was all clear in his mind. First we'd get some money set aside, and then we'd buy a house, and then a baby would come along and Dwayne'd be so solidly entrenched in my family that nothing could get him out.

"We have a place to sleep. Enough to eat. What more do you want? Most of the world's people would be out of their skulls with joy to have what we do."

"But I want us to get ahead," Dwayne said plaintively. "Have something to show."

"Things are always going wrong with houses," I said darkly. "They have to have new roofs and new furnaces, and any amount of money goes into things like fertilizer for the grass and something to cut the grass with after it grows. A house is just a black hole, sitting there ready to suck up any money you can lay your hands on."

"Well, I want one anyway. And it was your own brother, Jessie, who said buying a house would be a good idea. He showed me on a piece of paper about land values and tax savings and this and that. The way he pointed it out, you'd be crazy not to buy a house."

"Jordan!" I said, waking up to what was being said. "What's it to Jordan whether we buy a house or not?"

"Jordan has your best interests at heart. He worries about you."

"Like hell he does. Jordan is sly as a fox."

I knew if Jordan wanted us to buy a house, there was some reason we shouldn't I hadn't even thought about yet.

It took Dwayne over a month to pass his truck-driving test, but he did. And from that time on, he was away a lot, three, four, and sometimes even five days in a row. It all depended on the jobs he got and the distances he drove. I got used to seeing him set off in the early mornings for a run before it was light out, his old Budweiser cap pushed back on his head, clean underwear in his high school gym bag. He always looked glum starting out, but when he came back from a trip, running up the stairs to our room, flinging open the door with his arms wide, he was full of relief and joy. "I'm back! I'm back!" he yelled. "Made it, Jess."

I had the feeling he thought the minute he left the safety of our room, fate was after him, following, just ready to pounce. If he looked over his shoulder, there would be something so scary it would turn him to stone in an instant. But the top of our stairs was home base. Nothing could get him there.

He'd barely get inside the door, give me a hug, look around to see that everything was just the way he'd left it, and then he'd be down on the floor, rooting around in his gym bag, digging out the present he'd found for me in his travels. A plastic cow with its tail curled into a handle, convenient for tipping milk from its mouth; a silver-plated bracelet saying I LUV YOU; a satin pillow stuffed with balsam and bearing the message Greetings from Nashville, Tennessee, Home of the Grand Ole Opry.

"Here," he said, holding up the paper sack. "Something I found you in Truck Stops of America."

"Oh, what could it be?" I said, shaking the sack up and down. "I'll never guess."

Christmas, I could tell, had always held disappointment for Dwayne. With all those children in the family, the Hawkinses had probably been lucky to furnish them with hard candy. Dwayne had been starved of presents all his life.

So I always opened the sack he handed me with a cry of delight since I loved to draw that shy smile to his face. I knew what he wanted and slipped the bracelet on my arm, put the pillow on the bed, set the cow pitcher in the middle of the table.

On those homecomings, I rose to Dwayne's sense of occasion by cooking him what he most liked to eat—fried chicken, mashed potatoes and thickening gravy, turnip greens and corn bread. Peach cobbler for dessert with maple walnut ice cream on top. Dwayne didn't like to be faced with foods he'd never had to eat before, and since Eula's repertory was limited, he wasn't hard to please.

For the first couple of months Dwayne was driving a truck, he didn't say anything more about looking for a house, but he was only biding his time, waiting until we had a little money in the bank. Or maybe it was the early spring that made him impatient. In any case, after he'd been driving the truck for a couple of months, he added something else to the homecoming ritual. After I'd admired the present he gave me, he'd flop down on the bed and say, "Look at any houses while I was away?"

"No," I told him every time.

"You might just have a look, Jess," he said plaintively. "I am out there driving that truck as hard as I can."

"It's not because of me you're driving Humpin' to Please all over the Southeast," I told him quickly.

"Still. You could run around some with Bertha Penrose and look at a few places."

"I have better things to do," I told him. "And besides, you can't expect to raise the down payment on a house in just two months."

"We could work something out, I bet," Dwayne said, giving me a fishy look from the corner of his eyes.

"And you can leave Mama out of this," I said, though as soon as I spoke, I recognized my mistake. Dwayne would never have the courage to ask Mama for the down payment for a house. He was in awe of Mama and likely to remain that way. No, the person he'd ask would be Jordan.

"You can leave Jordan out of it too," I said, and saw by the way Dwayne quickly looked away that I'd guessed right.

"In fact you better just forget the entire thing for a long time to come. We won't be able to afford a down payment on a house until we're so old and decrepit we'll be in the market for a decent nursing home."

But Dwayne looked so depressed I relented a little. I told him the next time he came home for a few days we'd see what Bertha had to offer.

Bertha Penrose was the only real estate agent in Sweet Gum, staying in business mostly on retirees who had started drifting down from the North to the Virginia hill country in recent years. She was a stout, slow-moving woman who kept an atomizer in her pocket for spraying the air in front of her when she had to leave the safety of her car or office since, as she told us in the first three minutes we were with her, she was allergic to everything under the sun. House dust, cat fur, flower pollen—anything that could occupy airspace. She thought the spray from her atomizer dampened the air and therefore discouraged the dust, and she carried the atomizer in front of her through the dangerous air between office and car like somebody in the Middle Ages holding out a cross to ward off vampires. And because of all those allergies, she was reluctant to actually take us *inside* houses. She much preferred driving to some house that was on the market, idling in front with car's air conditioner working full time, describing what lay behind the closed door of the house by drawing the layout of the rooms on her dashboard with a stubby finger.

I found it quite lulling, myself, and sometimes took catnaps between one house and that next since I knew Bertha could offer us the Taj Mahal for $10,000 and I'd still say no. I had nothing to worry about. But Dwayne looked longingly at the houses we stopped in front of, craning his neck out the window to get the best look he could.

"How many doors does the living room in that one have?" he'd want to know. "How high are the ceilings? Basement dry?"

I was pretty sure that as Dwayne drove Humpin' to Please down to Savannah or up to Lexington he spent his time through dull stretches thinking up questions like those. He had so many of them Bertha finally had to break down and risk her life by showing us inside a few houses.

The first she showed us, at my insistence, were what she called modest houses, though I soon realized that *modest* was merely a real estate euphemism for run-down. These were houses with sagging porches and rotting roofs, floors covered with linoleum that uncurled at the edges, and kitchen sinks held to the wall by peculiar constructions of serpentine pipes. Dwayne's spirits sank lower with each of these houses we went through, and Bertha began wheezing pathetically, constantly forced to return to a water supply in order to refill her atomizer.

They both looked reproachfully at me, but I, in my perverse way, enjoyed pointing out the good features of these houses—the attic bedroom with sloping ceiling, the windows that faced stands of trees. A little work, I told Dwayne, and these houses would be fine. Yank off the roof, jack up the floors, and all would be well. But Dwayne could see only decay and early death in those houses.

The only one I genuinely liked was a log cabin, so far back in the woods on one of the mountains we had to drive up a rutted trail to get to it, a cabin somebody had built in order to be in a good position to shoot things from the porch. Bertha wouldn't dream of setting one of her feet inside the place, but she did give the keys to Dwayne so we could take a look.

The fireplace still gave off the smell of wet ashes, cobwebs were draped as thick as cloth over the upper reaches of the windows, the bathtub, sitting in the kitchen, had claw feet, and the gas stove sat on tall, spindly legs.

"My *grandma* had a stove like that she threw on a heap when I was six years old," Dwayne said, looking horrified. "I bet that thing would blow you up if you turned it on."

"But look how solid those logs are. This is a *real* house, Dwayne. Built by people with their own hands. Not some piece of junk."

"Gives me the creeps," Dwayne said. "I'd sooner spend

out my days in the room we have now than come to a place like this."

The house he fell for was in the development across Black Creek, a newly built house with a yard churned to mud by the builders, though none of this mud had found its way inside. Deep, thick beige carpet in every room except the kitchen. Three bathrooms, a Jacuzzi, microwave oven set at eye level.

"Oh shoot, oh shoot," Dwayne groaned as we went through the rooms. "This one's got everything."

"It also costs over a hundred thousand dollars," I reminded him. "It might as well be a heavenly mansion as far as we're concerned."

"But look here at this, Jessie," Dwayne said, calling me into the master bathroom to show the knobs in the shape of swans, turning them on and off like someone who'd never seen running water before.

"Don't you think . . . ?" he said, still bent over the faucets.

"No," I told him. I did *not* think.

"Jordan—" Dwayne started, but I cut him off.

"We are going to stand on our own feet," I said sternly. "You wouldn't want it any other way, would you?"

The truth was, I knew Dwayne wanted that house any way he could get it, but when I put it to him that way, he couldn't say yes.

Turning on the faucets one more time, he watched the water gush.

"I guess we could hold on a little while longer," he said

sadly. "Save up more money before we look again. Only, will you be happy, Jessie?"

I told him I thought I would be able to contain for some time to come any wild desire I might have to buy a house. And that's the way we left it.

16

*I*t was in the early spring, the busiest time of the year, with cows calving and sows farrowing, when Mama brought Lazy Boy back to the barn after a ride and he got spooked by a dried leaf rattling against the fence, taking Mama off guard and banging her into the side of the barn, tearing the ligaments in her knee.

"My own fault," she told me when I went to Clearwater after Sophie telephoned. "My attention was turned, noticing how well the pasture was coming along, and Lazy Boy doesn't miss a trick. Always looking for opportunities to pretend he's spooked. Makes him feel like he's a wild horse."

Her knee was bound up—Dr. Jacobson had come to

the house—and she was sitting on the veranda with her leg propped on a chair.

"Sophie says you're supposed to stay off that leg," I warned her.

I could tell perfectly well what she was intending to do, just by the way her head was set watching the barns.

"I can't just sit around here when there's so much to do. If my leg can't take it, well, hard luck to my leg."

"You want to be crippled for life?" I told her. "Fine. Go right ahead and hobble out to the barn, then."

"It's *March,* Jessie," Mama said, as though that settled everything.

It was easy for me to see at that moment what had allowed Mama to take over the farm after Daddy had his stroke, a woman who'd had nothing to concern herself with before except to decide what she'd wear to the Hunt Ball. I knew by the way she glared at me, beating the arms of her chair with closed fists. Nothing would stop Mama doing exactly what she wanted.

But I could be stubborn too. "I'm going to take over here, like it or lump it," I told her.

"You don't know the first thing," she said in alarm, but I turned my back and headed for the stable.

After I finished mucking out the stalls, I went to the hog sheds to take over the watering from Elroy and told him to go help Joe get a new fan belt on the John Deere so one of them could get started plowing under the winter wheat. I knew this was a top priority since the ground needed to warm up before spring planting. I knew more than Mama thought I did.

Later on I helped Elroy repair fence where deer had

broken it down, coming through the woods to get at the winter wheat, though every time I went to the house where Mama was doing the February accounts, she complained I was probably holding Elroy back more than I was helping him. I finally yelled at her to get off my back, and she subsided a little, but we both continued to glare at each other suspiciously.

That night I couldn't see any point in going back to Sweet Gum to sleep when I had a perfectly good room waiting at Clearwater, so after supper I went upstairs, turned the doorknob shaped like an eyeball, and entered the room that hadn't changed since Jordan and I were little. The bed with the ram's head, the bulgy green chair, the Chinese rug with the bald patches. Same walnut tree outside the south windows. Same cherry chest with one of the drawer pulls missing since Jordan and I had used it for a treasure once and forgotten where we'd buried it. Same smell of dusty quilts and old dry wood.

That night as I lay in bed I listened again to the rattling in the gutter that might have been a squirrel rolling acorns along its length, the noise that Jordan and I had made up stories about, telling ourselves it was ghost children playing with marbles—Bessie and Lucia, Grandfather Farquarson's little sisters who had died of diphtheria in that very room. We'd heard the story all our lives and imagined them in the long dresses and wide sashes they wore in their one photograph.

Sometimes we'd pinch each other and whisper, "It's little Bessie, come to get you," but the truth was we weren't afraid of Bessie or Lucia, they'd been so small when they died.

It was Daddy Jordan and I were afraid of as we lay side by side in the bed, listening to the boards settling against the nails and the rattling in the gutter.

Jordan said, "I think it's Daddy, can't you hear him? Coming down the hallway to get us."

I imagined his bulgy eyes and the gobbley noises getting more and more wild and angry, and I threw the quilt over my head.

Molly, lying across our feet, grew nervous when the house creaked, and her hackles rose as she lifted her head and stared at the door, making growlings deep in her throat. We knew she could hear Daddy's ghost out there in the hallway, shuffling up and down, looking for our door.

"If he comes in," Jordan whispered in my ear, "we have to yell 'Daddy, it's us!' so he'll remember."

But I knew he wouldn't remember because we'd been so little when he died. Jordan and I pulled Molly up to the pillow between us and held hands across her fur, all three of us watching the door for it to open the tiniest sliver.

But now I just lay listening to the rattling in the gutters while I brushed my feet against the sheets, thinking about Dwayne out there somewhere on the road to Raleigh, gliding along, beating out Reba McEntire on the steering wheel of the truck. I missed him. He seemed a lot farther away than North Carolina.

In the night, when I woke suddenly and stretched my legs to the foot of the bed looking for company, searching for Dwayne's long legs with the bony knees and the soft little tufts of hair growing along the ridges of his toes, I had a longing for him to be there in the flesh and not just part of some flickering picture in my head. I was surprised, how much I wanted him there.

I was up at first light to make a check of cows and hogs, the way Mama had always gotten up on spring mornings. I'd heard her more times than I can tell, padding along the upstairs hallway, the floorboard at the top of the landing giving off its complaint when she stepped on it.

Jordan and I had had chores to do too, before we caught the school bus in the mornings, but we always stayed in bed until the last minute and then went weaving drunkenly to the barns with our jackets hanging off our shoulders, our sneakers untied, cross as two cats.

But now, I liked coming into the stable, seeing the white breaths of all the horses making soft puffs of steam in the chilly morning air, listening to their sleepy snortings and whickerings which became more lively as they heard me in the feed room lifting the lids from the barrels of feed.

I liked having it all to myself—the barns, the pastures, the woods—and I knew why Mama had gotten up at first light to walk along the lane with her hands in the pockets of her jacket, the heels of her boots digging little new moons out of the ground with every step.

"If Daddy hadn't had that stroke, would you have turned out like Aunt Lillian?" I asked Mama, sliding a tray of toast and coffee across her lap as she sat propped on pillows. "Going to Atlanta to shop every three minutes, running all the time to meetings of the Heritage Society and the Garden Club?"

"I suppose your daddy could have taken care of the farm

without me," she said, laughing in a way that let me know she thought this was unlikely.

"You would have hated it," I said, sitting gingerly on the edge of the bed. "If you'd lived that life."

"Oh no I wouldn't," Mama said decidedly enough to end that conversation. "I'd have liked it just fine."

It made me feel shy, seeing Mama flushed with sleep, a little patch on one cheek where the folds in the pillow had left their mark. Even when we were little, Jordan and I hadn't come into Mama's bedroom except on Sunday mornings when she stayed in bed late, and it seemed strange to have her down helpless where she couldn't get away. All that opportunity, ticking by.

I watched Mama's knife move over the toast, spreading the butter, and all the things I might have said rushed through my head—"Were you in love with Daddy or what when you married him? Did you plan on having Jordan and me, or were we accidents?"—but when I opened my mouth, none of them came out. What I kept seeing, as I watched Mama's fingers move so gracefully over the toast, was that look I'd seen a thousand times when Mama's eyes happened to fasten on me unexpectedly—just the ghost of what she was feeling, and it was always the same thing. Pity.

Homely daughters should never have beautiful mothers. If I had any say-so in the way the world was run, that's one thing that would be outlawed.

While I sat picking the bedspread into peaks, trying to think what it was I most wanted to say to her, Mama gave a sudden little crow of delight.

"Oh, I wanted to tell you," she said. "Good news. Jordan

is thinking about setting up a law office here in Sweet Gum."

"What?" I said. "Why would he do that? He's got a perfectly good job in Richmond. He'd never make as much money in Sweet Gum."

"But working in a big law firm doesn't altogether suit Jordan. He could be his own person here. And Jordan would like that, wouldn't he? Never having to take orders from anyone else."

"Just where was Jordan thinking of living?" I asked, as things slid together in my head. "If he came back to Sweet Gum?"

"Why, here of course," Mama said in surprise.

"Clearwater?" I said, my heart starting to hammer dangerously.

Mama gave me a strange look. "You know sooner or later I'll need help in running the farm."

"And you expect *Jordan* to help?" I said. *"Jordan?* Jordan mucking around in horse shit and cow shit and hog shit? You must be kidding. If anybody's going to run this place eventually, it sure isn't Jordan. What's wrong with me?"

Mama looked startled. "I supposed since you married Dwayne . . . in fact Jordan's talked to me about buying you a house in town. And that might be appropriate when the two of you settle down a little."

"Oh he did, did he?" I said, beside myself. "Jordan said it would be nice if you bought us a little development house somewhere? Three bedrooms and a screaming baby in every one of them. No thank you. I'd rather cut my throat."

I could see it all, Jordan and Dwayne leaning over the motor of Jordan's car on Sunday afternoons, Dwayne innocent as a sheep, Jordan worming his way in as usual, hogging everything for himself when I thought he'd be content with having all the looks and being Mama's favorite and making all that money. But no. He wasn't content with having everything else. He wanted Clearwater too.

"When we were in high school, who was it out driving one of the tractors all during haying season?" I said furiously. "It sure wasn't Jordan. There he was in the shade with his feet up, reading a book."

"Jordan is allergic to alfalfa. You remember those rashes he'd get."

"I got rashes too. The difference was I ignored mine."

"Nobody asked you to suffer," Mama said, a closed look coming over her face. "Why did you work in the hay if it made you uncomfortable?"

"Because I believe in being stoic. I'd never have made it through my childhood if I hadn't been."

"Oh, please do not start in on that," Mama said, raising a hand to her brow. "I think I'll scream if I have to listen one more time to how I always favored Jordan, how you were a poor, unloved little thing, neglected and forlorn. You don't know how much that upsets me."

"It ought to," I said meanly.

"It is not true!" Mama said, turning her attention to her coffee. "It isn't true and it never was."

"That may be your story and you can stick with it, but it sure isn't the way I saw it," I told her as I stood up from the bed. "I should know my own feelings, shouldn't I?"

But Mama had turned her attention from me so completely a door thick enough to stop bullets might have just slammed between us. I always said too much, went too far, and couldn't seem to learn. That's the way Mama had been my entire life—tuning out anything she didn't want to hear. That was probably the way she stayed so young-looking. It didn't matter if *my* heart was broken. If she was tired of hearing what I had to say, I might as well clamp down hard on my tongue and shut up right there.

17

"*H*as Jordan said anything to you about coming to Sweet Gum to live?" I asked Dwayne when he got back from his run.

"I don't know," Dwayne said. "I wasn't paying attention."

"Can you see that? Jordan coming back here? I know he's going to end up sooner or later with some woman who'd go crazy in a place like Sweet Gum. Serve him right too."

I wanted Dwayne on my side, feeling indignant over the same things I did, but Dwayne was too sweet-natured.

"Wouldn't you like having all the family together?"

he asked in surprise. Everybody down the road from everybody else? That's what I like."

"Oh, you would. You would," I said darkly.

When Jordan drove from Richmond on Sunday, I watched him like a hawk as he cut up his roast beef. When he lifted his eyebrows in a questioning kind of way, as much as to say "What's the matter with *you?*" I went on glaring.

"Pass the horseradish" was the only thing I said to him the entire time. Only as we were carrying our dishes into the kitchen after dinner, I leaned close to him and said, "Want to come out to the barns with me, Jordan? Hose down the hog sheds?"

"Do you really need me?" he said, giving me an uneasy look. "I'm wearing good clothes."

"Oh, I'll manage," I told him. "You might as well sit in the shade like a gentleman and keep Mama company."

I went off feeling triumphant, hoping Mama had overheard that little exchange. It was only after I was in the hog sheds, hosing them down, that I saw what it had gotten me, that little game. A lot of hog shit, that was what. I didn't know who I was trying to fool. If Jordan took over Clearwater someday he could run it perfectly well without ever having to do the dirty jobs. He'd turn those jobs over to somebody else and do just fine.

And yet I seemed unable to change my tactics, going right ahead trying to impress Mama with how well I could do all those things she'd overseen when she was on her feet. Not that I was given credit.

On the afternoons I had to leave Clearwater early because Dwayne was getting back in town that day, Mama would inevitably say, "Oh, Jessie, aren't you going to take care of the horses this evening? I was counting on you for that. And Sophie was planning to have you here for supper. She's making scalloped potatoes only because you like them so much."

"Well, I can't help that," I said, heading for my car. "I did tell you Dwayne was getting back today, but you never listen to anything I tell you."

"I don't see any reason why you should cook when Sophie's already making supper. Dwayne could come here. I certainly don't begrudge him a meal, for heaven's sake."

Mama refused to understand that for Dwayne to come to Clearwater on the evenings he got back from a run would be a hardship. He wanted to have me to himself those nights, to give me the present he'd brought, to eat with his heels caught on the rungs of his chair without worrying all the time about what to talk to Mama about. But she refused to understand this.

However, Dwayne didn't appreciate the problems I had with Mama, either. I was caught between the two of them, and they both went out of their way to give me a hard time.

After those nights I spent in Sweet Gum with him, Dwayne always reached out a hand for me as I groped my way out of bed in the morning. "You don't have to go out there *now,* Jessie," he'd say. "Wait till after breakfast at least. I don't ever get to see you."

And then when I was at Clearwater, Mama would say, "Oh, why don't you just stay for supper here, Jess? Dwayne can go eat with his own family."

In late March, when all the sows were farrowing, things got even more impossible.

For two nights I stayed on a cot beside the birthing pens, or at least I set up a cot beside the pens. It wasn't much sleep I got, since I was kept busy keeping the smallest piglets warm between the folds of a blanket while I got their mothers used to being surrounded by ten or fifteen small pink snouts and twenty or thirty little slit eyes. With some of the new mothers farrowing for the first time, I had to be cunning, sneaking their babies to them gradually so they didn't freak out with the snorting and rooting and sucking all at once and crush a few of their young to death out of fear and annoyance. I had my hands full, with wild-eyed mothers and babies scrambling around in the straw, and didn't have much time to think about anything else.

Still, when Mama called me from the porch, I went to see what she wanted. She was established in her wicker chair, training her field glasses on the barns.

"I know Elroy's at the plowing because I can hear the tractor, but what I don't know is if Joe's started those calves on their shots yet."

"I've been with the hogs all morning, remember? I can't keep up with everybody and everything."

"But that's exactly what you do have to do," Mama said irritably. "If you want to take over my job, that's what it calls for. Joe gets bogged down, squandering the morning working on some engine we're not even going to need for three months while the calves are crying out for their shots."

"I haven't had a minute," I told her. "So far I haven't lost a pig, but do you even ask about that? No. All you can think about is Joe and the calves. Small thanks for anything *I* do."

"Very well," Mama said grimly, struggling to get to her feet and reaching for the cane I'd found for her in the attic, leftover from some blind ancestor. "I'll see to it myself."

"All right, I'll see to the goddamn calves," I said, pushing her back in her chair.

"And I won't have you using language like that to my face," she said furiously.

It was no wonder, with all this, that Dwayne slipped from my mind entirely. It was much later, when the sun was going down, I suddenly remembered he was due to get back from one of his trips that day, and of course I hadn't done one thing to get ready for his homecoming.

As soon as I remembered, I called out to Mama I had to leave right then, and rushed for the car.

But since I had to make a stop at Food Lion for chicken and frozen peas, it was getting dark by the time I drove up our street. Even in the fading light I saw Dwayne's truck, parked in the driveway, and I knew he'd come into an empty room without even a note waiting for him on the kitchen table.

"Dwayne! Dwayne!" I called out as I ran up the steps, but when I flung open the door there was nothing but silence to greet me. Though it was early dusk, there were no lights on.

I was relieved, thinking Dwayne had gone over to the Sunoco station to see his daddy and I'd have time to get the chicken in the skillet before he got back. I was just lifting the groceries from the sack, feeling cheerful, when I noticed, from the corner of my eye, a long lump in the middle of our bed. A lump with a tuft of red hair sticking out on the pillow.

"Dwayne!" I said, running over. "What's wrong with you? Are you sick?"

The blanket shifted and an eye looked out at me, but Dwayne didn't say a word.

"Is that you?" I said uncertainly, turning on the lamp.

But that moss green eye, watching me balefully, couldn't have been anyone's but Dwayne's.

"I got back last night and you weren't here," he said reproachfully, pulling the blanket from his face. "You haven't been here all day."

"Oh Lord, Dwayne, I'm sorry. I thought it was today you were supposed to get back."

"I told you when I left Tuesday. But you never listened, I guess. I said yesterday's when I'd be back."

"You knew where I was, Dwayne," I said, annoyed. "Why didn't you come over to Clearwater? Telephone at least?"

Dwayne just watched me with his mournful, bloodshot eyes.

"Well, couldn't you have done that? Couldn't you have come to Clearwater instead of lying around here feeling sorry for yourself?"

Dwayne shut his eyes. "I thought maybe you'd gone off and left me. How did I know you wanted to see me anymore?"

"Oh, for heaven's sake, Dwayne," I said. "I suppose you'd just lie in this bed until you starved to death."

"I knew if you wanted to see me again, you'd come back. So I just curled up and waited."

"I don't feel sorry for anybody who'd lie there in bed without doing a thing to help himself. What would you have done if I hadn't come back tonight, either? Gone hungry?"

"If you hadn't come back, I wouldn't have felt like eating. Everything would stick in my throat."

"Cut it out, Dwayne," I told him, scooping some shortening into a skillet and sliding it onto the stove to get hot. "You know you'd have gone to your mama's house and eaten everything in sight."

"No I wouldn't," he said, but he gave me one of his vampire smiles to show he felt better.

I was the tired one, with no patience left to spare, and while the chicken was browning, I took off my shoes and climbed into bed beside Dwayne. He didn't say anything, but after I'd been lying there a few minutes he reached down to the floor and handed me the beer he'd been drinking, and we finished it off that way, passing it back and forth.

When the chicken was tender, I made thickening gravy and cooked the peas and told Dwayne to come to the table. But before he would, he took a brown sack out of his duffle bag and handed it to me.

"I was planning on giving you this last night," he said, a note of reproach in his voice.

"Nobody said you had to bring me anything at all," I said as I reached into the sack and took out an ugly toy monkey wearing a miniature tee shirt saying Kiss Me, I'm Cute.

"Well?" Dwayne said, watching me expectantly the way he always did when he gave me anything. "Aren't you going to?"

"Going to what?" I said, setting the monkey down on the table with its arms in the air. I didn't know what Dwayne expected me to do with an ugly toy monkey with cheap plush fur, and I wasn't in the mood to have to act excited about it.

"Do what that monkey says," he said, grinning and sticking his jaw in my direction.

I gave him a quick kiss, but it made me cross to have to do it. I hadn't had more than two hours sleep in as many nights, I was so tired I felt light-headed, and there Dwayne was, expecting me to go nuts over an ugly monkey.

"Don't you like him?" Dwayne said, moving the monkey's arms up and down. "I thought sure you would."

"I'm just cranky," I told him. "I've been taking care of sows and baby pigs for two days, and I didn't get much sleep."

"If you weren't around, your mama would find somebody else to do all that stuff," Dwayne said. "She's got two people working full time for her and more on piecework. She'd get the job done."

Everything about Dwayne rubbed me the wrong way at that moment—the way he sat hunched over his plate so avidly, licking gravy off his finger, the way he pretended to shake hands with the monkey.

"What do you know about it?" I said. "What do you know about hired hands and how hard it is to find anybody with any sense to work for you? After all, it wasn't a problem you had to face in your family."

"What's that supposed to mean?" he said, an edge coming into his voice. "We were too shirttail poor to have anybody working for us, or what?"

"Interpret it any way you want to," I told him.

We finished eating in silence with the monkey on the table between us, its arms held above its head as though somebody held a gun to its side.

When we went to bed, all I wanted to do was sleep, but this wasn't the way we spent those nights when Dwayne got back from a run, and he was quick to let me know it. I'd no sooner settled in bed than I could feel Dwayne's hand, sneaking up the tail of my pajama shirt, his fingers sliding along my skin. I rolled away to my side of the bed, but Dwayne refused to take the hint. He slid along beside me and there his hand was again, groping its way in the dark.

He seemed to think just because he'd been gone for five days, driving around in a truck, I should give in to his every whim now he was back. What did he care I was so tired I couldn't even keep up with what day of the week it was? There he was, pushing on for what *he* wanted, just like everybody else I could mention.

Suddenly I flung myself away from Dwayne and turned on the lamp.

"Hey!" Dwayne said, outraged. "I'm blind."

"We always make love in the dark," I said. "If you want to this time, it's going to be in the light."

Dwayne's face was inches from mine, his eyeballs rolling under the closed lids.

"And with your eyes open too."

He rolled away from me and lay with his arm over his eyes.

"See? You can't, can you?" I said bitterly. "In the dark I

could be anybody, couldn't I? Not somebody with wall-eyes."

"Have I ever said a word about your eyes or anything else?"

"Oh, but there's a reason for that, isn't there?" I said meanly. "A very good reason."

Dwayne just lay with his arm over his face.

"Well?" I said, digging my elbow into his ribs. "Isn't that right? Isn't there a very good reason why you can put up with the way I look?"

"I'm tired," Dwayne said. *Tarred* was the way he said it. "I'm tarred as a dog. On the road five days and come back to this."

"And I've been up for two nights, but I came back here and cooked supper for you. And what did you do? Not even a word of thanks. Good manners is something you never so much as heard about in your family, obviously."

Dwayne grabbed my wrist under the sheet and stared at me across the pillow. "Don't say anything bad about my family," he said. "Don't do it, Jess."

So I went to my side of the bed, and he went to his, and we lay that way, clinging to the edges of the mattress, resisting the pull to the sagging middle.

18

*I*t was a perfect spring day as I drove to the farm the next morning, the air soft, the plum trees in bloom, but I couldn't enjoy a moment of it. I'd quarreled with everyone—Mama and Jordan and Dwayne—and I was so cross and unhappy I could hardly stand it.

When I got to the farm, it was to find Mama hobbling around on her bad knee and wouldn't be stopped no matter what I said, and one of the calves was so sick we had to have the vet. And after that, Mama told Joe off for not seeing to the calf earlier— he ought to have seen it was failing—and then Joe sulked.

It was a trying day, and I wasn't in the mood for trouble of any kind when I got back to Sweet Gum. All I wanted was to sit in a chair with my feet up and look out the window at the sky.

So I wasn't pleased, when I got to the top of the stairs outside our doorway, to hear somebody moving around in our room.

"Hell," I said under my breath.

I'd have to put up with Dwayne's bad temper or his silence if he still felt insulted and injured, and he probably still felt both.

But when I opened the door, I saw it wasn't Dwayne waiting for me but Eula, prowling through the shelves in our kitchen cabinet, her raised arms lifting her skirt high enough to show me the tops of her stockings, which made sausage-shaped rolls above her knees.

"Looking for something, Eula?" I said, but she clearly didn't know the meaning of shame. She went right ahead sliding the cans of beans and tomatoes across the shelf, snooping, I was sure, to see how richly stocked I kept our food supply. Was I feeding her boy well, or was I leaving him to go half-hungry? That was what she wanted to know.

"Just seeing if you had some coffee I could start in the pot," she said, her hands still busy.

"Make yourself at home," I said. "I guess you came looking for Dwayne."

"Oh, I know where Dwayne is. Over at Jolene's playing with the baby. Hanging over that crib looking his eyes out. Crazy about babies and always has been."

Oh ho, I thought. Dwayne hadn't wasted much time getting his mother into action, like a Civil War general maneuvering the big cannons into place behind the earthworks.

I took the coffee from the lower shelf on the left-hand side of the stove, the place where any reasonable person would have looked for it first, and measured some into the pot.

"Hon, it's you I've come to see," Eula said, showing her teeth in what she probably thought was a friendly smile. "Had to come to town to the grocery, so I thought, Well, why not go see my daughter-in-law? Pay her a little visit."

"You know Mama's torn the ligament in her knee," I said, to stave off any reproach for how I spent my time. "I've been over at Clearwater helping her."

I pulled out a chair for Eula at the kitchen table, and she sat, though I could tell her eyes were still roaming the room. I'd cut off her prowling before she'd gotten a good start.

"Oh, talk about knees," Eula said. "I've got rheumatism in my joints and headaches that split my head wide open. I hadn't been a well woman for ten years and nobody knows what I go through."

"Sounds like your life's not worth living," I said, not paying much attention to what came out of my mouth.

"Oh no, hon," she said, giving me a shocked look. "If the good Lord sees fit to keep me here on this old earth, I'll bow to His will. And my grandbabies give me the strength to go on. 'Granny, make me some sugar cookies. Give me a lap, Granny,' And I can't say no. My heart goes out to your mama, sitting by herself in that big house. Not even one little baby she can hold in her arms and love."

That was a subject I thought had been put on a back burner for a while in the Hawkins family, but clearly I was wrong.

"If Mama is pining away for a grandchild, she's been able to hold her tongue on the subject," I said.

Eula's eyes, under those hooded lids, were as fierce as an old crow's.

"It's Dwayne to think about too. Him over there right now, hanging over that baby's crib, trying to get it to pat-a-cake."

"Any time Dwayne wants to have himself a baby he can go right ahead," I said. "Only he'll have to leave me out of it."

"Course I know you're waiting until you can get yourselves a house," Eula said, ignoring my remark. "Dwayne's told me how you're saving up."

"That's what he told you, is it?" I said in as sweet a voice as I could raise.

When I handed Eula her cup of coffee, I set the milk and sugar within reach, knowing that her kind always took both, grasping even in small things.

"That boy working himself to death," she said. "Sacrificing himself. If me and his daddy had a thing set by we'd give it in a minute, but we haven't been as lucky as some. Worked ourselves down all our lives, but precious little to show. What gets to me is how those who do have it won't do a thing to help out their own children. What do they think they're waiting for? Planning on living forever?"

I watched Eula empty four heaping teaspoons of sugar and half the pitcher of milk into her coffee and stir it round and around. I felt light-headed from all I'd had to put up with the last few days and knew even before I opened my mouth I wasn't going to be responsible for what came out.

"All that money so near and Dwayne not able to touch a penny of it," I said, and laughed. "That does make you want to bite nails, I bet."

Eula drank the entire cup of coffee without once lowering it from her lips while her eyes glittered at me over the rim. When she finished, she set the cup on the table with a thump and got to her feet.

"You know, my boy could've married a whole lot finer-looking girl than you are," she said, spitting out the words. "Whole lots finer."

"So why did he marry me, then? Tell me that. Why did he marry me?"

But of course this was a question Eula wasn't about to answer. She swept from the room without a backward glance, shutting the door with a little click behind her. The moment she had, I snatched the cup she'd been drinking from and threw it against the wall, where it broke into smithereens.

When Dwayne came back at suppertime, I was waiting for him. I'd had Eula's voice in my ears for hours saying, "My boy could have married a lots finer-looking woman than you," and I was brooding, watching the light grow dimmer while I nursed a beer.

Dwayne switched on the light, and I could see his eyes going around the cold stove, the empty table.

"Looks like we better go out to eat," he said.

I just eyed him, cradling my can of beer in my hands.

"Western Sizzlin? Ponderosa, maybe?"

I didn't move.

"You're not still mad, are you?" he said in a plaintive voice.

"Why should I be mad? Just because your mother was over here telling me you could've married a lots finer-looking woman than me. Why should that make me mad?"

"You must've misheard her," he said, his ears turning pink. "She wouldn't say a thing like that."

I crushed the beer can in my hand so a few foamy bubbles fizzled through the slit. "She was here when I got back from Clearwater, prowling around in the kitchen cabinets. Telling me how we ought to have a baby, which is none of her business."

A soft, almost sweet look came over Dwayne's face. "She did that?" he said. "Bless her heart. Mama would stick her head in the mouth of a lion for one of her own."

"If she sticks her head in the mouth of this lion again, she's going to go around headless. Your mother is a dangerous old woman, Dwayne. She's got a mean streak too."

Dwayne turned pale, but I was not remorseful. I could feel the blood start to race, pounding in my ears.

"Mama told me from the beginning that sooner or later you'd throw it in my face," Dwayne said. "How you were a Farquarson. You'd never forget it, she said. But I never believed her."

"Oh, come off it, Dwayne," I said. "You know perfectly well your mother never told you not to marry me. Your mother was right in the middle of those plans you all made that afternoon when you were sitting around singeing the pinfeathers off a pullet or shelling a bushel of field peas. I might as well have been there in a ladder chair, listening to every word."

Even as I spoke, I knew that everything between Dwayne and me had been leading up to this moment, and now it was here, I couldn't stop myself and didn't want to, either.

"Pinfeathers?" Dwayne said, putting on a look of stunned amazement. "Peas?"

"Or some other homey task. Peeling peaches, maybe? The juice running off your elbows? Whatever you were doing when you hatched up the plan for getting your hands on Clearwater. Or half of Clearwater, anyhow. There *is* Jordan's share to take into account."

"Clearwater?" Dwayne said, groping for a chair and falling into it.

"Oh, stop it, Dwayne," I told him. "You can't act for two cents. I saw through you from the beginning, from the moment you said we should get married. You were as easy to read as a book. All you had to do, or so you thought, was marry an ugly woman no other man had paid attention to and put up with her until such time as a thousand acres came tumbling into your lap. Don't you think I *knew* that?"

Dwayne stared at me with his hands on his knees. "You think that's why I married you?" he said. "You really and truly think that's why?"

"I know it."

"You're joking me, aren't you?" he said, giving me a sick-looking smile.

"And you can stop that lousy play-acting too," I told him. "You're terrible at it."

Dwayne sat shaking his head back and forth.

"You wouldn't have married me if that's what you

thought. Never in a million years. Nobody in their right mind would do a thing like that."

I stood with my hand on my hip, my head cocked to the side, looking down at him.

"Well, of course I had my own reasons for marrying you, Dwayne," I told him. "I always was a jump or two ahead of you, mister."

"What reasons?" Dwayne said in that same stunned voice. I could tell it was a lot more than he'd bargained for, finding out the truth. If Dwayne had ever read Sophocles, he'd have known Oedipus could have told him a thing or two about that.

"Marrying you was like a slap in Mama's face," I said. "You didn't think about that, did you? All I had to do was marry you, and wham, I had Mama and Jordan where I wanted them. Up a cleft stick."

The fact that this hadn't worked out the way I thought it would when I first married Dwayne didn't stop me from saying these things. They were partly true anyway.

Dwayne looked straight ahead, into space. I could tell he was watching it all go rolling away, all those sweet green acres dotted with sleek cattle, the pastures and cattle growing smaller and smaller until they disappeared altogether into the far distance.

"So now we're even with each other," I told him. "Tit for tat. No hard feelings, I hope."

Dwayne didn't say a word. He didn't cast one glance in my direction. All he did was get up from the chair, take his jacket and Budweiser cap off the hook beside the door, and let it close behind him.

≈≈≈≈≈

I was sure he'd go straight to his folks' house, coming in the door saying, "Well, it's no good. She knows everything and, boy, she sure isn't too happy."

I could see them all gnashing their teeth, and I knew it would take Dwayne a while to recover from his disappointment. But I thought sure he'd be back later that night, ready to forget and forgive. I thought he might even be able to laugh about it some.

But Dwayne didn't come back that night, and he didn't turn up for breakfast, either.

I spent the day at Clearwater, and when I came back to our room late in the day through a rain, I was sure he'd be there. But the room was empty and had the feeling it had been that way for a long time.

I didn't want to stay there alone and was gathering up some books to take with me to Clearwater where I intended to spend the night, when I heard footsteps on the stairs. When I looked up, there was Dwayne standing in the doorway, his hair wet from the rain he'd walked through.

"Hey!" I said, smiling, trying to show him I didn't hold a grudge.

But Dwayne didn't smile back. In fact he looked awful.

"Are you sick?" I said, alarmed. "What's happened to you?"

He gave me a hunted look but wouldn't say anything.

"Oh, listen, Dwayne," I said. "Don't take it so hard. Neither one of us got exactly what we wanted out of the deal."

Dwayne brushed past me and began emptying underwear from his chest of drawers into his old gym bag.

"You're not starting a run tonight, are you?"

Dwayne nodded his head, ever so slightly.

"You look dead on your feet. You'll fall asleep at the wheel and not only die, but take an entire family with you."

Dwayne didn't seem to hear, but continued putting tee shirts in his bag.

"At least sit down and drink some coffee," I told him. "And I'll scramble eggs the way you like them."

He didn't say yes, but when I pulled a chair out from the table for him, he sat. When I put coffee in front of him, he drank. Encouraged, I got out the eggs and melted butter in a skillet.

"You go over to your folks?" I said with my eyes on the bowl where I was beating the eggs.

"No."

"Well, where then?"

He waited a long time to answer.

"I went down to Richmond to see Jordan," he said finally.

"Jordan!" I said, turning around to look at him. "What in the world for?"

But Dwayne had gotten up from the table, leaving half his coffee untouched.

"I got to go to Maryland, Jessie," he said. "If I tried to eat those eggs, I'd just throw them up."

"If you're sick, you oughtn't to go off in that truck tonight," I told him. "And it's raining too. You might as well stay here and get an early start in the morning."

But when I said this, Dwayne shuddered as though I'd

just doused him with icy water. He practically ran across the floor, grabbing his gym bag on the way.

It was only when he was already in the doorway, one foot on the landing, that he turned around and said, "You never did believe any of those things I said about you, did you? About how I felt. You never heard a word."

"What difference did it make what you said?" I told him, irked. "I knew perfectly well why you married me."

Dwayne pulled his cap low over his forehead and stepped through the doorway.

"And I guess you never did care a thing about me, either," he said in a voice I had to strain to hear.

"I like you fine, Dwayne," I said. "I always did get a kick out of you."

Dwayne turned to look me straight in the face, a look that sent a pain straight to my heart, it was so sad and beaten down. I never intended him to take it so hard, the loss of what he'd hoped for, and if he'd waited one more minute, I'd have begged him again to stay the night, safe out of the rain.

But the door closed, and I heard his feet on the stairs.

It was only when the downstairs door banged shut that I remembered his slicker and grabbed it from the hook by the door and ran after him. I never got a chance to give it to him though since just as I got to the foot of the stairs, I heard the truck motor start up. And so he was gone. The last time I saw Dwayne.

Part III

19

*T*he day after Phoebe told me she was my sister and we cried and got soggy arrowroot biscuit in our hair, I went back to the mainland and told Eddie I was going to have to take some time off from making salads in the Oyster Bar. A family crisis had come up I was going to have to attend to.

"Once I hire somebody else, you know you may not be able to get your job back," he warned, and I told him yeah, I knew. But money wasn't what I was worried about since Mama sent me a check every month anyway.

I looked for Agnes when I went to the Oyster Bar, but she hadn't come to work yet. I didn't have to see

her, though, to know what she'd say if I told her I was
going to the island to live with Phoebe for a while.

"You don't want to get mixed up in any funny stuff like
that," Agnes would have said, flicking a bony hip in my
direction.

Agnes was right, but I wouldn't have heeded her advice.
After all, Agnes didn't have a husband who had seemingly
disappeared from the face of the earth, as I did.

When I went to my room to pick up some clothes, I
heard Mrs. Chung shuffling around in the kitchen, and I
supposed she was there drinking jasmine tea and staring
out the window as she often did. I left my next month's
rent in her mailbox, put my clothes in the saddlebags of my
bicycle, and took off.

Pedaling around the final curve leading to Phoebe's
house, I saw a small figure coming down the road to meet
me. A figure with two heads. When I pedaled closer, I saw
that one of the heads was Phoebe's and the other was
Dion's, looking over her shoulder, riding her back in a
Snugli.

Both of them had the same wide smile, nothing but welcome, welcome, but I steeled my heart all the same, remembering what Keith had told me. Phoebe wasn't what
she appeared.

When I climbed off the bicycle, Dion lifted his arms to
me, and I took him from Phoebe, carrying him along. "See,
he knows me," I said, surprised.

"Well of course he knows his Aunt Jessie," Phoebe said.
"He's not a dope."

The room Phoebe had fixed up for me wasn't much
bigger than a good-sized closet, but I saw the moment I

stepped inside the doorway it would suit me fine. Daisies and roses, intertwined, wound their way from floor to ceiling among the brown blotches the water stains had made. My kind of place.

"I guess it's ugly?" Phoebe said uncertainly. "Dion picked out the pictures we put up. I put him on the floor with a pile I cut from magazines, and he patted the ones he liked."

From the walls, horses grazed, roses and delphiniums lavishly bloomed, two fat babies made a mess of a roll of toilet paper in the middle of a bed.

"Oh, pretty, pretty," I said, knowing what was expected of me. I hadn't lived with Dwayne all that time for nothing.

Phoebe gave me a quick little hug, in its speed reminding me of the way Minnie was apt to take a nip out of a hand, and I knew Phoebe would have been one of those children forever running into the house with a fat bouquet of wilting wildflowers to stick in your face, or she would make you shut your eyes and hold out a palm to have a snail slid onto it. You'd always have to be throwing things out behind her back, careful not to hurt her feelings.

When she'd said the day before, "Oh, Jessie, you can't go back to that little room in Anacortes now we've found each other. I want you here with me and Dion," I'd agreed, but not because I felt sorry for her. I agreed because I wasn't above taking advantage of another person's difficulties. Phoebe was probably the only person in the world who could tell me where Dwayne was, and she could do this only because she was wacko. A sane and ordinary Phoebe would have been useless to me.

"I found this old trunk to put your clothes in," Phoebe

said. "And look! I put the bed right under the windows so you can see out at night."

"I like it, I like it," I said, my voice already taking on a slightly testy tone. "You've thought of everything."

"I'm just so glad we've found each other again," she said, giving me one of her luminous smiles. "Oh, Jessie, I'm so glad."

"Yeah, me too," I said. "But now I need to unpack my clothes and have a few minutes to myself."

Phoebe looked crestfallen, but she didn't object.

"We'll be right outside," she assured me. "One call and we're here."

I knew she'd imagined us kneeling together in front of the trunk, folding my clothes and putting them neatly inside. Phoebe was going to want us to do everything together, and I knew I'd better make it clear from the start there were times I had to have a closed door between me and the rest of the world.

It didn't take more than five minutes to put away my clothes, and then I sat on the bed watching the sun sink over the milky water while the islands changed color from pale blue to lavender to a deeper sea blue, with none of the trees along their flanks or the rocks at their base visible since all contours were dissolved by that strong evening light. It wouldn't have surprised me if the islands dissolved completely, leaving nothing but the calm expanse of water stretching, as far as I knew, all the way to Japan. I was reminded of how undependable eyes were. And if an island could disappear, then nothing would be easier than for a person to be swallowed up. Now you see him, now you don't, swept away in the blink of an eye.

"I'm cooking supper," Phoebe called out hopefully. "Hear me, Jessie? I'm cooking."

"Fine," I said. "I'm glad to hear it."

"It's going to be a surprise."

The smells told me long before I came into the kitchen what we were going to eat that night, and it could have been one of those meals I was forever cooking for Dwayne's homecomings after a run in his truck. Fried chicken and lemon pie.

"Oh, that smells wonderful, Phoebe," I told her, and in spite of myself I was touched she'd gone to trouble. And I was surprised she knew how to do more than boil an egg.

Dion, thumping his heels on the high chair, grinned a toothy grin when he saw me, and even Sun and Moon, washing behind their ears as they sat on the rug by the door, gave me a moment of attention. Coming into the kitchen with the lamps glowing and the smells of rosemary and onion and lemon, I had a moment of something like longing. Is this what it would have been like, to have a sister?

"Bet you thought I couldn't cook," Phoebe said, laughing her tinkly laugh. "But surprise, surprise."

"I admit you did seem a little dreamy to me," I said diplomatically.

"Notice I do manage to keep the cats fed and the plants watered," she reminded me.

I waited until the coffee to say what I'd been saving up, deciding that would be the best moment.

"Phoebe?" I said then. "There's something I want to know so I'm asking you straight, and I want you to answer me straight. Do you know where Dwayne is?"

I caught it, or thought I did—that slight narrowing of her eyes.

"What makes you think I do?" she said, lifting Dion out of his high chair and unbuttoning her shirt so he could nurse. They made a pretty picture all right, Dion's full, rosy cheeks against Phoebe's white skin, and it seemed mean to be suspicious of someone who looked as childlike and simple and even innocent as Phoebe did at that moment. Nevertheless, I didn't quite trust her.

"*You* know a lot more about where Dwayne is than I do," she said.

"*Me?* I don't know anything."

"Anybody could do what I do if they just opened themselves up to it. People are scared of how much they might know if they let themselves. That's all."

Scared for good reason, in my opinion, judging by Phoebe, I thought. But of course I didn't say this.

"Oh, come off it, Phoebe," I said. "I've never known anybody able to do what you can. And you know it too."

"No," Phoebe said, shaking her head. "Look at the way people make up stories. Don't they seem as real as anything else? And dreams. Everybody has those. You see stuff that isn't there, don't you, when you dream?"

"But what you do is more than that. You can shut your eyes and put yourself inside Clearwater. You just open the door and step inside."

"I *remember* Clearwater," she reminded me. "The same way you do."

I managed to stop myself saying, "Yeah, but I really *do* remember it. You find your way there by some means known only to yourself."

"Still," I said carefully, "you do have special gifts, Phoebe."

"No I don't," she said, laughing, pushing that thick curly hair back from her forehead.

I couldn't tell if she believed this or was putting me on. What I was sure of was that I wanted something from her and she wanted something from me, and on that first night together as I sat sipping my coffee watching Dion's mouth slowly grow slack around the nipple as his eyelids closed, I thought what we both wanted was very simple. That was my mistake.

20

*E*arly in the mornings, first thing, Phoebe brought
me a cup of coffee, hot and strong, made with chicory
the way I liked it, and perched on the foot of my bed
while she drank her hot cocoa, a faint new moon of
chocolate slowly forming just above her upper lip.
Pulling her gown over her bent knees, she made
herself into a fat loaf shape, a bird with its feathers
fluffed out.

As I studied her the way I once had Jordan, that
pearly skin, the wide, direct gaze of those deep blue
eyes, I knew I could not have borne it, living between
the two of them if Phoebe really had been my sister.

I couldn't help being drawn to beauty the same as
everyone else, as willing to warm myself by that fire,

though it filled my heart with pain to do it. I tried to imagine what it would be like, living in Phoebe's body, lying content, like the smooth white center in a kernel of corn, covered with that loveliness. What would it be like, looking out at the world through those eyes? But I couldn't tell, would never know. One chance at life and it jinxed from the start. Even when Jordan was swimming beside me on his short leash, both of us inside Mama's body, he was gathering beauty for himself while I just floated with my thumb in my mouth, not knowing what was going on.

I would never know what it was like to be Jordan, never would know what it felt like to be Phoebe. I was stuck for good with what I had.

"Oh, doesn't it smell like home?" Phoebe said, shutting her eyes and drawing a deep breath. "Coffee and chocolate?"

This was not the right remark to make to me at that moment, caught up as I was in the sorrows of my life.

"When I think about home, I smell horse manure and pig shit," I said shortly.

"I smell hay and beeswax and roses, and when you wrapped yourself round in the dining room curtains there was Daddy's cigar smoke, the tiniest traces," Phoebe said, her eyes still closed.

"All you remember are the good things," I said unkindly. "In your memory it always seems to be spring with the jonquils and wild plum in bloom, Sophie singing in the kitchen, and the horses rolling in the new grass."

"What's wrong with that?" Phoebe said, giving me a hurt look. "What's wrong with wanting to be happy?"

"It always seemed shallow to me," I said. "No man can

call himself happy until he's on his deathbed, ready to check out. That's what the Greeks were always saying. You never know what's lying in store."

"Not all my memories are happy," Phoebe said. "Lots of them aren't. The very first thing I can remember, in fact, is standing under the apple trees on the other side of the pond when it was getting dark. I was too scared to move and just stood there saying 'Jessie? Jessie?' in this little voice."

"Oh yeah?" I said, wondering how much of this I was going to have to listen to, all those fictions about Phoebe's childhood and the part I supposedly had to play in it. "What happened then?"

"Oh, you came for me," she said happily. "You picked me up and wiped off my tears with your shirttail and carried me piggyback up to the house. Gave me a Hershey Kiss and said, 'Don't cry, Phoebe. I wouldn't ever leave you all alone in a scary place.' "

I looked at Phoebe holding her pink toes in her hands, tossing that golden hair out of her eyes, and thought, Honey, I would have left you out there till the cows came home. Would have dropped you in the deepest part of the pond. Pushed you in the pasture with the bull. If I'd had a little sister with a face like yours, do you really think you'd have lived to tell the tale?

"See?" I told her. "Even that story turned out to have a happy ending. You can't get away from it."

"You were such a great big sister to have," Phoebe said, squeezing my foot under the sheet. "I could always count on you."

"Uh-huh," I said skeptically, knowing there were gaps in

Phoebe's intuition that would allow a horse to pass through. It was strange to me how anyone so knowing could be so blind.

But I thought it was harmless, the cups of steaming coffee on my bedside table in the early mornings, the lemon pies and crème caramels giving pleasure to our evenings together. Why not allow myself to be spoiled a little? I'd done enough of the spoiling in the past, and where had it gotten me? I wasn't unwilling to be like one of the cats, lured to a warm fireside, coaxed from my wild ways by scraps of meat. I'd forgotten what could happen when I allowed my life to be intertwined with someone else's.

Of course I didn't tell Mama I was living on an island with someone who thought she was a long-lost family member, just as I'd never said that my purpose in traveling across the country by bus was to pick up through intuition or even magic some mystical sense of where Dwayne might be hiding himself. The uproar such an admission would make would reach all the way to Virginia as Mama and Jordan spent their spare time debating: which private mental institution would be most likely to make me comfortable and halfway content for the rest of my life?

Instead, I went to a lot of trouble to conceal my true whereabouts from Mama and Jordan, going to the mainland to collect letters, pay bills, post my weekly letter home, in one of which I wrote I'd quit my job at Eddie's and had gotten a job in a fish canning factory, a job working a swing shift with very irregular hours. I figured this explanation would cover my absences from Mrs. Chung's house in case they tried to telephone me there. I also said I'd become

friends with a nice, responsible divorcée with a car and
spent my free time riding around the countryside watching
snow-capped mountains emerge from the clouds. I wrote I
was getting out, doing things, enjoying myself and so could
almost never be found at home. Not once did I mention
Dwayne, and I certainly didn't say I thought I'd seen him
once, standing under a fir tree on the Mount Baker ski
slopes. I made up stories, in fact, as wild as any Phoebe was
making up for me.

But in spite of my efforts, I knew Mama and Jordan
were getting a little suspicious. They were together more
than ever, now that Jordan had given up his law practice in
Richmond and had started one in Sweet Gum. As he put it,
he did this because Mama needed one of us nearby, and
because it was something he'd always wanted to do—serve
the people he'd grown up with, a remark that made me
throw his letter across the room.

I started picking up an uneasy tone in their letters,
Mama asking me plaintively when I was going to decide to
come home, and Jordan, in his stiff little notes, repeating
the same ominous words each time: I need to talk to you. I
hated the thought of the two of them discussing me end-
lessly over their suppers, but of course they'd always done
that. Even if I dropped dead, it wouldn't stop them.

Sooner or later, I knew, they would find out I wasn't
staying at Mrs. Chung's any longer, would learn there was
no job in a fish canning factory.

And if Mama sent Jordan as an emissary, I knew he
could find his way to Mrs. Chung's, to Eddie's. He would
talk with Agnes, and she would remember my talk about a
psychic who lived on one of the islands. Jordan was a law-

yer, methodical and thorough. Sooner or later, he would find me. And then?

I could see him standing on the stoop of Phoebe's house, knocking on the door. Phoebe would open it, and they would stare into each other's face.

"Your eyes look exactly like my mother's," Jordan would say. "Your hair is the exact same shade as mine. Oh God! You must be my sister, the one I've been looking for all my life."

And they would fall into each other's arms with glad cries while I stood kicking my toe against the floor.

"Oh," Mama would say when she was told about this turn of events, "it doesn't surprise me one iota. From the moment Jessie was put into my arms, such a strange-looking little thing, I had the feeling something fishy was going on."

As I held Dion's hands and let him pretend-walk across the floor with his fat legs buckling under him, I kept an eye on Phoebe's face, at those widely spaced eyes that looked so guileless, so innocent. But no matter how guileless and innocent she looked, I knew she was sly enough to keep a secret. No matter how angelic Phoebe looked, she might be as sly as I was, and as cunning, though I still had confidence in my own powers, honed as they had been by years of longing.

21

I didn't even think the name *Dwayne* for fear Phoebe
would pick up my thoughts and harden herself into
deeper secretiveness. But I often saw it, the look of
anxiety Phoebe gave me, uncertainty marring the
perfect smoothness of her forehead.

"Is something wrong, Jessie?" she finally asked me
one evening as we sat side by side on the stoop,
watching as the sun touched the water and slowly
sank beneath it, our nightly ritual. "You seem sad."

"Do I?" I said.

We sat in silence as the sky turned from a rosy
peach to a clear faint yellow.

I could feel Phoebe weighing things in her mind,
considering and discarding.

"You know," she said finally, "if you really want to find Dwayne that much, you could without any trouble at all."

"Oh?" I said, trying to be nonchalant. "How?"

"Anybody could do what I do if they wanted to. Just shut your eyes and float. Slip into that empty place in the top of your head. That's all I have to do when I want to leave the here and now."

"My mind isn't like yours," I said. "What seems easy for you is impossible for me."

"You haven't even tried," Phoebe said. "Do what I tell you. Shut your eyes."

I leaned back against the house and uneasily let my eyelids close.

"Now what?"

"Float. Cut your ties. Don't hold on to anything."

"All I see is the dark," I told her.

"You're holding on. I can feel you doing it. What you have to do, Jessie, is cut yourself free from everything."

"I can't."

If I did, I feared I'd be like Phoebe, drifting around, imagining whole lives I'd never led but thought I had.

"You could do it, all right," Phoebe said. "You just don't want to. But that's okay. There's something else we can try. Another way to do the same thing. Tomorrow we'll see what happens."

Phoebe's idea of trying a new way of getting to intuition or second sight or whatever became clear the next morning when she insisted we climb into her little truck with Dion in his car seat between us, and sit there until I knew where to travel.

Phoebe let the motor of the truck idle, giving it a little

squirt of gas now and then to keep it content, while we waited.

"Well? Where to?" she said at last.

"How would I know?" I said, exasperated.

"We'll just sit here until you do."

The sea was a deep, troubled blue under heavy clouds, and it was depressing sitting there looking out with gusts of wind sometimes shaking the truck and rattling one of Dion's teething rings against the windshield. It was unnerving, and I was overcome with a feeling of strangeness when I told myself there I was, occupying the cab of a small truck with a woman convinced she was my sister, looking out at the kind of clouds that gathered only over huge bodies of water, so far from home I couldn't even keep up with what hour of the day it was back in Virginia.

"Let's go to the ferry, then," I said finally.

Wherever Dwayne was, I was sure he wasn't on the island. Anywhere the ferry might take us was more likely.

At Anacortes, the end of the line, Phoebe drove to the top of the ramp and took the only road. No choice. But when we came to a crossroads, she slowed, looking over at me.

"Left," I said.

After that I said, "Right."

Mostly I alternated, though once I said left twice in a row just to break up the symmetry.

Between us on the seat, Dion kicked his legs, the rolls of fat above his knees bouncing in his excitement. "Geeee," he said. "Gawwwww. Dadada. Olp."

"Let Dion tell us where to go," I said, blowing on the

fuzz that grew like baby-chick down over his head. "Maybe he knows."

But Phoebe wasn't in the mood to make light of our quest.

"Think about a cork bobbing on water," she said. "Let your mind float. Go free, go free, Jessie."

I shut my eyes on the green valley we were driving through, a valley in the shadow of mountains, and tried to let my mind slip its moorings.

"There's a turning coming up," Phoebe warned. "Right or left? Left or right? Feel it through the soles of your feet."

"Right," I said, not missing a beat.

"Now what?"

"Keep going," I said, cracking my eyelids enough so I could see the hemlock and Douglas fir, the road winding slowly upward. I knew we were on the Mount Baker highway somewhere, heading up toward snow.

When I saw a sign through my eyelashes saying Cleo's Coffee Cup, I called out quickly, "Stop here!"

"Great," Phoebe said encouragingly. "Look where you've brought us. Right to a café. See? How did you know where to stop?"

Hunger, I thought. "A little voice in my head," I lied.

As we came into Cleo's Coffee Cup with me holding Dion out in my arms like a present to the room, I noticed people looking up from their cups of coffee and slices of apple pie, all of them following Phoebe with their eyes as she made her way to a booth.

Living with Phoebe and seeing her all the time I sort of forgot how odd she was, but now I saw it reflected in all those upturned eyes. I realized she gave off some air of strangeness, as people do who make an excursion outside the walls of an asylum on a sunny day. It wasn't anything as obvious as the way she was dressed, though it was true she was wearing a horrible khaki sweater that reached halfway to her knees and zipped up the front with a large brass ring. Dangling around her neck were all her good-luck tokens, the crystal and the bear claw and the wood burl.

But it was something else, the expression on her face, I was nearly sure—the look of beatitude, her face suffused with an inner light as her eyes searched the ceiling. She was totally unaware of herself as a body moving among other bodies, an awareness I could never set aside for one moment myself since I could see with all too much clarity my own lanky, hangdog look, my walleyes under the heavy glasses, and I knew when the others saw me they thought, Lord! At least I look better than *that*. People watched me the way they would have an idiot, dribbling down her chin. One quick look and then away. But Phoebe's ethereal otherworldliness drew them. They couldn't take their eyes away from her.

Even after we had settled into our booth and ordered coffee and cinnamon buns, I was aware Phoebe was still being watched.

"Jessie," she said in that pure, sweet voice capable of cutting through a conversation like a small bell ringing in cold air, "do you pick up any feeling about Dwayne here? Do you feel his presence?"

Tipping her head back and closing her eyes, she rested her fingers gently on the tabletop as though waiting for it to levitate.

"Shhhh," I whispered, looking over my shoulder uneasily. "Keep your voice down, Phoebe. I don't pick up anything about Dwayne."

But even as I spoke, it was on the tip of my tongue to say, Sure. I see him. There he is, sitting in that far booth, wearing his old denim jacket and grinning like a fox over the rim of his coffee cup. Right there's where he sat. Apple pie is what he ate. If you touched it, that bench would still be warm.

When the waitress brought our cinnamon buns, which sat squat and fat on the plates, Dion said, "Dadadadada," eyeing them and opening and shutting his hands imperiously.

I broke off a piece of my bun, which he took neatly from my fingers without touching my hand and brought to his mouth ruminatively. Even while he chewed, his hands were demanding still, opening and shutting like fat pinchers. More, more, they said.

While I was feeding Dion, the waitress slid our mugs of coffee in front of us, and I saw with dismay Phoebe had slipped her hand over the waitress's arm and was holding her tight.

"Has a man come in here the last few days wearing a denim jacket?" she asked in that carrying voice that could be heard all around the room. "A man with red hair and wearing a cap with a bill pulled low? Has anybody come in from Virginia?"

"Oh, honey," the waitress said, "you know how many people pass through this place every week? And faces don't stay in my mind. If I ever have to get up on one of those witness stands, I'll make a fool of myself."

But after she'd turned away from the table and was half-

way to the kitchen, she suddenly came back to our booth.
"Tall?" she said. "Slender guy, maybe? Likes to joke
around? I do remember somebody like that."

"When?"

"Maybe a week? Aw, hon, I don't know."

"Any mention of where he was going?"

"Now that I couldn't tell you. I wouldn't have kept him
in mind at all only he had this funny way of talking. That
stuck with me."

"What do you think, Jessie?" Phoebe said triumphantly
as the waitress turned away. "And you saw him yourself on
top of Mount Baker, not twenty miles from here. See?
You've brought us to the right place. Just as well as I could
have done it."

Only a trick, I wanted to say. And that waitress just
wanted to please you. To chew the fat for a minute.

But at this moment Phoebe slid out of the booth, face
lifted heavenward, eyes shut, and began walking.

"Phoebe!" I hissed, but it was too late. There she went,
with one arm outstretched the way sleepwalkers do in mov-
ies, shuffling along slowly in the silence that had fallen over
Cleo's Coffee Cup. Everyone in the place had stopped eating and was watching her outstretched hand touch the
rounded corners of the booths.

I thought, Oh no. She will put that hot little hand of hers
down on someone's shoulder, she will rest it on the top of
someone's head, and I will be asked to take her away, to
take my strange friend and leave.

Phoebe, Phoebe, come back, I cried silently, putting
whatever force of telepathy I had into the thought, but I

could feel it going around and around in my head like a bee under a jar, not getting anywhere.

All I could do was watch with everyone else as Phoebe went without hesitation to the back of the room, to the very booth where I had made up a ghostly embodiment of Dwayne. On the bench I had imagined still warm from his body, she sat.

I kept my eyes on her, smiling a strained smile to show the others that whatever it was my friend was doing, it was perfectly all right, wasn't worth taking note of, while in front of Dion's waving hands I held a bit of cinnamon bun so he cried, "La la goooo uh uh daaaa," in a loud voice.

"Bun, bun," I said, waving it in his face to spur him on to new heights of expression while Phoebe, with that luminous smile on her lips, her eyes still shut, made her way unerringly back to our booth and slid into it.

"He was there," she said in a clear voice to the entire room, pointing with a stubby finger.

"Phoebe," I said firmly in the slightly raised but calm voice Mama had once used on Jordan and me to quell us in public places, "your coffee is getting cold and Dion is about to eat every last bite of your cinnamon bun."

Leaning across the table, Phoebe smiled so brightly in my face I felt my knees go weak. It was going to be up to me and no one else to get this woman out of the room without somebody asking, "What's wrong with your friend, dear? Is she not feeling well?"

I saw, in that moment, what Keith had had to contend with and why he had felt compelled to head for Alaska, leaving me holding the bag.

"He was in that booth," Phoebe said, informing the room. "And then he walked out the door there."

"Well, where else could he have gone?" I said crossly. "That door is the only way out."

But against my will, I felt myself slipping into the story, into the one we seemed to be making up piecemeal together, so I couldn't keep from leaning forward to whisper, "But where did he go then, Phoebe?"

Just as suddenly as Phoebe had entered the story, she slid right out of it again, shrugging as she picked up her fork and began eating what was left of her bun.

"You tell me," she said, washing her hands of the whole scene as though she had not just made a spectacle of herself, walking to that empty booth with arm outstretched, providing entertainment for a whole roomful of people.

"I don't know," I hissed.

"So *you* say." And Phoebe's smile, which had seemed so luminous just a moment ago, suddenly looked a little sinister.

"You know where he is," I said rashly, forgetting all I'd promised myself of patience. "You *know,* Phoebe, don't you?"

Phoebe seemed not to hear me as she lifted Dion from his high chair and pulled the zipper of her ratty sweater as high as it would go, a small, catlike smile on her lips.

Oh, I admit she looked like a child standing there waiting for me, the nape of her neck showing so white and vulnerable where her hair parted, but I didn't believe for a moment in her innocence. It was only the knowledge of what a bully I'd look, so much heavier and cruder than she was, if I slapped her on the face or kicked her in the shins, that kept me restrained. When I followed her out of the café, every eye watching our departure, I felt as shambling as a bear.

22

*A*s the ferry carried us back to the island, I sat on the deck in the wind with my hands in my pockets and glared at the water. I knew I'd been toyed with all day and was still being played out on a long line.

When Phoebe said, "Don't you think it's cold out here?" I only stared at her red nose, the circles under her eyes.

"If you're cold, go inside," I told her.

But of course she stayed where she was, pulling her thin sweater across her chest and wiping her nose on the back of her hand. Only Dion was happy, crawling the bench between us, making loud, conversational noises to himself.

"For heaven's sake, stop making that disgusting snuffling noise with your nose," I told Phoebe.

"No Kleenex," she said miserably. I found one in my pocket and handed it over, finding it typical that she couldn't even manage the most obvious necessities for herself.

"Those people in that café thought you were crazy." I told her cruelly. "Walking with your eyes shut like a sleepwalker. You made a spectacle of yourself."

Her eyes filled with tears.

"If I did, it was for you," she said in a small voice.

"No it wasn't," I said. "You were playing some kind of game with me all day."

"I wasn't," Phoebe said, trying to sound indignant, but it was the little smile at the corners of her mouth that gave her away.

"You enjoyed yourself!" I said, outraged. "You liked making us both look like crazies."

When she laughed, I sprang away from the bench and marched over to the railing where the wind whipped my hair all around my face.

"You look funny when you get mad, Jessie," she called out in a merry voice, and I felt even more injured and abused as I held tight to the railing, turning my back.

Acting, acting, it was probably all acting with Phoebe, all those times when circles appeared under her eyes, the times she looked so pitiful and downcast. Because of her beauty she could always wring hearts, could always draw a protector to her side.

Just as she was doing, I became aware, at that very moment. Across my shoulder, I could see a white-haired man wearing a Harris tweed jacket stop in front of her, take it from his shoulders, and wrap his jacket around her.

"Sweetheart, you look frozen," I heard him say. "Let me buy you a cup of coffee."

Phoebe shook her head, but the man brought her coffee anyway and sat beside her while she drank it, making his knees into a trotting horse for Dion to ride.

When the white-haired man lifted Dion in his arms and led Phoebe inside the cabin, out of the wind, I was left alone at the railing to nurse my bad temper. I was the one wronged, but who noticed? Who cared?

I could have died of exposure on that deck before anybody would have given me his coat or brought me a cup of coffee. I'd known all my life if you're ugly, people don't take note of your living, breathing self. Some big, bulky *thing*. That's all they see.

I knew if Phoebe had really been my sister, no power on earth would have kept me from tormenting her. I knew exactly the bruised look that would come into her eyes, the pale lavender circles that would appear under them, the wounded look that would have made Mama scoop her up and hold her tight, glaring at me, the ugly hulk in the corner, eyes as magnified behind my glasses as a grasshopper's, looking on helplessly while Mama said, "Oh cruel! What a black-hearted beast to torment your little sister so."

While we ate supper, I held a dignified silence, but later on, when I was lying in bed watching the daisies and roses in their snakey ascent from floor to ceiling, battling their way through the brown splotches, I relented when Phoebe rapped her timid one-knuckle rap on the door.

"Come in," I said.

Of course she looked remorseful—head bowed and bare feet sticking from under her gown—sad and apologetic.

"Are you still mad?" she said in an uncertain little voice.

"Not anymore," I said, patting the bed to show she could sit there if she liked, that I bore no hard feelings.

She perched at the foot of the bed with the tail of her gown drawn over her knees, clutching her toes.

"I really did get the feeling Dwayne had been in that café," she said.

"Oh well, what's done is done," I said. "No hard feelings."

"You sure?" she said, giving my a shy smile, "Oh, I'm glad, Jess. I hate it when you're mad."

When she leaned over the bed to hug me, I hugged her back, though all the time I was wondering if I could surprise her secret out of her while she was asleep.

If I whispered in her ear, "Tell me everything, Phoebe. Tell all you know about Dwayne," I wondered if she would talk without knowing, and I could snatch from her what I needed and depart like a thief in the night.

23

*I*n the days that followed, Phoebe and I made it up together: this was the way sisters should behave.

In the kitchen we worked side by side, chopping and sautéing and mashing down dough. We took long walks along the water, filling our pockets with smooth black stones circled with white lines that made delicate designs, and when we got home, we laid the rocks out on the kitchen table and admired them, congratulating each other on especially beautiful finds. When we went to the store for groceries, we pointed out the tops of the distant mountains, so clear against the blue sky, and when all the mountains were visible, making themselves known in the way the gods sometimes descended from Mount Olympus to the ancient Greeks, we knew it was a lucky day.

Sometimes we packed a picnic, catching the ferry to San Juan or Orcas where we drove along the water or spread a blanket under a madrona tree to let Dion crawl between us, keeping him entertained as we might have an energetic dog. I noticed the way Phoebe always tossed the last crust of her sandwiches into the bushes for the Steller's jays and her way of saying "Ohhhh" in a downward slide when we came around a curve in the road, opening a view to water or to the sight of an eagle riding a thermal high above our heads. I got used to these habits of hers.

My way of pleasing Phoebe was to throw all the moldy food out of the refrigerator or to scrub the kitchen floor with Lysol, while her way of pleasing me was to leave pressed flowers tucked next to my pillow, or a little piece of driftwood shaped like a goose on a windowsill in my bedroom. Once she left a square of paper containing Dion's palm print in green paint, a surprise for me to find when I opened the covers to climb into bed.

When I took our dirty clothes to the basement and dumped them into the washing machine—Phoebe's small socks along with my big ones, Dion's rompers and my blue fleece nightshirt along with Phoebe's gown with its dainty tucks—I saw as I lifted the damp clothes later into the dryer they were all intertwined and intermingled together in the way, I knew, Phoebe wanted our lives to be.

As though we'd agreed between us, we didn't talk about Clearwater or what had happened under its roof in earlier times, but on a morning in June, I woke thinking that at home it would be time for the first cutting of hay, and I wished I were there driving one of the tractors, cutting a long, satisfying swath through the alfalfa.

But as soon as I thought of this, I remembered Jordan was living at Clearwater again, sitting every night at his place at the dining room table. There he was, entrenching himself deeper and deeper, while I was three thousand miles away on a speck of island, doing something that couldn't have been explained to a living soul in any way that would make sense. Sitting out far, far in left field playing with the ants while Jordan was at the plate, hitting one home run after another.

In spite of my best efforts, I don't have a sweet nature, and there were times, living with Phoebe, when my true nature showed itself and I fell easily into a quarrel.

Over cleaning the stove, for instance. Phoebe had let the stove get into a squalid state, but when I pointed this out, she played the child, all helpless and abused. She had too many things calling for her attention, she just didn't notice things like dirty stoves.

So I held my breath as I sprayed oven cleaner into that cavernous space where spills had become baked on as shiny as obsidian, feeling more and more cross, and paying no attention to what Phoebe was doing.

"As soon as you finish that," Phoebe said, in such a happy voice it immediately made me even more cross, "we can take a picnic and watch the summer dances at the Indian reservation. I've got the sandwiches all made, and you didn't even notice what I was doing, did you?"

"You can go if you want to," I said, grinding my teeth. "I'm here in the middle of a job that's been neglected so long it's a crime."

"We don't have to go this minute. I'll wait till you've finished."

"You didn't ask me before you started making those sandwiches. Not a word about whether *I* wanted to go watch some Indians hopping around in the dirt."

"I only wanted to surprise you," she said, her voice quivering, her eyes growing round with hurt and loss in exactly the way I could have predicted.

"Okay, you've surprised me," I said cruelly. "Now I'll surprise you by telling you to take Dion and go without me."

"It wouldn't be any fun if you don't come," she said, sitting down in the middle of the kitchen floor with her arms around her knees, rocking back and forth. In another minute she'd probably have her thumb in her mouth.

"Then it won't be any fun," I told her, going ahead and finishing with the stove, walking around Phoebe to get to the toilet to empty the bucket of black water before I stripped off my rubber gloves and got busy on the refrigerator, opening little pots of leftover food and sniffing.

"Oh, listen, you're not going to do that *now,* are you?" Phoebe said. "That can wait. There's not a reason in the world you can't come with me unless you're deliberately being mean."

"Oh?" I said, taking some dubious baked beans to the garbage and dumping them in.

"Not unless you want to make me miserable."

"Tell me," I said, taking the top from a container of spinach soup, "is there any reason why you can't take your sandwiches and go on by yourself? I don't mind if you leave Dion with me."

"I most certainly will not!" she said. "I'm taking Dion and I want you to come too."

"And if I don't want to come?"

"You're just saying that because you know I hate it."

"Only what you want counts?"

"That's not what I said! You're twisting things around. All I want is for us to go out in the sun and enjoy ourselves. All in the world! And the only reason you're saying no is to get me upset."

It was true it gave me a kind of perverse pleasure to force Phoebe to show her true colors. All the helpless little-girl stuff was nothing but a ploy she used to draw people to her and to keep them with her once she had. She was good at this, no question about it. A genius, maybe, in what she did best. But anyone who grows up an outsider is expert at seeing through other people's games, just as I'd seen through Dwayne from the beginning. So I wasn't fooled for a minute.

I looked straight at Phoebe, she looked back at me, and we stood like that for some time, neither of us giving in. But my eyes glazed finally, and I felt a little light-headed from looking at one spot so long.

"Okay. I'll go for a ride," I said. "But I won't go to any Indian dance."

As we drove along in the truck with me dangling toys in front of Dion to keep him amused, Phoebe kept up a cheerful talk, one that I replied to with nothing more than yes, no, and maybe. I knew she was talking a lot because she was nervous. She knew I'd given in suspiciously easily, and she had the unhappy feeling she couldn't depend on me, that I was biding my time before turning on her in some fashion she hadn't yet forseen.

When we got to the reservation, Phoebe parked beside

some cars and slid out of the cab to open the door for me, reaching out her arms for Dion.

But I sat where I was, looking down at her.

"Well, come on," she said nervously. "I can hear the drums, can't you?"

"Have you forgotten?" I told her. "Didn't I tell you I wouldn't go to the dance?"

"But there's no reason not to come," Phoebe said, tears filling her eyes. "You'll enjoy yourself, Jessie. I promise."

"You don't seem to understand the English language," I told her. "Is there some meaning for *no* I haven't heard yet?"

"If you don't go, I won't either," she said, heading back around the truck, but I slammed her door and locked both.

"Oh no," I said. "You wanted to go to the dance, and I wouldn't think of standing in your way. "I'll look after Dion so you won't have to lug him around."

Phoebe sent pleading looks up at me, but I remained firm. I would have continued saying no if I'd been killed for it. If I gave in once to Phoebe, she'd have me so tied to her in no time I'd be like a fly made into a bundle by an energetic spider.

Phoebe hung around the truck for another minute or two, but she saw she didn't have any choice but to carry through on what she'd started, so she finally walked off in the direction of the drums, casting one more tearful look in my direction to see if I'd relent.

The moment she disappeared between the cars, I kicked open the door of the cab and climbed out with Dion in my arms, as cross as two sticks.

The sound of the drums drew me, and I wanted to see

the dance. I wanted to be part of the fun. But I couldn't do it.

Taking a blanket from the truck, I carried Dion to a quiet spot under some small trees and put him down to crawl, feeling aggrieved and hard done by, a state I'd spent much of my childhood in. It was the way, I figured, Joseph's brothers had felt all their lives until they finally got the gumption to sell off the favored brother into slavery and got that load off their backs. They'd probably laughed all the way back home.

For the next hour, I chased Dion around, dragging him back by the straps of his overalls when he headed into the bushes, shaking dirt and rocks out of his hands when he tried to eat them. I was tired out and frazzled when Phoebe came back looking fresh and excited.

"Oh, you should have come, Jessie," she said. "They wore these masks, these eagles and bears and wolves and things. I almost forgot they were people, they were so good at making those animals come alive."

I snatched Dion from the blanket and headed for the truck.

"Did you have fun?" Phoebe called out as she gathered up the blanket. "Did you and Dion enjoy yourselves?"

"We had a fun time," I said. "F-U-N fun."

"You would have liked the dancing," Phoebe said. "It was magic the way they turned themselves into eagles and bears. Creepy almost."

"Um," I said, annoyed enough to bite nails.

I noticed the sidelong looks Phoebe gave me as we drove back to the house, and I was nearly sure she knew exactly how angry I was.

But when she dug the sandwiches from the sack and gave me one, I took it. I was too hungry to say no.

"I just hope the mayonnaise hasn't gone off from sitting in a hot truck all this time," I told her meanly. "If it has, we'll both get good and sick."

"Tastes fine to me," Phoebe said.

Even by suppertime I hadn't forgiven Phoebe, and it was only after I'd set Dion's bowl of oatmeal and mashed banana within grabbing distance so he'd emptied the mess over the floor for Phoebe to clean up that I felt eased at all.

I never let Phoebe come with me on my weekly trip to Anacortes, where I went to pick up my mail and pay bills, though she always wanted to. It was my day off, the only time I could be sure of having time to myself. But when I rode off after breakfast to catch the early ferry, I didn't mind leaving it a matter of some mystery what I did all day.

All I did, in fact, was to go to Mrs. Chung's and read my mail while I sat with my feet propped on the windowsill before I concocted my weekly letter home which, as a piece of fiction, often took some time to construct. When I'd finished those chores, I often took a nap, soothed by the familiar ugliness of Mrs. Chung's room, greeting as an old friend the green patch of mildew that always renewed itself just above the westernmost window no matter how many times it was wiped away, and welcoming the pink parasol that shaded the glare of the light bulbs in the ceiling.

Once, I rode my bicycle past Eddie's, considering going in to see if Agnes was around since I would have welcomed the easy way she always said, "Why *hi*," and the way she had of going to the heart of any question. But it was just this that made me decide not to look for her at Eddie's after all since I knew perfectly well, without listening, what Agnes would have to say about my life with Phoebe. She would be right in everything she'd have to say, her commonsense arguments indisputable, but in the predicament I found myself in, common sense would get me nowhere. I had gone so far beyond common sense in my life it was no use even giving a longing look backward. So I pedaled by Eddie's without a lingering glance.

The most anxious time I had on those days I spent in Anacortes was the opening of Mama's weekly letter. As I lifted it from the mailbox, I took note of whether the envelope was thick or light, whether the stamp was centered neatly in the corner, or whether it was slapped on crooked with a hasty hand. I wanted to prepare myself, to have advance warning if the news turned out to be bad.

No matter how long I put it off, sooner or later I'd have to sit in the chair by the window, tear open the envelope, and read about the handsome old Georgian house—fallen into disrepair—that Jordan had bought and was converting to use as a law office. I skipped hurriedly through the progress reports on plumbing, plastering, refinishing of floors, and read, with dismay, Mama's description of the upper floor which he was converting into what she called a "fine little apartment." I could see myself put to pasture there in a few years, the sister at loose ends, aunt to Jordan's two or three handsome children and sister-in-law to his pretty Mary Washington wife.

The day I emptied Mama's letter into my lap and another, from Jordan, fell out on top, I looked at the paper, neatly folded into a square, and had the feeling this was the one I'd been waiting for, the one I'd feared getting.

"You're not living at Mrs. Chung's, your so-called job in a fish canning factory doesn't exist, and if you don't get in touch with us within three days, we're going to inform the police," This, or something like it, was what I expected to hear, the message in Jordan's handwriting falling from the envelope like a snake spilling out of a chink in a wall.

What he actually wrote, though, was this:

> *Jess, your letters to us are very strange, and personally I think you make up a lot of the things you choose to tell us. Mama's worried to death, and I've reached the end of my patience. Mama doesn't know I'm going over her head this way, but I'm telling you, Jess, you must give up whatever it is you're doing out there and come home. It's not because of Mama's health I'm saying this. Her health is fine.*
>
> *Jordan*

This was such a Jordanish letter it made me want to spit. That note of prissiness and piety—*I know what's good for you and you'd better listen.*

I had no trouble at all seeing the little scene where Jordan would usher me into his new office, which still smelled strongly of paint, pull out the chair at his wide desk and sit with fingers coming together in a peak so the sleeves of his jacket would slide back to reveal crisp white cuffs and small, very discreet gold links.

"There is something I must tell you," he would say. "I'm sorry to be the bearer of such bad news, but I thought you should know Dwayne's body has been found miles down the river in a swamp. In the pocket of his clothes, falling off his decaying body, a note was found, almost miraculously preserved. A note containing one word only. A word you can probably guess. In block letters, during those last moments of his life, Dwayne spelled out your name."

"Oh, screw you, Jordan," I said, leaping up from my chair and walking wildly around Mrs. Chung's little room. "Screw you, screw you, and I hope you die."

It took me a long time to calm down enough, but I finally gathered myself in hand sufficiently to write one of my little fictions home. I said I'd just returned from a camping trip with friends to the Olympic Peninsula, where my knapsack had been ransacked by a very large marauding raccoon. I was planning to come home soon, but I was enjoying myself so much I would stay a little longer. But by the end of the summer, I would certainly come home to Virginia.

This, I hoped, would keep them off my back a little longer.

24

*A*s always, when I came back after a trip to
Anacortes, I half expected the island to have
disappeared while I was away, sliding without a trace
under those still waters, and I watched for my first
sight of the headland with anxiety. It seemed, as I saw
it looming on the horizon in the evening light, I was
coming to Delphi where the voice of the oracle rose
from the cave and where the sacred snakes, milk fed,
pale as fog, slipped into the crevices of the rocks and
disappeared into the labyrinths.

I didn't feel easy again until I was pedaling my
bicycle over that very solid pavement, with the smell
of gorse rising from the ditches. It was only then I
could believe in the island once more, in the mountains

shimmering across the water, the sunlight on the shiny leaves of the trees, and I knew that in the small house where paint peeled back like tongues from the windowsills, Phoebe and Dion would be waiting for me.

But on that evening I opened the back door onto an empty kitchen and a house that felt empty. When I called Phoebe's name, the only answer I got was one of Dion's chortles from upstairs.

"Hey, Dion," I called as I climbed. I had a sense of *déjà vu* even before I opened the door to Phoebe's bedroom, knowing I'd been through that scene before.

When I flung back the door, it was just as I had expected, with Phoebe no more than a lump in the bed, the covers pulled so high I couldn't see even her hair.

Oh no, I thought. Here we are again, back to square one.

"Phoebe," I said, yanking back the covers, "I can't leave you five minutes, can I, without you going into a funk again."

She looked at me with those faraway, unseeing eyes, and angry as I was with her I had to admit that whatever strange quirk she had in her brain, it was no joke. That unseeing look in her eyes scared me so much I grabbed the collar of her shirt and shook, the way a dog shakes a rat.

"You want to come with me?" she said in her distant, little-girl voice. "Pick poke salit in the draw?"

"Stop it!" I yelled. "You're putting me on, aren't you?"

Of course she didn't say anything, and I dropped the covers back, picked up Dion, and went downstairs to make a pot of tea and to feed Sun and Moon who were walking the kitchen cabinets, their tails waving.

While I set the mugs on a tray, Dion wrapped his hands in my hair and chortled happily.

"Baby," I said to him, "what are we going to do about your mama?"

I couldn't help thinking Phoebe went into these declines just to scare me, to keep me on the hop.

It was hard to see how somebody like Phoebe—lying in the bedroom that moment thinking she was five years old again and living in a place where she'd never set foot— could have a baby like Dion who was laughing happily as he pulled my hair, but that was just a throw of the genetic dice, the kind of chance Mama must have spent some of her life brooding about too.

By the time I got Phoebe settled against pillows with a mug of hot mint tea in her hands, I'd decided what I had to say to her.

"Phoebe," I said, sitting on the edge of the bed, "we are locked out of Clearwater, both of us, and there's no way we can get back inside."

Phoebe opened her eyes a fraction to look at me and shut them again.

"No, you listen to me," I told her sternly, Mama's voice coming through clear and strong, Mama at the end of her patience. "We can't get back there anymore. The front door is locked, the back door is locked, and the side door is locked. No way in. Those doors are going to stay locked, and here we are, outside. No way of *ever* getting back. I mean, those keys will never be in our reach again."

"Cellar door?" she whispered. "I bet they forgot the cellar door."

"Nope. The cellar door is locked too," I said heartlessly.

"It's getting dark," Phoebe said in a small, lost voice. "I'm scared, Jessie."

"It is *not* dark," I said. "Open your eyes, dummy. And anyhow, it's both of us locked out here. I am too."

I was feeling my way, guessing every step. But I wasn't ready to have Phoebe grab my hand and say, "You're going to leave me here, all by myself. I know what you're thinking, and I can't *stand* it."

Her eyes looked wild, and I sat very still, trying to exert some kind of calming influence, wondering what I was supposed to do.

For just a moment I had a glimpse of what it must be like to be Phoebe, scurrying in terror like some soft-bodied little animal looking for the protection of shell, hole, tree root. Other people's skin. Other lives. I saw what it must be like for her, diving into that protection.

"I mean it," I said sternly, though it hurt me to do it. "I'm locked out too. You aren't the only one."

And though I'd said this for Phoebe's benefit, I saw that what I'd just said was true. I *was* locked out of the Clearwater I'd most like to return to, the time when Jordan and I were so close we spoke the same secret language. It wasn't ever going to be like that again.

Feeling the old grief, it wasn't surprising, when Phoebe put her hand over mine, I intertwined my fingers with hers and held on.

"So here we are together," Phoebe said. "Just us. Even when you were mean to me, I always *loved* you, Jessie."

"Yeah, I have you too," I said, not able to stop myself echoing her words.

"You mean it?" she said. "Is that the truth?"

She tightened her hold on my fingers and thrust her face so close to mine that my eyes went out of focus and everything grew fuzzy.

"Sure," I said, though I didn't know if I was telling the truth or not.

"Well, I'm glad," she said, looking relieved, slipping her hand from mine as she leaned against the headboard. "I think maybe Keith's gone for good."

"Aw, no," I said. "He'll be back in the fall."

"Today I got a check from him in the mail, and he didn't write even a note. Not even 'Love, Keith.'"

"Maybe he didn't have time to write," I said. I could see Keith on the deck of a boat, up to his knees in silvery fish, wading through with his arms flailing.

"Keith knows it would scare me, getting something like that through the mail."

It scared me too. I'd known, when Keith paid me that visit, that his eyes were focused on far distances, but I'd hoped I was wrong. Keith had managed to dump Phoebe into my lap, but I had the feeling I was the end of the line. In Phoebe's mind, sisterhood was probably a lot more dependable than anything else she could have relied on.

"Don't worry about Keith," I said. "You want a guarantee he'll be back? Okay. I'll give you a guarantee."

"I'm going to stop crying now," Phoebe said, giving me a luminous smile that did nothing whatsoever to cheer me up. "I know you won't let me down."

Uh-oh, I wanted to say. Don't even think such a thing. You call yourself a psychic and you don't have even an inkling of what's going through my head this minute?

I drank some of my tea, gone lukewarm, feeling suddenly

exhausted. If I'd just survived a ride on a wild horse, I wouldn't have felt much weaker.

But Phoebe seemed to have forgotten all about her scare and hummed to herself as she sat, hands clasped behind her head, looking out at the fast-sinking sun.

"Jessie?" she said. "Do you really want to know where Dwayne is?"

I got a jolt, but I was too wary by that time to let her see it and didn't even bother to answer that question for a long time.

"Oh, I suppose so," I said finally in an offhand way.

"If you really want me to, I'll try to find where he is."

"Don't go to any trouble," I told her. "Just, you know, if something turns up."

"I'm going to try. Really."

"That'll be nice," I told her, and finished drinking the rest of my tea in one big swallow.

25

*T*hose days I spent with Phoebe, slowly drawing toward autumn, were like the days spent in bed when you've had a fever, a time when you've taken a little retirement from your life, just lying there watching things flow by.

I didn't know what Phoebe was thinking, and maybe she didn't know what I was thinking, either. We were both given to bouts of brooding when we would sit, idle, on the front steps, staring out at the water.

Not once did Phoebe mention Clearwater—that door remained closed, and I certainly didn't try to open it again. What we did was what two women alone together are likely to do. We went on a binge of cleaning the house, emptying cups without handles and plates with cracks into the trash, rubbing beeswax into the wood-burning stove so it gleamed, carrying rocks we found on the beach to the yard and encircling the flower beds with them. One day we took the ferry to San Juan and went to the hardware store where we bought a bucket of peacock blue paint and two brushes. By nightfall, the sitting room floor looked like the sea on a summer's day when the sunlight turns the water translucent.

Together we painted Dion's room a brilliant white to catch the light, and against that white background, we tacked up bright pieces of cloth so he'd have something pretty to look at in the early mornings when he pulled himself up by the bars of his cot and stood swaying, talking to himself.

After we'd finished tacking up the cloth, we stood back to admire what we'd done.

"Reminds me of quilts. Texas Star?" Phoebe said, her voice suddenly faltering a little, and I knew exactly what she was thinking about. The quilt that had lain over Mama's bed all the years of my childhood.

"But my favorite is Beulah Land," I said, not missing a beat.

Beulah Land was the quilt Aunt Lillian always got on the guest bed when she came to visit, the one made by Mama's grandmother, the oldest quilt we had in the house.

"This winter when we're shut inside, we can piece us a quilt together," Phoebe said. "We'll sit in front of the fire like two old white-haired women, piecing on our quilt, and Sun and Moon will take baths on the rug, and Dion will be walking everywhere on his own two legs."

"The only kind of quilt the two of us could make together would be a crazy quilt," I said, and Phoebe smiled, showing teeth as even and white as a child's milk teeth.

I found Keith's address, the one he'd left with me when he went to Alaska, among a jumble of things I'd dumped into a bag when I came to the island, and I wrote him a note asking when he'd be coming back, saying I could stay with Phoebe only a little longer. But I dropped the note into the mail without much hope it would do any good. After all, Keith had known very well what he was escaping from when he went away, and he had probably taken one look at me and figured I wasn't somebody likely to lead an adventuresome life.

So, not relying on Keith, I tried to get Phoebe interested in advertising herself as a psychic reader and making money that way. I urged her to put up notices in health food stores and vegetarian restaurants in Seattle, to put a classified ad in the newspaper.

"There're hordes of people out there looking for somebody like you," I told her. "All you'd need would be for two or three to find you, and they'd spread the news like wildfire. You'd have so many people waiting around in your driveway to see you, somebody could make a fortune with a concession stand. You wouldn't even have to set foot outside the house."

"Jessie! You know I can't do that!" Phoebe said, horrified.

"Real oracles are very rare in today's world," I told her. "In fact they're nonexistent. And nearly everybody's looking for one. Besides that," I added, making an appeal for altruism, "look at all the good you could do for people. I'll bet there's not a person in the world who doesn't have at least one question he'd give almost anything to have answered."

"I can't believe you're saying this," Phoebe said, looking panicked. "Don't you know how I am? How I'd be swamped by all those people in a week? I'm not like the ones who read palms and give tarot readings. All I have to do is look into some people's faces, and I already know too much. There I'd go, sliding into their lives. All those birthday parties. All those spankings and tears. All those goodnight kisses and fear of monsters in the closet."

"What if you just saw three people a day?" I said. "And you charged each one a hundred dollars? You'd be rolling in money for very little work."

"You *want* me to go crazy?" Phoebe said wildly. "Is that what you want?"

"Okay, okay," I said, making the gesture with my hands that meant no dice.

"Phoebe?" I said when she'd calmed down a little. "You know, you did put that notice in the laundrymat in Anacortes. The one I found. How come you did that if you have such a horror of the whole thing?"

"Keith," she said, a look of unhappiness passing over her face. "He talked me into doing that. The very same way you're talking right now."

"Yeah, well, but was it so terrible? *I* saw your notice, after all."

"I know you did," she said in a quiet voice. "Are you glad?"

I saw how I'd slid into that trap, pushing myself down the chute.

"Well of course," I said, since there wasn't anything else I could say.

"But you can see why I can't go around sticking up notices everywhere," she said.

I couldn't argue with her. Of course it was impossible for Phoebe to become a professional psychic reader. Not only would she go crazy, but so would the people who came to consult her. She'd certainly changed my life, doing exactly what Keith warned me she would, burrowing her way into my life the way a wood louse burrows under tree bark.

So I gave up trying to change Phoebe's life and settled instead into uneasy accommodation, waiting to see what would happen. There were even times, as we sat side by side on the top step watching the sun sink nearer and nearer the water while Dion crawled on the grass at our feet, when I had moments of thinking of us as two sisters, taking our ease together. It didn't seem so farfetched.

Anybody walking past on the road, seeing us from a distance, would probably think we sat together in silence because we were so much in accord we didn't have to talk. I remembered how it had been when Aunt Lillian came to visit us at Clearwater, she and Mama going for long walks over the farm, so deep in conversation they probably didn't see a thing they passed. Or drinking scotch on the veranda in the late afternoon with their shoes kicked off, sprawling lazily, totally at their ease. That's the way Phoebe and I sat on the front stoop, our eyes fixed on the islands changing color out there in the water. If we didn't feel like talking, we didn't bother to say anything. Just then, sitting side by side with Phoebe on the stoop, I felt she was like a little rock I'd found on the beach and had carried in my pocket next to my skin for so long I'd forgotten it was there.

The morning when I woke with a heavy, thick feeling in my head and a sore throat, I couldn't believe it. I was never sick, hadn't been sick to take any note of since I was ten and stepped on a hornet's nest hidden in the grass in the lower part of the orchard where it was grown up with weeds. My legs swelled up from all the stings, and for several days I felt feverish and awful, lying on a sheet Mama kept sprinkling with water while I read *Robin Hood* and glared at Jordan every time he came in smelling of horses and looking pleased with himself.

I didn't want to be sick and had no intention of it, so I got out of bed in spite of the way I felt and went downstairs where Phoebe had Dion in his high chair and was measuring the coffee for the pot. When I'd pulled out a chair and sat in it, I knew I wasn't going to be able to eat any breakfast. Phoebe handed me a cereal bowl, but I sat looking at it, having no intention of filling it with shredded wheat.

Phoebe gave me a sharp look as she spooned oatmeal and applesauce into Dion's mouth.

"You don't look so good," she said. "You sure you feel okay?"

"Of course I feel okay," I said. "I always feel okay."

"You look like something the cat brought in. What you ought to do is lie down."

"Well, I'm not going to," I said crossly. "I believe in telling my body what's what. You give in on one thing, and it starts taking advantage."

When Phoebe handed me a cup of coffee, I worked on it, thinking the heat would do something for my sore throat, but there was something wrong with the taste.

"What did you put in this coffee?" I said. "It tastes awful."

"That's not the coffee," Phoebe said. "That's you. You've got the summer flu whether you admit it or not. You always were wrongheaded as a mule."

"Summer flu!" I said in contempt. "What kind of sickness is that? You could look all day in a medical dictionary and not find any mention of summer flu."

"What Sophie calls the miseries."

"As soon as I wake up, I'll be fine," I said.

But the sight of Phoebe eating her cereal, the milky smell, the sound of crunching, made me feel queasy, so I went into the sitting room, picked up the book I was reading, and sat on the sofa. My head felt heavier and heavier, and I couldn't seem to keep my mind on what I was reading, my eyes going back over the same few sentences. Without intending to, I found myself slipping lower and lower on the cushions, and after a while I decided I might as well take a quick catnap. I'd probably feel fine when I woke up.

Later, when I did wake up, I saw that Phoebe had dragged a chair across the room so she could sit four feet from my head, watching my face.

"You look like a vulture," I said. "What're you doing, waiting for me to die?"

"I just thought I better keep an eye on you," she said. "You look kind of out of it."

I was dismayed to find my head still felt heavy, my throat still hurt.

"I don't know what good you think watching me every minute is going to do," I said.

"If you went to bed, you wouldn't have to stick your feet up on the sofa arm," Phoebe said practically, and I had to admit she had a point.

"Well, maybe I will stretch out for a few minutes," I said.

My bed, under the intertwining roses and daisies, looked good to me, and I was relieved to be back on it, though I would never have admitted this to Phoebe.

When I woke up, sometime in the afternoon, there was a cold glass of lemonade with the ice still clinking, sitting beside my bed. It was exactly what I wanted, and after I drank it, I went back to sleep, feeling a little better.

At suppertime, Phoebe stuck her head in the doorway to ask what she could get for me, and when I said vanilla custard, she went off and made some, bringing me a bowlful, still warm, the way I liked it. She'd even sprinkled a little nutmeg on top, the way Sophie always did.

I could hear Phoebe downstairs in the kitchen, talking to Dion while she fed him his supper and ate her own, and I liked the companionship of it, listening to the murmur of Phoebe's voice and Dion's imitation talk while I sat leaning against my pillow, looking out my window at the sky which had gone the clear pale yellow it turned after the sun went down. I ate my custard very slowly, and it was a comfort to my sore throat.

Maybe it was because I felt a little light-headed because of the fever, but I felt content at that moment. Even, in spite of everything, happy. If I'd been given the choice at that minute: in all the world where would you choose to be right now? I would have picked the exact spot where I was, lying in Phoebe's little room, watching the islands take on the purple color they turned before they went a deep blue as darkness fell, letting the last bite of Phoebe's custard slide down my throat, listening to Dion make his fussy fake crying noises as Phoebe changed his diaper and put him in his nightshirt, ready for bed.

Phoebe brought Dion to the door of my room for him to wave good night, and in his long nightshirt he looked like some creature trying to fight its way free of a cocoon. In Phoebe's arms, Dion struggled, drawing up his knees to his chest and with one powerful kick thrusting them out, his arms reaching toward me while Phoebe held on, braced against the doorjamb.

"Wave to Aunt Jessie," she told him, and he did. Or at least he gave me his version of a wave. One of his hands, eye level, opened and shut like a sea animal taking in water and forcing it out again. He was used to having me bounce him up and down and kiss him on both fat cheeks as a bedtime ritual, and he wanted what he was used to. The whole thing.

"Not tonight," Phoebe told him. "Aunt Jessie's sick."

But Dion let out a roar when he was carried off to his crib, and I was pleased he missed me and wouldn't take disappointment lying down. You had to be tough in this life, and I thought Dion would generally get what he had his heart set on. He'd go barreling after it and nothing could stop him.

By the time Phoebe got Dion settled for the night, it was dark outside, and I turned on the little lamp by my bed so all the world seemed to have shut down to this one small place. In the rosy light, I looked up at the ceiling and kept getting very involved with all the lines and cracks in the plaster, some of the cracks big enough so the shadowed part was green and mossy-looking with mold. I thought about what it would be like if I weren't any bigger than an ant, say, and stepped off the plaster into that world of mossy green. All of the world looked altered to me because of the fever. If my legs had held me up, I would have gone out somewhere for a beer; I would have taken a walk along the beach. I didn't want to sleep anymore; I wanted to *do* something.

I thought about the time when Jordan and I had scarlet fever at the same time—we were five—and how the world had seemed different that time too, with my brain heated up with fever. How the light had seemed to shimmer in colors I'd never noticed before, and how I could hear the deathwatch beetle clicking away in the wall and thought at the time what she was saying made perfectly good sense.

It had been the same for Jordan. Lying side by side on the bed, we more than once had the strongest feeling we'd just floated right off the sheets and were hovering somewhere near the level of the lowest big branch of the walnut tree outside our window. We held hands while we floated around, and it seemed we passed thoughts between ourselves without saying a word. It was our very best time together, when we were cut adrift by that fire in our heads.

Later on, though, when we didn't have a fever any longer and were getting better, we were so cross we couldn't stand it, and there was no limit to the mean things we tried to do to each other. Jordan sat on Rosie, my stuffed poodle, so she would smother, and I threw his Cowboy Jim off the bed where Jordan couldn't get him, and broke into little pieces all the bright-colored crayons Jordan wanted to use to draw pictures with, leaving him only white, black, and gray intact.

When Phoebe came into my room after getting Dion to bed, she looked a little frazzled. "You want some more custard?" she said, hovering just inside the doorway.

"It was great," I said, "but I couldn't eat any more."

"Well, I guess you want to go back to sleep," she said, showing a lot more tact than she usually did.

"No," I told her, "but you probably don't want to be around me much. What I've got is catching, no doubt."

"Oh, I never catch anything," she said, instantly looking happier as she hightailed it to my bed and sat on the foot with her arms around her knees. She'd just been waiting for an invitation. "I can't even remember when I was sick."

"That's what I said too," I told her. "So you better not be cocky about it."

Phoebe laughed, leaning back to wave her feet in the air. "If you don't want to sleep, I know what. Let's play rummy."

"Oh Lord, Phoebe," I said, but she'd already slid off the bed and was running to her room for the cards. I had this picture in my mind of long, hot summer afternoons with the cicadas twanging from all the trees in a deafening kind of way, while on the veranda with wet towels over our heads, Jordan and I slapped the cards down on the stones, both of us half-asleep with boredom.

When Phoebe stationed herself cross-legged on the bed, shuffling the cards between her fingers so fast they were blurs, I slipped into that old rhythm again. Somewhere, somehow, Phoebe had spent a lot of time playing cards, I could see that. As Phoebe tipped her head back to laugh when she got the cards she liked, I could see exactly the way she'd been at ten, with the sort of wiry, monkeylike quickness some children have, winning all the games in whatever place she'd played them. Teamed together, we'd have been unbeatable.

Phoebe won more of the games than I did, but I played her hard, forgetting about fever and sore throat until, suddenly, I felt so exhausted I had to lie back against the pillows, leaving my cards fanned over my stomach.

Phoebe made a little sorrowful noise and grabbed my foot under the sheet the way she might have grabbed Dion's. "I forgot you were sick," she said. "I should have stopped ages ago."

"I forgot too," I said. "But that's the point, isn't it? I didn't want to just lie here feeling bad."

"You don't look so good right now," Phoebe said. "You'd better go right off to sleep."

I knew I must look terrible with my hair matted up from sweating so much, my nose shiny, my lips a little chapped. But I didn't care. I knew Phoebe didn't mind what I looked like. She was probably less aware of herself in those ways than most dogs were, so how could she be expected to take note of other people? It was very restful to just lie there knowing I looked terrible but not caring, and I thought that was the way it ought to be with the people you lived with. That's the way it had been with Dwayne, I remembered suddenly with a little pang of loss, and that would have been the way it would have been with Phoebe too, if we really had grown up together.

"Just a minute," Phoebe said, sweeping up the cards into her pocket. "I'm going to get you some water and some aspirin, and what else? Something to read in case you wake up in the night?"

"I don't think I'm going to feel like reading in the middle of the night," I said, but Phoebe took one of my books from a stack sitting on my chest of drawers and put it beside my bed. It was *Being and Nothingness* which I'd found in a secondhand store and thought maybe I ought to read sometime though I'd never gotten around to it. I wasn't going to get around to it that night, either, but I thought it was sweet of Phoebe to pick the fattest book she could find so, no matter how long I might lie sleepless, I could have entertainment if I wanted it.

Phoebe set out everything in a row, water glass full to the brim, two aspirin lined up with the edge of the table and book beside them, but still she hesitated, trying to think of something more.

"You sure you'll be all right?" she said. "I could sleep in here on the floor right by your bed. It wouldn't be any trouble at all."

"I'm fine," I said. "If I need you in the night, I'll wake you up."

"Promise?"

"Sure," I said. "But you've done all you can do, Phoebe. Water, aspirin. That's all that can be done."

"I wouldn't mind a bit sleeping right there," she said, pointing out her spot. "I'd *like* to do it."

"I know you would," I said, as patiently as I could. I didn't have the energy for Phoebe's zeal.

"Sure?"

"Phoebe, I've got to go to sleep," I told her, the only thing that got her to move away from the doorway.

"I'm right here," she told me, sounding a little disappointed. "One peep and I'll be there in nothing flat."

The next few days, while I stayed in bed, Phoebe cooked me what I liked to eat and brought me a fresh glass of water when I'd done no more than take a sip or two from the old glass. She played cards with me even when I was cross and no fun to play with, and when she went for a walk down the road with Dion in his Snugli, she brought me back handfuls of pretty rocks, spreading them over the bed until I felt weighed down by her desire to entertain me. She liked having me down helpless so she could take care of me. When I was feeling better but still got suddenly tired at unexpected moments, all this got on my nerves and I shouted at her a few times, the way people shout at too-exuberant dogs who won't learn not to come putting their dirty feet on your trousers legs or clawing at your feet.

But Phoebe wasn't any more curbed than a dog would have been. Still, it wasn't too hard to get used to, just lying in bed watching the light change in the sky outside my window, telling Phoebe I thought I could eat a little chicken broth made with lots of onions, or asking for an extra pillow, a lamp that cast a better light. It's not hard getting used to ordering somebody else around. I could see how, if Phoebe had really been my little sister the way she claimed, I'd have taken full advantage of my seniority and would have had her in my service in no time. I probably couldn't have stopped myself.

On one of those evenings when Phoebe was sprawled at the foot of my bed, slapping cards down on the bedspread between us, she said, "Jordan used to cheat at cards. You know that?"

"Yeah," I said. "He'd open his eyes just a little too wide. That's how come I could always tell. The little sneak."

"Aw, he wasn't sneaky otherwise," Phoebe said. "Just at cards."

I snorted. "You must've been blind, then," I told her. "Look at the way he was around Aunt Lillian. Buttering her up. Turning on the charm full throttle. I couldn't stand it, the way he'd stand around just looking beautiful, knowing she was watching him and was going to reach out any minute to give him a hug."

I forgot entirely in the heat of the moment that Phoebe had never set foot at Clearwater; it was hard to keep that in mind when there was Phoebe, reminding me of the way Jordan cheated at cards.

"Jordan just likes to please people," Phoebe said. "What anybody wants to hear, that's what he gives them."

"There's another name for that," I said. "Two-faced is what I'd call it."

"Even when he cheated at cards, it was a joke. Entertainment. What's so terrible about that?"

"Everything!" I said, glaring at her. "Everything's wrong with it. Do you think for one minute it was other people's feelings Jordan cared about? Himself! That's the only person Jordan ever considered."

"I think you're too hard on Jordan," Phoebe said. "He's good-natured. He'll always do what he thinks he *should.*"

"Says you," I told her. "But I know what I know." I managed to refrain from adding, Which is more than you do. It was crazy to suppose that Phoebe, who had never laid eyes on Jordan in her life, could know something hidden from me, who had known him not only from the moment of his birth but even before that.

Phoebe and I shared more stories together in those days while I had the flu than we ever had before. Mostly what Phoebe told me were tales of her travels in the Northwest and down to California, the people she'd come across, the odd things that had happened. These tales were rambling and full of the names of people I had a hard time keeping separated, and they never seemed to have much point to them. To tell the truth, I dozed through some of these, coming awake again only when Phoebe's voice fell silent.

But there was one story she told that I listened to closely. She told of a time when she was ten or eleven and went out ice skating on a frozen pond, all by herself on a full-moon night. It was the sight of the full moon shining over the islands that set her off, that made her remember that other time, when the ice had creaked and groaned, how through the ice she'd seen black water stirring as though something swam along with her, flowing right under the blades of her skates.

"Weren't you scared?" I asked, but she shook her head, shutting her eyes to get it clear in her mind just how it had been.

"I had the feeling that whatever it was under the ice was

enjoying itself," she said. "I didn't think about it swallowing me up. Or at least not after the first minute or two. And the moon kept me company, doing curls over the ice to keep up with me."

"A fish?" I said. "It must have been a fish swimming around."

"Too big for a fish," she said. "Just some big black thing."

I could have told her the story didn't sound a bit like Virginia. Our pond at home never froze solid, and even if it had some unusual winter, not a one of us knew how to ice skate. I was touched that Phoebe gave away more than she seemed to realize in the telling of the tale. And I saw too the little shiver she tried to pass off as a shrug and knew she'd been more afraid than she was letting on, sliding over that dark water all by herself on a cold winter night. I reached out and squeezed her toes, in the way she often squeezed mine, to try to show I understood.

Later I held it in my mind, as clean and pure as a piece of ice—that one little story about Phoebe's childhood that might have held the truth.

26

"Jessie?" Phoebe asked one night after Dion had gone to sleep and we were sitting at the kitchen table having second helpings of devil's food cake. "Why is it so important to you to find Dwayne? Because you love him so much?"

"I need to know what's happened to him," I said, making a face. "Is that so hard to understand?"

Phoebe cut a sliver of cake with the side of her fork and carried it slowly to her mouth.

"You *don't* love him then?" she said, a stricken look on her face.

"People do get married for other reasons, you know," I told her.

Phoebe's fork, with its bit of cake, waited suspended halfway to her mouth.

"Phoebe, Phoebe," I said with a sigh. "I might as well tell you. Dwayne married me because of Clearwater. I knew from the very beginning that was the reason. He was a poor boy growing up with a horde of brothers and sisters, and all his life he could see that big house on the hill and those rolling green pastures. I don't really blame him for what he did."

Phoebe sat watching me as she chewed, her eyes never wavering a moment from my face.

"You don't have to look at me like that," I told her. "I know what you're thinking."

"Are you one hundred percent sure that's why he married you?" she said.

"I may be ugly, but I'm not stupid too," I told her.

"But if you *knew* that about Dwayne . . ."

"Why did I marry him?" I said, feeling a bitter little smile at the corners of my mouth. But with Phoebe watching me so closely, I felt like the inside of my head was scoured, I couldn't say I'd married Dwayne in order to get back at Jordan and Mama for a lifetime of pain. I couldn't go into all that for Phoebe's benefit or for anybody else's.

"Let's just say I had my reasons," I said.

"Jessie—" Phoebe started in, but I cut her off before she could get started. I didn't want to hear her say how sorry she was for me, and all the rest. Pity was the one thing I couldn't stand.

"I wasn't taken in by Dwayne for a minute," I said. "So you can just stop what you were going to say before it gets any further out of your mouth. You don't have to feel sorry for me."

"I will if I want to," Phoebe said, sticking out her lower lip so I could see perfectly well what she would have looked like pouting when she was three. "You think you know everything."

"Not everything," I said, feeling a little smug now that I'd gotten her on the defensive. "But I know plenty about certain things."

Phoebe picked up my cake plate and carried it off while I was still licking icing from my fingers.

"Not nearly as much as you think you do," she said darkly, dousing the cake plates under hot water.

"And the same could be said for you too," I told her.

We were in a huff and walked around for a while avoiding looking at each other, every move we made deliberate like two people on a stage, pretending to be at home there. But it was going to be daylight for quite a while yet, it was too soon to retreat to our bedrooms, and so we both came to rest eventually on the front stoop the way we did most evenings, to watch the islands change color as the light faded.

For a while we sat as far apart as we could get on the step, our heads turned in opposite directions, but Phoebe kept making throat-clearing noises and jabbing around with a stick she picked up, making invisible writing in the air between us, and I recognized what she was doing as heavy-handed playground stuff, one kid trying to worm his way back into the good graces of the others after doing something embarrassing like crying or going to pieces at being teased and yelling, "I hate your guts and I'd laugh if you everyone dropped dead in your tracks."

"Dion get off to sleep okay?" I said in a stiff voice, still keeping my gaze fixed on the farthest island.

"I put him down in his crib, he talked to himself for about two minutes, and that was it. Out like a light."

We sat in silence a little while longer, but of course we couldn't keep it up, not after we'd started talking.

"Jessie?" Phoebe said in a dreamy voice, leaning forward with her chin in her hands, a faraway and even mournful look on her face, giving off even in one of her milder moments what I thought of as a kind of aura of uncanniness. "Do you miss Dwayne?"

It was a question I didn't want to answer, a question I didn't even want to think about.

"Well, yeah," I said reluctantly. "I guess I do."

It was that shy smile he had when he handed me one of the presents he'd bought me in his travels. The way he'd said, "We're married now, Jessie. You can tell me anything." Those two sharp teeth that showed when he smiled a wide smile. All of those memories struck pain to my heart.

"What was the best part, when you two were together?"

"I always had fun with Dwayne," I said. "He could make me laugh. I could forget myself when I was with him."

I hadn't thought about it in exactly that way before, but I knew as soon as I spoke that what I said was true. And I felt a sudden great longing to see Dwayne's face and that slow smile, to hear him say, "Hey, I'm back!" in that delighted kind of way.

"You aren't big on fun," Phoebe said. "Somebody else needs to get you started."

"I know how to enjoy myself," I said, feeling insulted. "I'm easy to please."

"Easy to please?" Phoebe said, sounding astounded. "You?"

"What's so hard to believe about that?" I said, becoming not only insulted but upset too. "The least little thing can please me. Listening to Dion make believe he's talking, watching Sun and Moon using each other for pillows. Anything."

"I always thought I got on your nerves a little bit, the way *I* get a kick out of whatever comes along."

Phoebe often did get on my nerves for exactly this reason, but I wasn't about to admit it.

"Of course you don't get on my nerves by *enjoying* yourself," I said. "As far as I'm concerned you can enjoy changing the cat boxes, scrubbing up Dion when he makes a mess of himself. What's it to me? Why should I care?"

Phoebe gave me a sad look. She hated it when I yelled at her and every time I did, I ended up feeling I'd done something terrible. So when she said, "I miss Keith, Jessie," with her eyes welling up with tears, I felt even worse. There I'd been carrying on about Dwayne without once giving a thought to Keith and the fact that Phoebe might be missing him.

"Oh, he'll be back before long, I'm sure," I said, sounding a falsely cheerful note the way people feel compelled to do with children. "As soon as bad weather starts, he'll be back right away."

"You think so?" she said, looking a little more cheerful.

"Sure," I said. "Why not? Why shouldn't he come back?"

"People disappear," Phoebe said, turning sad eyes full on

my face. "They go away and that's that. They never do come back."

I wanted to ask her who she had in mind. I wanted to know about those past desertions. But it seemed more important to be reassuring.

"They may go away," I said, "but that's not the end of it. Look at Dwayne and the way I came out here trying to find him."

"I wasn't thinking about Dwayne and how you might be feeling," Phoebe said sorrowfully. "I wasn't thinking about that at all."

When she put her hand over mine, lying on the step between us, I didn't try to pull it away as I'd done that first time I came to see her. It had never struck me before, how much we had in common, but now I saw it was true that I had been the selfish one, ignoring Phoebe's pain. So I left my hand where it was, under hers, as we sat watching the one star we could make out, a faint light in the darkening sky.

27

*T*hose golden days at the end of the summer when the days had already gotten noticeably shorter, were good ones. I'd gotten used to Phoebe and her ways and didn't even notice it any longer when she got that spacey look in her eyes. Everybody had irritating habits, as I knew very well, and it either got so you couldn't stand them any longer, not another minute, or you got used to them and stopped noticing so much. She put up with me when I was cross, and I put up with her when she was spacey. It seemed fair enough.

And I liked waking in my room with the roses snaking up the walls, listening to Dion talking to himself as he pulled up to hang onto the top bar of his crib, listing drunkenly on one side and then the other until his knees gave way and he sat with a plop on his mattress. I just lay looking at the way the roses wound themselves around and around the daisies, with no end and no beginning, and waited for the sound of Phoebe's feet on the stairs as she carried up coffee on a tray.

If I thought about it at all, I supposed, vaguely, that when Keith came home I'd go on back to Virginia. And if he didn't come back, well, there wasn't any reason I shouldn't stay until Thanksgiving, as long as I could keep Mama and Jordan off my back. Maybe I'd stay until Christmas. There wasn't any big hurry that I could see.

I had the feeling that, every day, the bones that used to be Dwayne bleached a little whiter in whatever wild brushy place they'd come to rest; if Phoebe was keeping any secret from me, I'd come to believe that was what it was. When we sat across from each other at the supper table, lingering, listening to the distant sound of the ocean, the water sliding between the smooth stones, I didn't even feel the urge to say very quietly, so softly Phoebe might answer before she thought, "Do you know where Dwayne is, Phoebe? Would you just tell me where he is?"

If Phoebe knew where Dwayne was, she had her own reasons for keeping quiet about what she knew. I was willing to let it rest there.

So I wasn't expecting it at all, the morning I woke early to the click of my bedroom door being opened, the soft padding of Phoebe's bare feet across the floor, her hand on my shoulder, her voice in my ear saying my name, though I pretended to be still asleep. I knew by the urgency in the way she shook my shoulder that she had something to tell me, and I wasn't ready to face whatever it was.

"Um?" I said, slipping back into sleep for four seconds, five.

Phoebe climbed into bed beside me, as she did every morning, and I could smell the coffee, rich with chicory, though I kept my eyes shut.

"Jessie?" Phoebe said again, nudging me in the ribs with her elbow this time so I struggled to sit and took the mug she offered me.

"I think maybe I know where Dwayne is," she said, and although I heard the words perfectly clearly, I just sat there with my eyes closed, acting like I hadn't. But I could feel my heart quickly starting to gather speed.

"You want me to tell you?"

"You think he's dead," I said, my eyes still closed.

"No," Phoebe said. "I don't think so."

But I still didn't say, Well, where is he, then? Having waited so long for Phoebe to answer that question, I felt wary. Maybe it was the old story, fate keeping from you your heart's dearest wish until you act like you didn't want it anymore. And besides that, I felt the question came trailing a lot of other things behind it. I wanted to just stay right where I was, with the blanket pulled up against the early morning chill, the mug of coffee held tightly between my hands.

And yet I asked Phoebe the question. There had never been any doubt I would.

"If you want to see him, you should go back to Anacortes," Phoebe said, not looking at me. "I think you ought to go to your room in Mrs. Chung's house."

"You make it sound like a scavenger hunt or something," I said. "What in the world would Dwayne be doing in Mrs. Chung's house?"

"I had a dream about him," Phoebe said, mashing the edge of the sheet into accordion pleats. "In that room."

"Doing what?"

"Standing there in the doorway. I don't know."

"But what does it mean?" I asked. "Could you see his face? Was he happy or unhappy? Was he waiting there for me?"

"Getting a picture like that isn't like reading the newspaper," Phoebe said. "I don't know what it means. I don't know why he was standing there. I just saw him, is all. And when I woke up, I had this strong feeling about it. That if you wanted to see Dwayne, you ought to go back to that room."

As always with Phoebe, I felt she was holding back on me, that there was much more she could say if she just would. But maybe I was wrong, and she'd told me everything she knew. My heart started racing at a dangerous clip, so fast it seemed to flutter in my throat. Still I held back.

"What do you think, Phoebe?" I wanted to know. "Is it going to be good news or bad?"

Phoebe didn't answer right away, working at a crack in the rim of her tea mug with a thumbnail. "You don't have to go back if you don't want to," she said at last. "Dwayne must've had a good reason to want to disappear or he wouldn't have done it. You could just let him go, Jessie."

The look she gave me was anxious and troubled, but I didn't know whether it was because of something she knew and wasn't telling, or because she could see how upset I was getting.

"Phoebe?" I said. "Is there some reason I shouldn't go looking for Dwayne?"

She went on working at the crack in her mug with her thumbnail without speaking, and I could see she was torn between two alternatives and didn't know which way to go. Phoebe could never be direct, could never just say what was on her mind and be done with it. I could see how hard it was for her, caught always on the cusp between what she knew through her five senses like everyone else, and what she knew through some other way, as the rest of us saw only occasionally and always with doubt and uncertainty.

"You could just stay here," she said in a small voice I hardly heard. "We could just stay here together, you and me and Dion. I've been happy like this. Have you?"

"Yes," I said. But even as I spoke, I was looking out the window, seeing what kind of day it was going to be. Sun or rain. Already I was thinking about the ferry schedule.

And of course Phoebe could follow the line of my gaze. She'd always known my moods.

"I'm scared if you go off you won't come back," she said in such a small voice I had to strain to hear.

"Oh, don't act like a four year old," I said in exasperation. "Why wouldn't I? If Dwayne is in Mrs. Chung's room, then I'll bring him back here with me. He's always been crazy about babies. He'd like to come."

But still Phoebe sat pleating and unpleating a little portion of the sheet. "Well, but then you'd both leave," she said. "You'll go back to Virginia . . ."

"Oh, look, Phoebe," I said. "Don't you remember what I

told you about Dwayne and me? About why we married each other? It's not some great reconciliation scene we're talking about here. I just want to know that Dwayne's okay. That's all. He might not want to see me at all. In fact he probably won't." As soon as I spoke, I felt sure that what I'd just said was true, that if for some reason, so odd I had no hope of guessing what it might be, Dwayne was in my room in Mrs. Chung's house and I found him there, he'd only give me a hurt, baleful look and storm out again. The thought of this filled me with dismay, and I watched with gloom as Phoebe bunched the sheet and tightened her fist around it.

Phoebe looked miserable too, and I noticed how she kept turning her face away from mine, but I couldn't see why she was upset. She wasn't the one who would have to face an angry Dwayne. As far as I could see, she would spend a perfectly pleasant day on the island, fooling around with Dion. She didn't have any reason to look so depressed.

"I think we might be able to make the eight-thirty ferry," I told Phoebe. "If we hurry." Already I was sliding to the floor, reaching for my jeans.

Phoebe didn't move right away. She just sat with the sheet in her fist as she watched me get dressed. I could tell by the way she was clamping her teeth on her bottom lip there was something more she wanted to say, but I didn't want to hear it right then so I bustled around, being active and practical. After a few minutes, Phoebe got slowly out of bed and went downstairs with the empty coffee mugs in her hands.

I went into Dion's room to get him ready for the day,

and he laughed when he saw me coming through his doorway as he bounced against the bars of his crib.

My own spirits weren't high, in spite of my show of
energy, and as I lifted Dion into the air, my hands around
his very solid little body, I put my face against his plump
cheek and sniffed that sweet baby smell, touched by sorrow
thinking what a short time he was going to be so open to
the world. Life was full of such hard things, I knew. And as
I hugged Dion close, feeling sorrowful, I thought maybe I'd
picked it up from Phoebe, that ability to feel behind the
edges of things, to go beyond ordinary knowledge.

When I came into the kitchen with Dion in my arms, I
expected Phoebe to give me one of her sad looks, but instead she'd turned efficient, setting out bowls for cereal on
the table, buttering slices of toast.

"I'll take care of Dion," she said. "You just eat your
breakfast."

"You eat some too," I told her, pushing the toast in her
direction, but I saw she didn't eat any.

While I ate, Phoebe held Dion in her lap, entertaining
him by letting him hold a pencil gripped in his fist like a
dagger and bearing down on a piece of paper.

"Dion's drawing you a picture," she told me. "Or maybe
he's writing you a letter. Which is it, Dion?"

When she held his hand in hers and moved the pencil
across the paper, he laughed and kicked his legs.

"We'd better hurry if we're going to make it," I said,
wiping my mouth on the back of my hand.

Phoebe folded up Dion's letter and slipped it in the
pocket of my jeans as we were leaving the house. I felt it

was a piece of good luck she was giving me, a little talisman to carry into danger.

The sun was shining when we left the house, but the high, puffy clouds in the west could bring in rain before I returned, and after I put my bicycle in the back of the truck, I tossed my slicker on top of it, trying to prepare myself for any possibility.

On the way to the ferry, Phoebe kept her eyes resolutely on the road, but it was her silence that let me know she was in low spirits.

"Listen, Phoebe," I told her. "I don't know why you're so down at the mouth. I'll be back on the six o'clock ferry, one way or the other. It's not the first time I've gone off for the day. What's so terrible about it?"

"I could come with you," she said, but I could tell by the way she said it, she knew I was going to say no. Which I did. It seemed pointless to bring Phoebe and Dion along with me. And besides that, I knew if Dwayne was in Anacortes, I wanted to see him alone.

At the ferry slip, Phoebe walked down to the water with me, holding Dion in her arms. "I'll be here," she told me. "Six o'clock."

I told her fine. I'd see her then.

When she put her free arm around me in a clumsy embrace, I gave her a quick hug back, leaning down to do it.

"Jessie?" Phoebe said in my ear, still holding me tight, but I had my eye on the ferry, ready to run if they started throwing the ropes from the pilings, and wasn't prepared to listen to any last thing she might have to tell me. All Phoebe could do was to stand on tiptoe to give me a quick kiss on the cheek before I sprinted for the ramp, pushing my bike along, getting on board just as they were loosening the ropes.

When I looked back, Phoebe was waving one of Dion's hands between hers, but already she was a small figure growing smaller by the moment as the ferry backed out of the slip, and it gave me a pang to watch the gulf widening between us. I thought she looked brave, standing there waving, and I was struck by how hard it must be for her, knowing as much as she did, caught between what might come about and what would, for sure. It had never been any fun, being an oracle. The Greeks had let me know that a long time ago.

28

*A*s I drew my bicycle up the steps of Mrs. Chung's house, I looked at the window on the second floor, but it was impossible to see anything of the room from that angle—only the light reflected from the glass. Leaning my bike where I always did against the railing, I took my mail from the box, knowing I was putting off opening the door, climbing the stairs. I hoped Mrs. Chung would emerge from her kitchen, kimono billowing over her shoulders, but the house was so quiet I could hear the ticking of the ornate ormolu clock Mrs. Chung kept on the mantel in her living room.

It was only when I was climbing the stairs, easing down on each step as quietly as I could, that it struck me what a crazy thing I was doing. Say that Dwayne *was* alive. Say, even, that's he'd run off from Virginia and had traveled across the country until stopped by the ocean, climbing off a plane in Seattle or a bus in Bellingham. Even if he'd done this, how would he know his way to my room in Mrs. Chung's house? And why would he suddenly appear there after having hidden out for months? I knew the story made no sense.

But the power of Phoebe's suggestion was so great that even with all my doubt, when I stood in front of the door to my room, hand on the knob, I couldn't bring myself to fling it open. Instead, I tapped on it with my fingernails and pressed my mouth to the crack.

"Dwayne?" I said, in such a small voice it was nearly a whisper.

There was no reply, not even the sound of the creaking of a board as someone who has been leaning on one leg gently shifts weight to the other.

So I took a firmer grip on the knob, swung the door open, and stood dazed by the light streaming through the big window, bouncing from the shiny top of the table, glinting from the footboard of the bed.

"Dwayne?" I whispered again. But I knew unless the light itself was an immanence of a ghostly Dwayne, he was as absent from this room as he had been from any other since that night he'd stepped out the door of our room in Sweet Gum and disappeared into darkness.

Even so, I flipped up the spread to see if he might be lying underneath the bed in the middle of the dust balls, I opened wide the door of my closet, lifted the latch of every cabinet.

But of course Dwayne wasn't in any of these places. Phoebe was wrong. And I was full of relief to see that Phoebe too could have a dream that was only a dream, her vision as dim or defective as anyone else's, her intuition as uncertain. Not even Phoebe, I saw, could escape the desire to tell the story as she wanted it to be. She'd wanted to please me, to give me what I wanted in return for my telling her I loved her. And desire had twisted things, as desire always does.

"Well, well," I said to myself as I walked around the familiar space, running my hand over the windowsills, the chair backs. It had been ten days since I'd been in that room, and I was glad to see it again in all its ordinariness, with my copy of *The Trojan Women* lying half-concealed under the bed, the cannister painted with pink rosebuds holding my Indian tea, my red flannel shirt draped carelessly over the back of a chair.

It came back to me, strongly, the life I'd lived before I went to the island to live with Phoebe, a life I hadn't considered for weeks. And as I thought about the way it had been when I lived in that room at Mrs. Chung's, the life I'd lived with Phoebe faded a little, wavering in my mind. From that distance, it seemed even stranger than I'd thought and less explicable—a life completely impossible to explain to another soul.

Of course I remembered the roses and daisies snaking up the walls of my bedroom, I remembered the way Dion chortled when he saw me in the early mornings, I remembered Phoebe's face under the thick curly hair, the way she could look at one thing, unblinking, for a long time the way a cat can. But all of these pictures dimmed a little, as though a cloud were passing over.

I couldn't pretend it wasn't mainly relief I felt, not having to face Dwayne again, much as I wanted to know what had happened to him. It was that first moment I feared, the look in his eyes, and I was glad to sit with my feet propped on the windowsill without anyone to look at me reproachfully or happily either. There I'd stay until it was time to catch the ferry back to the island, and when I saw Phoebe again, I'd say, Guess what? You're not such an oracle after all. Maybe you're even losing your gift of second sight and can turn out to be like everybody else. What do you think about that?

After a while, I got hungry and opened a can of soup, warming it on my hot plate, eating with my thumb hooked over the rim of the bowl.

Taking *The Trojan Women* from under the bed, I opened it to the place I'd reached the last time I'd come to Anacortes, just near the end, with Hecuba left all alone, husband, sons, daughters, grandchild all killed by the Greeks, and she and her women on the point of being taken slaves. I saw my favorite line, the one that always sent a wave of sympathy through me: "Lo, I have seen the open hand of God;/ And in it nothing, nothing, save the rod/ of mine affliction . . ." I was letting my eyes play that line over when I heard the front door open and thought, Oh Lord, I must have forgotten to lock it behind me, and Mrs. Chung will have a fit. She depended on that door being kept locked against the world.

There was the shuffling sound of someone turning

around in the downstairs hallway, and then a heavy tread, starting up the stairs.

The Trojan Women slipped to the floor as I leaped to my feet, counting the footsteps as they climbed—seven, eight, nine—and I could feel the little hairs on my arms rising. These weren't Mrs. Chung's light, hesitant steps. These were loud and heavy, though slow and uncertain. A man's footsteps beyond doubt.

"Dwayne!" I cried, in horror.

The footsteps were on the landing, coming down the hallway toward my door, finding me out, and I feared the waterlogged clothes, the algae clinging to that red hair, those white cheeks.

I sprang across the room, moaning, prepared to bolt, ready to do anything except be trapped in that room with my back against a wall as a ghostly Dwayne stared at me with accusing eyes.

In panic, I flung open the door. "Dwa—?" I started to say, but the word died on my lips.

Instead of a dead Dwayne, I was inches away from a very solid and very much alive Jordan, looking straight at me, astonished.

"Jessie! Thank the Lord!" he said. "I thought I might have to knock on every door."

"Where did you come from?" was all I could think of to say.

"Where do you *think?*" he said. "Outer space?"

He dropped his suitcase just inside the door and put his arms around me in an uneasy hug. His clothes were wrinkled, there were shadows under his eyes, he looked wild. All I seemed capable of doing was standing and staring.

There was a battered look about Jordan that diminished even his good looks.

"I want to know what's going *on* with you," he said, in a not altogether friendly way, as he flung his all-weather coat onto my bed.

All I seemed capable of focusing on was his tie, which was lying diagonally across his shirt, one end hanging over his shoulder like a tongue hanging from a mouth.

"Every time Mama tried telephoning, your landlady said you weren't there. Finally she admitted you hadn't been here for weeks. 'In weeks I not see your daughter' was how she put it, to be exact. Can't you just see Mama? How wild she went? And that restaurant where you used to work? They said you'd quit early in the summer. The fish canning factory where you *said* you had a job? Never heard of you. So what's going on? What's happened to you, Jess?"

"Would you like some tea?" I said. "Coffee?"

Jordan looked at me as though I were out of my mind. "I don't want anything out of you except sense," he said. "Can't you even sit down? I keep having the feeling you're going to bolt for the door, any minute."

Even as he spoke, Jordan was pacing my room, peering from the window, running a finger over dusty chairs. But when I sat on the edge of the bed, he sprawled in the bamboo chair, looking a little dazed and disoriented. He was obviously having a hard time believing he was where he was, just as I was having a hard time believing it was Jordan sitting in the wobbly bamboo chair in exactly the spot I'd imagined him sitting more than once.

"It doesn't look to me like you've been in this room for

weeks," he said. "So how does it happen I have the good fortune to find you here today?"

"That's a very long story," I told him. "And you'd just sneer even if I told you."

The look he gave me was long-suffering.

"I told Mama all along those stories in your letters were made up. 'I know how Jessie's mind works,' I kept telling her. After all, how many stories of yours have I listened to from the time we were babies, practically? I ought to be able to tell when you're laying one on. But Mama couldn't believe you'd do a thing like that. Telling deliberate falsehoods."

"Look, Jordan," I told him. "If I told you the truth about what I was doing this summer, you'd never believe me. You'd probably think I'd lost my mind."

"Try me anyway," he said, leaning back in the chair, making a peak of his fingers balanced above his stomach in just the way I'd imagined him doing, sitting at his mahogany desk in the office of his beautifully restored Georgian house in Sweet Gum.

"No way," I said. "Why should I stick my head in that noose? Just to have you laugh at me? Forget it."

"Listen, Jessie," he said, leaning forward in his chair, fixing me with those steely blue eyes of his that were so much like Mama's, "I just flew across the entire country, through a storm that tossed the plane around like a Frisbee, drove up here from Seattle without knowing where I was coming to or how I'd find you once I got there. Hardly a wink of sleep all night. But I don't suppose you think all that deserves any kind of consideration, do you? You think it's perfectly all right for me to spend my time coming to find you just so I can hear you say, 'Why, hello, Jordan. What brings you to these parts?' "

If this was a plea for my sympathy, I wasn't about to fall for it. "Let's get one thing straight, Jordan," I said. "*I* didn't ask you to come out here, did I? I'm not responsible for something you decide to do on your own hook. So if you and Mama got all upset over nothing, well, it's your hardship, not mine."

I couldn't get it out of my head: Jordan and me playing poker on hot summer afternoons, trying to fake each other out, Jordan becoming more alert as I got bored and careless.

"All right, let's take it from here," Jordan said, his eyes fixed on the ceiling in a patient kind of way. "You go tearing off on a Greyhound bus, zigzagging across the country like a drunk dog on a cold trail, end up in some little town three thousand miles away from home where you don't know a soul; take some two-bit job you quit, write letters home full of made-up stuff, and then you sit there, calm as a newt, and say everything's just fine and you can't understand why I should come to see you or ask what the hell's happened to you."

"Oh, you're so prissy, Jordan," I told him. "Not only do you have to beat me out of every little crumb of goodies in my life, but you have to act so self-righteous about it too."

Jordan gave me a furious look, raking his fingers backward through his hair, a look of fire in his bloodshot eyes. "Just what's that supposed to mean?" he said. "What did I ever beat you out of?"

But now I'd turned sullen, not wanting to go into all that. I just sat staring without blinking at his forehead, in a way I knew from past experience he wouldn't stand for long. In less than five seconds, he'd jumped up from his chair and stationed himself over by the window, leaning against the sill, a position that allowed him to look down at me from a superior height. "Let's try this again," he said in exactly the way he probably talked to clients who were being difficult, getting themselves tangled in the threads of a story that careened around from one direction to another. "Why did you come out here in the first place, leaving home in such a hurry, spending five nights on a Greyhound bus?"

"Why, I just wanted to see the country," I said, and laughed. "People do. All the time."

Jordan stood stony faced, leaning back against the sill. I saw he was prepared to stand there waiting all day if he had to, squeezing information from me like toothpaste from a tube, and I remembered, too late, this was the way he'd always beaten me at any game we'd ever played that required long, careful thought. I'd get impatient and play any old piece down on the board just to get some movement going, and then Jordan would quietly clobber me, wiping my pieces off the board one by one in a methodical kind of way.

"Well, okay," I said, shifting uneasily on the bed. "To tell the truth, I was looking for Dwayne. I didn't believe he'd drowned, I felt he was alive somewhere in this country, and if I came to the right place, I'd know it. Intuition would tell me."

As I said this I could hear how crazy it sounded, and I hated to admit this craziness to Jordan, but I saw I was going to have to toss him a bone of the truth for him to gnaw for awhile, hoping it would hold him back from the rest.

"I knew it!" Jordan said. "That's what I told Mama at the time, that you'd gone charging off with some half-baked notion like that in your head, and she said no no, you just needed a rest from Sweet Gum for awhile." Jordan thumped the windowsill in pleasure at his own cleverness. "Well, did it work? Did you get the feeling Dwayne was around here somewhere?"

I shook my head. "I didn't get the feeling he was here any more than that he was in, say, Flagstaff, Arizona, but I'd come to the end of the line. Next, it was Canada or the ocean."

I wasn't about to tell Jordan I thought I'd seen Dwayne on the ski slopes of Mount Baker and was even less likely to tell him a psychic had sensed his presence in Cleo's Coffee Cup. I wasn't about to give him ammunition like that to shoot me down with.

"What I just don't understand," Jordan said in a soft voice that instantly made me uneasy, "is why you wanted to find Dwayne at all. After what you did to him, Jessie."

"What I did to him?" I repeated in confusion and disarray. "What did I do to Dwayne?"

I felt I'd fallen into a trap, sliding my checker carelessly onto the square, seeing too late how Jordan could now jump four of my hapless men. This was so much Jordan's style, to let me think I was in the clear before wiping me off the board.

"Oh come *on,*" Jordan said, fixing me with those blue eyes. "Marrying Dwayne was just a game of some kind for you, wasn't it? A joke? Don't you think I know, after all this time, the kinds of things you think are funny? You got a kick out of marrying poor old Dwayne and flaunting him in Mama's face. That's just exactly the kind of thing that would make you laugh. Don't I know that? Hell, Jessie, I *know* you. You didn't give a thought about what you were dragging Dwayne into. How he was going to get hurt. All you could think about was how *funny* it was. Well, if it gives you any satisfaction, I've never seen anybody as torn up as Dwayne was after you told him what you did. That you married him as a joke of some kind."

"Whoa!" I said. "Just a minute, Jordan. Why do you think Dwayne married me anyway? Answer me that. It's a one-sided story you're telling, and not the truth at all."

"If you don't think it's the truth, it's too bad you couldn't have tuned in on the scene when Dwayne came to visit me in Richmond just before the wreck. When he broke down, going on about how much he loved you, I guess you'd have roared with laughter, wouldn't you?"

Intent on my own version of the story, I wasn't listening to Jordan's.

"So why did Dwayne marry me, then? You haven't answered that. I'll bet Dwayne didn't tell you, did he?"

Jordan gave me a hard, intent look. "He married you because he loved you," he said. "Why else?"

"Hah!" I said triumphantly. "Now I know it's nothing but a big fat lie you're telling me. You've got the story all wrong from beginning to end. Dwayne never loved me, not for a minute. It was because of money and Clearwater he married me, not another reason. I knew that from the word go."

Jordan fixed me with angry, bloodshot eyes. "That's exactly what Dwayne told me when he came to Richmond in a state. 'Jessie thinks I just wanted money.' That's what he said. But let me tell you, Jessie, you might as well have picked up a gun and shot Dwayne as told him what you did. All he could talk about was wanting to disappear off the face of the earth. That's how he felt. I know he loved you. I'd attest to it with my dying breath."

I sat staring at Jordan, not able to take my eyes away, a lot of things going through my mind. I shook my head feebly, trying to deny every word he'd said, but the words wouldn't come to my lips.

What I kept seeing was Dwayne's face and his shy, sweet smile as he handed me the present he'd brought from his travels, Dwayne looking up at me with that same smile while I sat in the pecan tree doing nothing but throwing green pecans down on his head, Dwayne's eyes, the sad way they'd looked before he'd walked down the stairs from our room in Sweet Gum for the last time. And as I watched these scenes, all I'd thought about them started shifting.

"Are you *sure?*" I said to Jordan. "You might've heard wrong . . ."

"Jessie, I heard him," he said. "I'm not deaf and I'm not crazy."

But it wasn't what Jordan said but something else that convinced me, the way Jordan looked at me, his eyes just a little to the side as though what he'd had to say embarrassed him—not the wide-eyed directness that usually meant he was hiding something.

"Oh damn!" I said, clutching my elbows in my hands, struck with misery.

What I could see with perfect clarity was the languorous, sleepy look in the back of Dwayne's eyes as he joined me on our twangy old bed, and I was overcome with longing to see it again, that way Dwayne's face softened when he looked in my direction. A lot of the things I'd said about Dwayne to other people hadn't been anything but hurt pride talking. I could see that.

"So Dwayne *did* drive his truck into the river, then," I said, my lips starting to tremble. "He's dead."

Moments passed, Jordan holding his silence while he studied the floor, moments when I quit bothering to breathe. "No," he said finally. "He's not dead."

"Then where is he?" I said, looking wildly around the room as though I expected Dwayne to unfold himself somehow out of Jordan's suitcase or spring up from underneath his coat.

"Why should I tell you that?" Jordan said. "Don't you think you've hurt him enough?"

When I sprang up from the bed, it was because I longed to dig my fingernails into Jordan's handsome cheeks, to pull out that golden hair by the roots.

"Just who do you think you are, anyway?" I shouted at him. "God or somebody?"

Jordan watched me, not blinking an eye. "What do you want to see Dwayne for?" he said.

"I have a question for you, Jordan. Do you think, in your whole life, you've never made anyone suffer? Yes or no. Have you?"

"What kind of question is that?" Jordan said warily, knowing a trap when he saw one.

"Just a plain question," I said. "And you know perfectly well what the answer is too. Take me, for one. You think you've never made me suffer? What about the way I've had to live all these years with your good looks and your charm. And then, after all that, to hear you say you didn't even believe I was your true sister. How do you think that made me feel?"

Jordan's face seemed to expand, to grow fuller as color flushed his cheeks. The little smile at the corner of his lips was the same one he'd smiled when he was ten and told Mama he didn't have a thing to do with the bowl-deep dent that had suddenly appeared in the back fender of her car. Of course he hadn't backed into the walnut tree. Who, him? If Jordan ever found himself in front of a firing squad someday, that same faint little smile would accompany him into the next life. Embarrassment—that's what that little smile hid.

"I don't know what you're talking about," he said. "Saying you weren't my sister."

"At that party I went with you to at your fraternity house. Your last year in law school. You said you'd always figured the hospital where we were born got the babies mixed up. Your exact words, Jordan, because I heard you."

I was sure Jordan would deny it, would say I was making it all up or was dreaming, and I was ready with what I was going to reply to that, telling about standing behind the column, about watching Jordan lift the bourbon bottles out of a sack. I was ready with the whole story, down to the last detail.

But Jordan didn't deny it.

"All I meant was we're different. Well, aren't we? Haven't you ever thought it's a little odd, the two of us being twins?"

I'd much rather he'd have denied the whole thing. Much rather he'd said, "Oh, that was just a joke." I could see he'd probably forgotten all about the time when we'd had a secret language of our own.

"Practically all my life," I told him bitterly. "But whether or not you like it, Jordan, you're stuck for life with me as a sister. I'm stuck with you too."

"Oh, come on, Jessie," Jordan said in a disgusted voice. "What do you think I came all the way across the country for, trying to find you?"

"Because Mama wouldn't let you rest until you did."

"It wasn't just Mama, though. *I* care about what happens to you too."

"Well, fine," I said. "Now you've found me. Now what?"

Jordan walked over to the bamboo chair and dropped into it with an unhappy look on his face. I knew he felt he deserved more credit than I was willing to give him. He *had* made a trip all the way across the country, trying to find me. He *had* been worried. And yet here I was, accusing him of things he'd rather not think about, refusing to show any gratitude for his efforts. I could see the struggle going on, whether he should plead harder for his case or let it ride.

"Jessie," he said finally. "I don't know if I should do this or not, but I'm going to tell you something. Dwayne's on his way to Virginia. He's going home."

"He is?" I said, stunned.

When I looked into Jordan's face, I saw for a moment the ghost of the boy he'd once been, running across the school ground at recess to grab my end of the rope in a tug of war, helping me out for no reason except he wanted to.

"If you want to see him, that's where he'll be."

There were so many questions in my mind I didn't know where to start. "Where's Dwayne been all this time?" was the one I chose. "When everybody thought he was dead?"

"Different places," Jordan said. "Traveling around, trying to forget what had happened. I'd get a postcard every once in a while, from New Orleans or Kansas City. All over. But all he ever said was, 'This finds me well. Hope it finds you the same. Dwayne.' But then one day he telephoned, out of the blue, wanting to talk. Well, wanting to find out about you is what it amounted to. When I told him you'd come out here, he got me to tell him all I knew. He said he was going to take the next bus heading west. I told him I thought he was crazy, but nothing would stop him. Once he got out here, he was afraid to knock on your door. Too scared to do it."

"Dwayne was out here?" I said. "He came to find me?"

I couldn't believe it—that Dwayne would care that much. When I thought of all those things I'd said to him that last night before he went out in the rain to climb into the truck, I wanted the floor to open up and let me slide through.

"That's what I'm saying," Jordan said, sounding a little testy, and I could see that this whole scene was more than he'd bargained for, that the whole thing tired him out.

"If I go back home, I'll see Dwayne?" I said, still incredulous.

"I told you, Jessie. He knew I was coming out here to see you, and whatever happened after that . . . well, I think he has his hopes."

I could see Dwayne clearly, pushing up the bill of his cap with the palm of his hand as he ran to meet me, smiling wide enough to show those two pointed teeth. In one way, I wanted to grab Jordan's hand and pull him out of that chair and drive instantly to the Seattle airport, breaking the speed limit all the way. And I also just wanted to sit weakly on the bed clutching my elbows, scared to move.

It was typical of Jordan that he now considered the conversation about Dwayne finished. He brushed down the sleeves of his suit jacket with his hands, brushing away what seemed to me invisible bits of lint, and twisted around so he could look out the window at the bay and beyond the bay to the faint line of snowcapped mountains.

"I don't guess you know this," Jordan said, still not looking in my direction, "but you left Mama in a hole when you came tearing out here the way you did. She'd gotten used to having your help on the farm, and she could use some, but you know how proud she is. She'd never say anything to you about it. Too proud to open her mouth."

At an earlier time, I would have felt guilty, but now I just looked Jordan straight in the eye. "What's the matter with you?" I told him. "You're living right there. Why couldn't you make yourself useful?"

"As you like to remind me, Jessie, working on the farm isn't exactly what I do best. You're better at that than I am. I don't mind admitting it. And Dwayne would be useful on the farm too, if you get together again. Mama and I could help you find a house somewhere nearby . . ."

"Oh you could, could you?" I said, the old familiar rage exploding. "You'd pack me off to live like a tenant farmer while you made yourself comfortable at Clearwater. I can just see it. But I have news for you, Jordan. If I come back home again, it's going to be on my terms, not yours. And that goes for Dwayne too," I added.

"I just thought you'd be happier, having a place of your own," Jordan said, his eyes growing wide, looking full into mine. "That's all I was thinking."

I doubted very much if that was all. I knew that wide-eyed, innocent look of Jordan's too well. But I tried to give him the benefit of the doubt. It was possible I was jumping to false conclusions and maybe Jordan was being merely the dutiful brother and son, trying to keep everybody happy. This was a possibility, though one I'd never believe in. I knew that too.

I spoke to Mama briefly on the telephone, telling her both Jordan and I would be coming back the next day and warning her if Dwayne appeared on the doorstep, she was to tell him I was on my way home and he should wait right where he was. For once, Mama accepted what I had to say without a word of fuss; I could have told her I was arriving back with a suitcase full of poisonous snakes and she probably wouldn't have said more than "Oh?"

Jordan and I made reservations for a late afternoon flight, the soonest we could get, and went out to eat.

It crossed my mind that I was certainly going to miss the six o'clock ferry back to the island. I knew I wasn't going back to the island that night at all. But although I thought about this, I didn't dwell on it. There were so many things on my mind that Phoebe wasn't uppermost. I was sorry she'd have a trip to the ferry in vain, but I couldn't do anything about it. If she'd been a reasonable person with a telephone, then none of this would be a problem. I'd suggested to her often enough that a telephone might be a useful thing to have, but Phoebe being Phoebe, she'd always shrugged her shoulders. So what could I do? I'd make it up to her later.

When Jordan and I were sitting across from each other in the restaurant, drinking wine, I didn't know where to start, which thread to pull that might unravel the whole ball. Jordan was tired, slumped in his chair, and I sat turning my wine glass around in a tight little circle. But finally I asked Jordan about the night when Humpin' to Please had gone into the river and Dwayne had disappeared.

"Dwayne can't even swim," I told Jordan. "So how did he get out of that truck and make it to shore?"

Jordan took a long breath. "Driving his truck into the river wasn't anything Dwayne intended," he said. "When he came down to Richmond after you told him what you did, he was beside himself. Said he was going off on one last run, and then he'd abandon the truck somewhere. He'd go to New Orleans, cutting out and running like a horse with a horsefly on his rump."

When the waiter brought us our salmon, Jordan got to work on it, but I had no appetite for food and sat toying with my fork. After a few minutes, Jordan went on with his story.

"So Dwayne did get back in the truck and take off. I couldn't do a thing with him. I still don't know to this day exactly what was in his head. But I do know it was a rainy night, remember that? And the pavement was slippery. And besides that, Dwayne didn't have his mind on what he was doing. One way or another, he told me later, he found himself on a long hill leading down to a bridge across the river. He felt it too late, when the truck started gathering momentum. Too late to shift down to a safer gear. Preoccupied as he was, he knew the brakes couldn't hold a big truck on a hill like that. They'd burn right up. So there he was, barreling down, faster and faster. Dwayne said he was tempted to just turn loose of the wheel and let fate do whatever it wanted to. But it was the thought of all that deep cold water down there that changed his mind. Maybe he didn't care if he died or not, but he didn't care to die that way. So he threw all his weight against the cab door, got it open, and then he was rolling over and over as he went into the ditch. By the time the crash came, the truck hurtling through the railing, he had gotten to his feet, and so he saw the headlights disappear. Swallowed up. Afterwards, he said, it was so still and quiet he could hear a cricket singing somewhere at his feet."

I could see Dwayne, standing in the wet ditch, the rain soaking through his clothes, the darkness thick around him.

"Well, as he stood there, it came over him what had happened was a sign of some kind. He felt maybe he'd died after all, and his old life was sitting down there at the bottom of the river. But he was miraculously resurrected. Given a new chance. Another life. All the time he was walking the six miles to the nearest gas station, limping along, he had the feeling he wasn't the same old Dwayne at all, but somebody else altogether. Something had happened to change his life."

"How was he different?" I wanted to know, but Jordan couldn't answer that.

"He seemed the same to me," he said. "When he got to the station and telephoned, I came to get him. Lord! He was a big mess, the way his clothes were ripped up and his face all scraped. That's all I could tell. How banged up he was."

I could see it all, the whole scene from the top of the hill where Dwayne lost control of the truck, to the gas station he came to in the middle of the night. But then I remembered something.

"You weren't in the truck with Dwayne, were you?" I said, thinking about Phoebe's vision of that scene with Dwayne pumping the useless brakes of the truck while a tall, thin somebody sat there and watched.

"Of course not," Jordan said. "Why should I have been?"

"No reason," I said. But I knew Phoebe hadn't been exactly wrong in what she saw after all, since Jordan had been involved with Dwayne every step of the way. In spirit, he was right inside that cab.

"And you kept your mouth shut, letting everybody think Dwayne was dead. That was a mean trick, Jordan."

"It's what Dwayne wanted, so how could I say no? He said his mama would know he was still alive anyway since, without a body stretched in front of her eyes, she'd never believe he was dead."

"Yeah, well, Eula probably didn't think he was dead," I said. "But it caused me enough grief."

Jordan kept his eyes on his plate, restraining himself from reminding me how much it was my fault that Dwayne wanted to disappear in the first place. And it *was* my fault; I acknowledged that. But even so, I also knew there was nothing simple about it since everything had started before I was born, when Jordan and I were pushing each other around with miniscule elbows while we were still swimming together in the womb.

During coffee, Jordan asked me again what I'd been doing during those weeks after I'd quit my job at Eddie's and was writing those made-up letters. As he asked me this, Phoebe's face slid into my mind for just a moment, Phoebe's face, lit by one of her luminous smiles, and Dion, laughing as I lifted him from his crib, showing his four teeth. It was on the tip of my tongue to say, "Jordan, there's someone in the world who has Mama's eyes and a nose like yours and who knows every rock at Clearwater. Someone you could claim as your long-lost sister." But there was no way I could explain Phoebe to Jordan, no way to make any of that even remotely believable. So I just shook my head.

Jordan looked at me over the top of his coffee cup, but for once, he didn't press the point. I could tell by the way he was sitting, hunched down over his plate, that he didn't want to hear any more strange revelations, any more peculiar news. He just wanted to finish his meal in peace and go off to a comfortable motel and go to bed with the blanket pulled to his ears.

It came to me too, looking at Jordan across the table, that we were going to be spending the rest of our lives in each other's pockets, practically, and it would be wise to ignore certain remarks, certain sharp glances. There were things we should have better sense than to say, if we were going to survive together. But I also knew that old closeness with Jordan, that way we'd been when we were little, was gone for good. I would always be wary of Jordan, he would always be baffled by me.

29

*I*t was late that night when I finally got back to my room in Mrs. Chung's house after settling Jordan in a motel, and I was thinking about packing, of what I would take with me the next day and what I wouldn't bother with, when I threw my jeans over a chair and a small piece of paper fell to the floor. I couldn't think what it was, that little piece of paper folded over and over. It wasn't until I'd picked it up from the floor that I remembered Dion sitting in Phoebe's lap, his fat hand held in hers while they wrote me a letter, both of them laughing with their heads bent over the table.

And as soon as I saw that picture, remembering the morning which now seemed light-years away, I was flooded with another picture that forced me to make a little involuntary cry before I could stop myself.

There Phoebe was, sitting in the cab of her truck, jingling the keys to entertain Dion as she happily watched for the six o'clock ferry to come into the dock. "Jessie's coming," she said to Dion. "Look! See her yet?"

She waited while all the cars drove up the ramp and away, while all the people walking or with bicycles made their way off the ferry, sitting there unmoving while the ferry backed away from the slip and headed off to San Juan and Orcas. And this was a scene that repeated itself when the eight twenty-seven ferry came in. And the ten forty-two. Only by this time Dion was asleep in his car seat, so Phoebe had nobody to talk to. I had put all this out of my mind earlier, caught up as I was with Dwayne's story, but now I knew how disappointed Phoebe must have been when I didn't return on any of the ferries.

I looked at my watch, but it was after midnight—long past time for the last ferry to the island. And I felt caught up in one of those bad dreams where all the doors you tug on so desperately are locked.

In my agitation I unfolded the piece of paper, Dion's letter, and smoothed it over my knee as though I expected those squiggles to make sense, looking as I so often had for revelation, for magic.

As I stared at the lines on the paper, I saw there *were* words making their uncertain, wavering way over the paper, words as uneven as a child might have written them.

"I NO NOW WHY DANE DISAPEARED," the words said.

I stared at them, at this message from afar, and at first

they made no sense. All I knew for sure was I had a powerful feeling Phoebe was as close as my elbow, that for
Phoebe, time and distance weren't obstacles to be overcome but could be sailed through as easily as air.

"I NO NOW WHY DANE DISAPEARED." I read
again, and this time intuition of how to read those words,
as though they were in a secret code, suddenly came to me.
I felt the message fly directly from Phoebe's fingers to my
heart.

Of course Phoebe had known Dwayne loved me, long,
long before I could even entertain such a notion myself.
And because of this, I knew why she'd asked with such
anxiety if I'd loved him since all along she must have felt a
kind of kinship with Dwayne: If I was so blind about him,
wouldn't I be just as blind about her? I might as well face
the truth. Phoebe had *known* I was going to make that
mistake all over again even while she still held hope she
might be wrong, that even her terrible intuition could go
haywire.

She'd held those two things in her head that morning as
she ran the tip of the pencil over the paper, Dion's hand
held in hers. That "NOW" she put on paper occupied both
times, the early morning as she sat at the table and this
middle-of-the-night present as I sat on the edge of my bed,
knowing I was too late to say, "Oh, Phoebe, I'm sorry I
didn't come back when I said I would. It doesn't mean
what you think it does."

I could easily imagine her waiting for the six o'clock
ferry, watching as it emptied, knowing even before the last
person climbed the ramp that I wasn't going to be on it,
that it was all turning out just the way she thought it would

and I had left her for good. If that's what she thought,
would she disappear too, as Dwayne had, taking Dion with
her?

I lay in bed trying to get a message through to Phoebe in
the one way she understood. Wait, I told her. Wait right
where you are and don't move a muscle. I never meant to
abandon you. It's not the way you think it is.

I tried to see the scene where I'd step off the early morning ferry, going straight to Phoebe's house and telling her
the moment I opened the door, "Pack your suitcase for
Virginia, Phoebe. You're going to come home with me."

But in spite of my best efforts, I couldn't lift the heavi-
ness that had settled around me like a winter cloud.
Phoebe had probably known from the beginning that it was
what I hoped to get from her that drew me. It had never
been possible to fool Phoebe. Not about anything that mat-
tered.

Before daylight the next morning I was knocking on the
door of Jordan's motel room, having decided to take his
rented car with me to the island. I had to wait for him to
pull himself out of bed—he'd always been slow to wake up
in the mornings—but he finally opened the door, swaying a
little, his hair wild, his eyes squinted nearly shut. But when
I told him I needed to borrow his car keys for a few hours,
that I had some things to take care of, he didn't hesitate to
hand them over.

"I'll be back in time to get us to the airport," I told him.
"You might walk around town. See the sights."

He nodded, but in a sleepy kind of way that let me know

all he was going to do was climb back into bed and stay for hours. "What time is it, anyway?" he said groggily.

"Early," I told him.

But for my purposes, it wasn't early. It was late.

In spite of the early-morning chill, I rode outside on the deck of the ferry, looking over the water that was first pearly gray and then rosy as the light grew stronger just before sunrise. I had the feeling that by standing on the deck, I was urging the ferry on to make speed. I had this picture in my mind: just as I got off the ferry I would see Phoebe's truck, with Phoebe riding tall in the cab and Dion waving from his seat, and behind them the bed of the truck would be loaded high. But when she saw me Phoebe would grin. She would open the door of the cab, I would swing up, and Phoebe would turn the truck around at the ferry slip and head for home. And after that? Beyond this picture, I couldn't see. But I told myself that maybe Phoebe and Dion and the two cats would travel across the country, and Phoebe could live where she'd insisted she'd grown up.

But when the ferry pulled into the slip at Phoebe's island, her truck wasn't among those waiting to drive on board, and as I drove, as fast as I dared, down the familiar road, I didn't pass her truck there, either.

In spite of the beauty of the early morning, the air so clear that trees and houses looked magnified, I had a feeling of dread, a dread I tried to set aside. I wasn't a Phoebe, to know beyond what my senses could tell me.

But when I drove into the driveway leading to Phoebe's house my heart sank, and I knew that what I felt was foreboding. The house had a closed, shut-in look, and I was sure it was empty. The knob to the back door turned under my hand, but this didn't surprise me. "Phoebe?" I called, without hope.

What struck me at once, when I stepped into the kitchen, was the absence of Sun and Moon who were nearly always hanging around. And then I saw that their feeding dishes, which usually sat pushed against the base of the cabinets, weren't there. I knew at that moment that my foreboding was justified, that the house was indeed empty. There was evidence everywhere of how hastily Phoebe had left—the drawers of the chest hung half-open, a diaper bag was kicked halfway under Phoebe's bed. When I saw one of Dion's teething rings lying on the floor, I put it in my pocket.

Only my room was untouched, and I couldn't bear to look at that order, at the rocks that lined my windowsill, at the roses and daisies winding their way up the walls. I shut the door on all of it.

I didn't see why Phoebe had to leave in such haste, why she couldn't have waited until the early morning, at least. I didn't see why she had to leave me to wander around the abandoned rooms, feeling guilty and disconsolate.

What I had in my mind was Phoebe driving a long dusty road in the shadow of stark mountains. Phoebe on her way to Alaska. That's what I thought. But even about this I was far from sure. What I felt was that the earth had swallowed Phoebe, as it had seemed to swallow Dwayne months before.

"Phoebe," I said out loud to whoever or whatever might be listening, "if you knew so much, didn't you know I loved you even if you are beautiful? You're my sister, as much as anybody could be. Hear me saying it?"

Maybe, wherever she was, Phoebe plucked this message from the air. I hoped she was able to do this, but I couldn't tell. My powers didn't extend so far.

Before I left the house, I took Phoebe's message to me from my pocket and spread it on the kitchen table, using the sugar bowl to hold it in place. The last thing I had to say to her. I locked the door when I left, knowing that if Phoebe returned she'd have her own means of getting back in.

30

*O*n the airplane, I pushed past Jordan to get what I wanted—the window seat. He was already pulling off his jacket and folding it neatly before lifting it into the rack above his head, then, when he sat, lifting the creases of his trousers as he carefully extended his legs, pushing the recline button on his seat arm.

"It seems about twenty years since I flew out here," he said. "Hard to believe it was only yesterday."

I couldn't believe that by early dark I would be in the backseat of Mama's car as she drove Jordan and me from the airport, turning off the highway to the road that would carry us up to Clearwater where the lights would be shining from the dining room windows and where Sophie would have left a baked ham keeping warm in the oven.

Maybe Dwayne would be waiting in his pickup under the walnut trees, the door open so he could stick his feet out into the cool, while Ricky Skaggs sang about love to keep him company. When he heard the car start up the hill, he'd leap out of the truck, pulling the bill of his cap up and down the way he did when he was excited. And before Mama could bring the car to a good stop, before I could get the door open, there he'd be, bending down, his face turned a little sideways so he could see in the window, grinning his vampire smile and saying, "Hey, Jessie? Hey, Jess?" before I could get out a word about sorrow or remorse.

Though the day had started sunny, the clouds had rolled in by the time we reached Seattle, and when the plane rose it was through clouds that shut us into darkness almost like night while drops of water whipped along the glass as the plane rocked and plunged like a spooked horse.

Jordan linked his fingers across his stomach and shut his eyes, unimpressed with the elements, but Jordan's conscience was either easier than mine or not as active. Vengeance had always seemed to me to play a perfectly legitimate part in the scheme of things, though I was a lot less sure about justice. I wouldn't even try to deny my own guilt, however. When I thought about Dwayne, when I thought about Phoebe, there it was, staring me in the face.

I slid down in my seat and put a hand across my eyes, feeling like Jonah hiding in the hold of the ship during the storm while up above everybody was running around trying to decide who it was God was after. I knew if God wanted to get me there I was, surrounded by nothing but air and with a downdraft bucking us all around.

But as the plane climbed the clouds thinned, the light coming through the little window growing stronger and stronger until, suddenly, the clouds dissolved to nothing but wisps of pearly smoke as we rose into sunlight so dazzling I had to shut my eyes.

When I opened them again it was to stare straight at the snow-covered dome of Mount Rainier, with the sunlight golden on its crest, so close, such an amazingly huge *thing* floating above the clouds, serene, indifferent, as removed from the concerns of this world as a smiling Buddha. Who could guess, standing at the soggy, drippy, dark foot of that great heap of rock and snow what a wonder there was, up far out of sight, above the clouds where the sun was shining.

"Look! Look, Jordan!" I said, shaking him by the shoulder.

But Jordan was slow to bestir himself, and by the time he leaned across me to peer out of the window the plane had slid past that golden dome, and it was lost far, far behind us.

About the Author

Mary Elsie Robertson's previous novels are *After Freud, The Clearing, Speak, Angel,* and *Family Life.* She was born and raised in Arkansas, lives in upstate New York, and teaches in the MFA Program for Writers at Warren Wilson College and, for one semester a year, at the University of Arizona.